致敬译界巨匠许渊冲先生

许渊冲译
楚 辞

ELEGIES OF THE SOUTH

译

许渊冲

中国出版集团
中译出版社

译序

半亩方塘一鉴开，天光云影共徘徊。
问渠哪得清如许？为有源头活水来。

——朱熹《观书有感》

中国文化是"天光云影共徘徊"的一片汪洋大海，而它的"源头活水"就是《诗经》和《楚辞》。《诗经》是中国最早的现实主义诗集，编于公元前六世纪，地区包括华北的黄河流域，东起富庶的齐国，西至强盛的秦国，中原地带有人口稠密的郑、卫等国。在华北，儒家把远古传统、神话、巫术逐一理性化，把神人化，把奇异传说化为君臣父子的世间秩序。《楚辞》却是中国最早的浪漫主义诗集，作于公元前三世纪，地区是华南的长江流域，当时主要是版图广大的楚国。楚国保持和发展着绚烂鲜丽的远古传统，弥漫在一片奇异想象和炽烈情感的神话世界中；而楚文化的代表，是把个体的人格情操和想象的神话世界融合为一，开创了中国抒情诗光辉典范的屈原（约公元前340—前278）。

从屈原起，开始了中国诗人个体创作的时代。屈原的作品，最初是单篇流传的。现在所能看到的版本，最早是东汉王逸的《楚辞章句》，前十篇的次序如下：一、《离骚》，二、《九歌》，三、《天问》，四、《九章》，五、《远游》，六、《卜居》，七、《渔父》，八、《九辩》，九、《招魂》，十、《大招》。后面还有几篇汉时人作品。一般说来,《楚辞》只收战国时期的楚国作品,所以本书只译了《楚辞章句》的前十篇。

《诗经楚辞鉴赏辞典》序言中说:"今传屈原二十余篇作品,可以分成三类,构成一个序列。首先应说《九歌》十一篇,它本是楚地的祀神乐曲,经屈原加工润色,刮垢磨光,成为精美的诗篇。这组诗的抒情主人公或为神祇,或为主祭者。诗是代言体,尚非诗人的咏怀。它们更多地展现了诗人从继承到创新的创作轨迹。其次是《天问》,它是屈原根据神话、传说材料创作的古今无两的煌煌大篇,着重表现了诗人的历史观与自然观,显示了哲理与抒情的两重性。第三是《离骚》《九章》等作品,是屈原的政治抒情之作,它们有事可据,有义可陈,情感充沛,形象鲜明,气象磅礴,达到了思想与艺术的完美结合。《天问》《九歌》和《离骚》……各自代表了楚辞的最高成就。"

《离骚》是我国古代最早、最辉煌的长篇抒情诗,其气魄之宏伟、抒情之深刻、构思之奇幻、辞采之绚烂,在古典诗歌的宝库里首屈一指。屈原在楚怀王时曾担任过"左徒"的要职,一度得到怀王的信任。他主张改革内政,联合东方富庶的齐国,抵抗西方强盛的秦国;但秦国的使臣贿赂了楚国的大臣,大臣向楚王进谗言,楚王不但不接受屈原的意见,反而把他放逐。所以他在《离骚》中写道:

怨灵修之浩荡兮,终不察夫民心;
众女嫉余之蛾眉兮,谣诼谓余以善淫。

关于"离骚"二字的意义,司马迁说是"离忧",班固说是"罹忧",王逸说是"别愁",本书的译名采用司马迁和王逸的说法。《离骚》既是政治抒情诗，又是伟大心灵的悲剧，全诗可以看作是由"述怀""追求""幻灭"三部分组成的三部曲。他"述怀"的名句如：

民生各有所乐兮，余独好修以为常；
虽体解吾犹未变兮，岂余心之可惩？

他"追求"的名句如：

吾令羲和弭节兮，望崦嵫而勿迫；
路漫漫其修远兮，吾将上下而求索。
……
前望舒使先驱兮，后飞廉使奔属；
鸾皇为余先戒兮，雷师告余以未具。

诗人的理想冲不破现实环境的束缚，所以感到"幻灭"；但是远游自疏的念头又终于被眷恋故国之情所压倒。例如：

陟升皇之赫戏兮，忽临睨夫旧乡！
仆夫悲余马怀兮，蜷局顾而不行。

这四句诗，显然受了《诗经〈周南·卷耳〉》的影响："陟彼砠矣，我马瘏矣，我仆痛矣，云何吁矣！"后来甚至影响到元代马致远的《秋思》："古道西风瘦马"，使马和思乡之情紧密地联系起来，甚至成为与乡思有关的意象了。

《离骚》在艺术表现上的最大特色，就是比兴、象征手法的运用。"比兴"在《诗经》里已开其端，但是大多作为

III

特定的修辞手段。《离骚》却将这种手法扩展到诗篇的整个艺术构思上,借以塑造出一组组富于象征色彩的意象群来。朱自清说过,"比体诗"有四大类——咏史(以古比今)、游仙(以仙比俗)、艳情(以男女比君臣)和咏物(以物比人)。《离骚》中借男女恋情来比喻君臣离合的很多,如上面引用的"众女嫉余之蛾眉兮";借仙比俗的也不少,如上面引用的神话意象群:羲和、望舒、飞廉、雷师;以物比人,主要是用香花芳草比喻忠臣,用野花杂草比喻奸臣;以古比今如:

夏桀之常违兮,乃遂焉而逢殃。
后辛之菹醢兮,殷宗用而不长。

就是用夏商灭亡的前车之鉴,来警告楚王。但是楚王不听忠言,国事日益混乱,楚国危亡在即,屈原悲愤交加,最后在夏历五月五日投汨罗江而死。后人缅怀他进步的理想,卓绝的人格,不幸的遭遇,在他离世的每个周年纪念日举行龙舟竞渡,象征性地要挽救诗人的遗体,这种风俗长达两千多年之久,甚至传到了日本、朝鲜、东南亚,由此可见他的事迹感人之深。

《离骚》可以和西方荷马的史诗《奥德赛》及但丁的《神曲》先后媲美。荷马比屈原约早500年,《奥德赛》描写特洛伊战争的英雄奥德修斯,在回国途中经历的海上风险,他过人的智力和身受的痛苦。《离骚》写的却是诗人追求理想的天路历程,他高尚的品德和离乡背井的内心悲哀。奥德修斯追求的是现实生活,是回到故国和妻子家人团聚;屈原寻求的却是理想的君主或美人,如洛水的宓妃,有**娀**之佚女、有虞之二姚等。

但丁比屈原约晚1500年。茅盾在《世界文学名著杂谈》中把《神曲》和《楚辞》作比较说："但丁的《神曲》的基本思想是基督教的禁欲主义，……也有异教的传说和神话。同样地，屈原所'上下而求索'者，虽然是尧舜的'纯粹'，可是他也喜言'巫俗'。《神曲》是'梦的故事'，而《离骚》和《九章》也是神游的故事。《神曲》开头的文豹、狮子和牝狼是象征或隐喻的，《离骚》等篇的椒兰凤鸠也是隐喻。《神曲》托毗亚德里采为天堂之向导，但丁是把这个纯洁的女子作为信仰象征的；同样地，《离骚》也托言求'有娀之佚女'。《神曲》包罗了中世纪社会的政治现象，交织着中世纪哲学和科学的思想；屈原在他的一气发了一百八九十个疑问的《天问》内，也颇有包举一切……古代文化的气概。不过有一个大不同在，即但丁是站在自己的立场上肯定地批判了一切，而屈原则是皇皇然求索。"

有趣的是，钱稻孙把《神曲》译成中文，用的就是"骚"体，如《地狱》曲一的前六行：

方吾生之半路
恍余处乎幽林，
失正轨而违误。
道其况兮不可禁
林荒蛮以惨烈
言念及之复怖心！

这真是中西文化交流的一段佳话了。

《九歌》是祭祀神灵的乐歌，相传是夏朝的音乐，流传于楚国民间。屈原流放时，看到民间祭祀的歌舞之乐，感到乐曲很美但歌词鄙陋，于是就在原来的基础上加以润色，创作了一套新的歌词。这就是流传至今的《九歌》，共十一篇，前九篇祀神，第十篇《国殇》祭鬼，第十一篇是尾声。有人认为第一篇《东皇太一》是总的迎神曲，最后一篇《礼魂》是总的送神曲，所以只写祭祀，没有颂神。第二篇本是《云中君》，据闻一多考订，认为是错简，《东君》应当在《云中君》之前，因为在《史记》《汉书》中，"皆东君、云中君连称"，二者本是"依农业社会观念，象征着两个对立的重要自然现象——晴与雨的"。《东君》是男巫扮太阳神的唱词，而第十一、十二句是女巫唱的。太阳神的形象，从红日东升到丽日当空，到夕阳西下，都是雄伟而壮美的，祭祀场面也写得非常热闹。《云中君》是写云神的，第一、二句有人说指女巫，有人说指朝霞；第三句可和雪莱的《云》比较，最后两句是女巫的唱词。《湘君》和《湘夫人》两篇合起来是一个整体，由男巫扮湘君，女巫扮湘夫人，男女对舞对唱。《湘君》写湘夫人的心理活动，由希望而失望，而怀疑，而痛伤，而埋怨，入情入理，曲尽其妙。《湘夫人》则写湘君赴约、失望，怀想，盼望，望之不见，遇之无因等情节，开头四句借景引情，情景交融，是历代诗家所推崇的佳句；《大司命》是扮寿命之神的男巫和人间凡女的对唱，是神凡恋爱的悲剧。《少司命》一说是写送子娘娘；郭沫若说是写爱情女神失恋，所以说："悲莫悲兮生别离。"《河伯》写黄河水神对洛水女神的相思。《山鬼》写巫山神女的相思之苦，徐悲鸿还画了《山鬼图》。《国殇》则是追悼秦楚交战阵亡将士的哀歌。

《九歌》虽是祭祀用的乐章，但主要内容却是恋歌。古代的祀神祭节，也正是青年男女欢会游乐的大好时光，用恋歌作祭词是自然的事；因为祭神的目的是为了得到神的保佑，所以用恋歌来娱神、悦神；而《九歌》中的恋歌如《湘君》《湘夫人》《少司命》《山鬼》等，艺术形式完美，对后来两千多年的文学有深远的影响。

《九章》就是"九篇"，包括九篇内容与《离骚》近似，篇幅较小的作品。第八篇《橘颂》的风格与其他各篇不同，说到"嗟尔幼志""年岁虽小"，有人认为是屈原早期的作品。这是一首咏物诗，赞美橘树，同时借咏橘来自喻，比喻自己的品德，像橘树一样，是"独立不迁"，"苏世独立"，"闭心自慎"的。这首诗写得不即不离，不离开橘，又不局限于橘，而是把橘和自己结合起来写，写出了诗人自己的品格。其他八篇梁启超说是"《离骚》的放大"，不过主要是用写实的方法，反映诗人一些具体的生活片段，及当时的思想情绪。如《史记》没有记载屈原流放的地点，《抽思》写他初放汉北，《哀郢》写他流放郢都以东，《涉江》写他从今天的武汉一带，流落到荒凉的湘西，《怀沙》写他从湘西奔赴长沙，最后死节，这四篇填补了流放地点的空白。

《九章》之中，《惜诵》可能是屈原流放后写的第一篇，接着可能是《悲回风》《思美人》《惜往日》。《哀郢》可能作于公元前289年，那时秦将白起攻陷了郢都。"乱曰：曼余目以流观兮，冀壹反之何时？鸟飞反故乡兮，狐死必首丘；信非吾罪而弃逐兮，何日夜而忘之！"梁启超认为是"最沉痛的"文字。"这等作品，真所谓'一声河满子，双泪落君前'。任凭是铁石人，读了怕都不能不感动哩！"《涉江》是屈原流放江南时所作，抒情才悲戚深沉，叙事则历历如见，议论则引古证今，随文变幻，各达极致。《抽思》一篇写得情意缠绵，如怨如慕，充摄诗篇灵魂的，是屈原高尚的理想：

"望三五以为像兮,指彭咸以为仪。夫何极而不至兮?故远闻而难亏。"《怀沙》是屈原临终的作品,通篇以赋为主,比兴兼施,灵感因岁序景物而生发,事理借形象比喻以辨明;熔思想美、艺术美、自然美于一炉。梁启超说:"他最后觉悟到他可以死而且不能不死,他便从容死去。临死时的绝作说道:

知死不可让,愿勿爱兮。
明告君子,吾将以为类兮。

《天问》是哲理诗,思想、历史价值很高。诗人提出了170多个问题,问到宇宙起源、天地形成、天象变化、洪水灾难、四方异物、神话传说、历史变迁等。鲁迅在《摩罗诗力说》中赞叹道:"怀疑自遂古之初,直至百物之琐末,放言无惮,为前人所不敢言。"《天问》素以难懂著称,闻一多《天问疏证》中精义较多。《天问》的形式在两千多年的古典诗史上是独一无二的;在国外,则有《旧约·约伯记》可以比较。

《远游》是中国第一篇游仙诗。梁启超说:"《远游》一篇,是屈原宇宙观、人生观的全部表现,是当时南方哲学思想之现于文学者。"《远游》写凡人修炼得道而神游太空,不同于《离骚》写的神话人物游天。因为《远游》表现的主要是道家思想,和屈原的思想不同,有人认为不是屈原所作;也有人说屈原思想不限一家,某一时期具有道家思想是可能的。《远游》之前,诗人的思想表现在下列句中:

惟天地之无穷兮,哀人生之长勤;
往者余弗及兮!来者吾不闻。

《远游》中的道家思想，主要表现在仙人王子乔的下列句中：

道可受兮，而不可传；
其小无内兮，其大无垠；
……
虚以待之兮，无为之先；
庶类以成兮，此德之门。

得道之后，诗中最后一段也有描写：

下峥嵘而无地兮，上寥廓而无天。
视倏忽而无见兮，听惝恍而无闻。
超无为以至清兮，与太初而为邻。

《卜居》和《渔父》是两首叙事诗，采用对话的形式表达作者的思想。梁启超说："《卜居》是说两种矛盾的人生观（此孰吉孰凶？何去何从？），《渔父》是表自己意志的抉择。"如屈原说："举世皆浊我独清，众人皆醉我独醒。"而渔父则劝他"与世推移"，并且唱道："沧浪之水清兮，可以濯吾缨；沧浪之水浊兮，可以濯吾足。"王逸说这两篇都是"屈原之所作"；又说《渔父》是"楚人思念屈原，因叙其辞，以相传焉"。无论作者是谁，作品思想都与《离骚》是一致的。

《九辩》的作者是宋玉（约公元前298—前222）。王夫之在《楚辞通释》中说："辩，犹遍也；一阕谓之一遍。"所以"九辩"就是"九遍"，就是分成九个乐章的组诗。宋玉在诗中把自然的季节、楚国的政治气候、个人的身世，有机地融合在一起，而以秋天的萧瑟之气贯穿全诗，达到了情景交融的境界，使"宋玉悲秋"成了文学史上的习语。诗中多是低沉幽怨的哀音，也有高亢激昂的调子，那多是从屈原的作品中改装过来的。屈原为自己的政治理想不能实现而愤慨，宋玉却是为个人的失意而痛苦。《九辩》洋溢着忧郁美，第一乐章被古人誉为描写悲秋的绝唱："悲哉，秋之为气也！萧瑟兮，草木摇落而变衰。"宋玉在诗中表现了对事物的怜悯感，自己才华出众的优越感，发泄苦闷后的痛快感。他创造了情景交融的美感，包括天上地下多层次的空间美，季节转换的时间美，社会生活的动态美，内心矛盾的传神美，双声叠字的音乐美。尤其是最后一个乐章，用了"抟抟""湛湛""习习""丰丰""苃苃""躍躍""阗阗""衙衙""锵锵""从从""容容"等叠字，取得了难以形容的效果，前无古人的成就。后来汉武帝、魏文帝、李白、杜甫、李贺等写悲秋诗，没有一个人不受宋玉启发的。

《招魂》和《大招》，有人说是屈原所作，招的是楚怀王的魂；有人说是宋玉所作，招的是屈原的生魂。楚国巫风盛行，有病垂死的人，可以请巫招魂；所以宋玉托上帝的意旨，借巫语招屈原的魂，寄托楚人对他的厚望，盼他还朝的深意。《招魂》开始一段写屈原自诉洁身服义，君主却不察知他的盛德。于是上帝告诉巫阳，把灵魂招还给屈原。以下便是巫阳招魂之辞，可以分为两大层次。前一层次把天地四方的害人事物，写得神怪无以复加：长人，十日，雕题，黑齿、蝮蛇、封狐、雄虺、木夫、土伯等，都不同于儒家后来加工修饰过的神话，而是险恶壮美的形象。后一层次列述宫室、起居、饮食、燕乐、声色之美，王夫之说："盖人君待贤之礼，自当极致其丰。"所以极尽夸张、想象之能事,写得淋漓尽致。如"美人既醉,朱颜酡些。娭光眇视,目曾波些。""士女杂坐,乱而不分些。放陈组缨,班其相纷些。"王逸说"外陈四方之恶,内崇楚国之美",是希望楚王觉悟,召屈原来挽救危亡的。后一层次的欢乐气氛,是和前一层次诡怪可怕的景象形成对比,在艺术上达到平衡的。《招魂》最后一段和开始一段对应,用第一人称代屈原写魂归来后,将和楚王射猎于云梦,真是怀念屈原的最好诗篇。《文心雕龙》说:"《招魂》《大招》,耀艳而深华。"可见这两篇的词采之艳,意蕴之美,"衣被词人,非一代也!"梁启超说:《招魂》可和歌德的《浮士德》先后争辉。

《楚辞》在中国流传了2000多年,直到19世纪才有西方译本。1852年,在维也纳出版了普费兹梅尔博士的德文译本。1870年,在巴黎出版了德尔韦侯爵的法文译本。最早的英译文,是1879年《中国评论杂志》第七期309到314页上发表的派克英译的《离骚》,译文却得到剑桥大学翟理斯教授的赞赏,但他认为开始很好,后面就难以为继了。牛津大学霍克思教授认为:派克释义多于翻译。现将他的译文摘抄在英文序中,以见一斑。

1884年,翟理斯教授在上海出版了英文本的《中国文学精华》,其中选译了《卜居》《渔父》和《山鬼》三篇。他的译文优雅可读,但是过分欧化,现将他译的《卜居》也摘抄在英文序中。1895年,英国皇家亚洲学会的《亚洲学刊》第二十七期847到864页发表了理雅各英译的《离骚》。他的译文忠实地翻译出了王逸的解释,可能还参考了德尔韦侯爵的法译本,显然比派克的英译本更加准确,但和他英译的《诗经》一样,一点不能引人入胜,读来毫无诗意,仿佛他译《离骚》只是责无旁贷,自己完全没有兴趣。理雅各之后,日本还出版了质量很高的《离骚》日译本。

有个德国学者艾尔克,在1914年曾把《招魂》译成德文,到1923年又把《大招》译成英文。到1939年,他发表的《古代中国的死神》中,包括了他英译的《大司命》和《少司命》。他的译文基本上是逐字直译,对开始学习中文的外国学生倒还有用。现将《招隐士》中两行摘抄在英文序中,以见一斑。

1918年,韦理出版了他英译的《中国诗选一百七十首》,其中包括《九歌》中的《国殇》;1919年,他又出版了《中国诗选续集》,其中包括《大招》,霍克思认为是光辉灿烂的译文。1946年,韦理再出版了《中国诗选》,这两篇都收在其内,《国殇》修改较多。

1928年,英国皇家亚洲学会《华北分会学刊》第59期231至253页,刊登了比亚拉斯的《屈原的生平和诗作》一文,其中包括他英译的《东皇太一》《山鬼》《天问(前12行)》《惜诵》《卜居》《渔父》几篇,完全是机械式的直译,毫无文学价值可言。此外,他还曾将部分《楚辞》译成德文。

1929年,在新加坡出生的华侨、英国爱丁堡大学博士、厦门大学第一任校长林文庆,在上海出版了英译《离骚》。英国汉学大师翟理斯,印度著名诗人泰戈尔,都为林译本写了序。翟理斯说:"《离骚》是一篇奇妙的抒情诗,可以和古代希腊诗人品达比美争辉。诗篇是公元前300多年写的。我在1872年第一次读到的时候,诗句有如闪耀的电光,使我眼花缭乱,觉得美不胜收。"他还说林译使英国显得瞠乎其后,停滞不前了。泰戈尔说:"这篇政治抒情诗是一首哀歌,使人栩栩如生地看到一个伟大民族的心灵,如何渴望在道德精神的基础上,建立起一个稳定的社会。……我们感到整部

诗篇弥漫着时代末日的悲哀,并发现希望的曙光也是如梦如幻。读读下面这四句诗:

汩余若将不及兮,恐年岁之不吾与。
朝搴阰之木兰兮,夕揽洲之宿莽。

我们仿佛听到黄昏的微风发出了临终前的叹息,诗句的字里行间吐露了生离死别的衷情。"但是霍克思的看法不同,他认为林译只适宜学生用来做中英对照本,译文不如理雅各的准确,而且同样缺乏文学价值。现将林译摘抄两段在英文序言中,以见一斑。

1947年,英美出版了白英和西南联大师生合译的《白驹集》(古今中国诗选),闻一多参加了选题,包括《九歌》《涉江》《离骚》几篇。霍克思认为译文清新可读,除了韦理的译本外,《白驹集》要算最好的,它不会使读者望而却步。但白英把有韵的骚体译成散文了。

1953年,北京外文出版社出版了杨宪益夫妇合译的《离骚》等诗,包括《九歌》《九章》《卜居》《渔父》《招魂》《天问》在内,除中间两篇外,全部译文押韵。霍克思说这是匠心独运的一座丰碑,但像蒲伯译的荷马史诗一样,并不忠实于原文。

1955年,韦理又出版了他英译的《九歌》,霍克思认为译文是无价之宝。1959年,牛津大学出版社出版了霍克思自己译的《楚辞》,包括王逸《楚辞章句》中的全部作品,内容最为广泛。他的译法介乎直译与意译之间,从微观的角度来看,比前人更准确,但从宏观的角度看来,却只能使人知之,不能使人好之、乐之。

1975年，纽约出版了柳无忌等编译的《葵晔集》，其中选译了《离骚》《湘君》《大司命》《哀郢》《橘颂》五篇。1984年，美国哥伦比亚大学出版了华逊编译的《中国诗选》，其中选译了《离骚》《云中君》《湘君》《山鬼》《国殇》五篇。柳无忌和华逊都把有韵有调的《楚辞》译成无韵无调的分行散文；也就是说，最多只能传达原诗的意美，但是不能再现原诗的音美和形美。而《楚辞》的英译本如果只有意美而没有音美、形美，那就会使人觉得奇怪：怎么能把《离骚》和《奥德赛》及《神曲》、把《天问》和《约伯记》、把《招魂》和《浮士德》相提并论呢！

《诗经楚辞鉴赏辞典》序言中说："在一个民族文化中，如果只有山峦而没有高峰，只有江河而没有大海，只有大合唱而没有最强音，是断难彪炳于世界文化之林的。"屈原就是中国文化史上的第一座"高峰"，大合唱中的第一个"最强音"。而散体译者却把《楚辞》译成"山峦"，译成"大合唱"了。而我认为，英译《楚辞》一定要再现原诗的意美、音美、形美，才能使这座高峰屹立于世界文化之林。

目录
Contents

译序 / I

离骚 / 002
Sorrow after Departure

九歌 / 042
The Nine Songs
    东皇太一 / 042
    The Almighty Lord of the East
    云中君 / 044
    To The God of Cloud
    湘君 / 046
    To the Lord of River Xiang
    湘夫人 / 050
    To the Lady of River Xiang
    大司命 / 054
    The Great Lord of Fate
    少司命 / 056
    The Young Goddess of Fate
    东君 / 060
    The God of the Sun
    河伯 / 062
    The God of the River
    山鬼 / 064
    The Goddess of the Mountain
    国殇 / 068
    For Those Fallen for the Country
    礼魂 / 070
    The Last Sacrifice

天问 / 072
Asking Heaven

九章 / 112
The Nine Elegies
    惜诵 / 112
    I Make my Plaint
    涉江 / 122
    Crossing the River
    哀郢 / 128
    Lament for the Chu Capital
    抽思 / 136
    Sad Thoughts Outpoured
    怀沙 / 144
    Longing for Changsha
    思美人 / 154
    Thinking of the Fair One
    惜往日 / 160
    The Bygone Days Regretted
    橘颂 / 170
    Hymn to the Orange Tree
    悲回风 / 174
    Grieving at the Whirlwind

远游 / 186
The Far-off Journey

卜居 / 206
Divination

渔父 / 212
The Fisherman

九辩 / 216
Nine Apologies

招魂 / 240
Requiem

大招 / 268
Great Requiem

许渊冲译楚辞

离骚

帝高阳①之苗裔②兮，	我是颛顼古帝远末的子孙，
朕③皇考曰伯庸。	已故伟大的伯庸是我的父亲。
摄提④贞⑤于孟陬⑥兮，	我出生在虎年的正月里，
惟庚寅吾以降。	庚寅那天我出生了。

皇⑦览揆⑧余初度⑨兮，	父亲揣度我出生时的情形，
肇锡⑩余以嘉名。	开始给我取个美好的名和字。
名余曰正则兮，	为我取名叫"正则"，
字余曰灵均。	给我取字叫"灵均"。

纷吾既有此内美兮，	我不仅有美好的内在品德，
又重之以修能。	又富有行事的才能。
扈⑪江离与辟芷兮，	江蓠和芷草披在我肩上，
纫⑫秋兰以为佩。	秋兰连缀佩在腰间。

---

① 高阳：传说中远古部落的首领，名颛顼，号高阳氏。
② 苗裔：远末的子孙。
③ 朕：古时候不论贵贱都可以称"我"为"朕"，这里指"我"，到了秦始皇的时候，"朕"才变成皇帝的专称。
④ 摄提：古代纪年的一个术语，全称摄提格，相当于今天所说的寅年，即虎年。
⑤ 贞：正。
⑥ 孟陬（zōu）：孟，古语开始的意思；陬，夏历的正月。
⑦ 皇：指其父亲，也就是上文的伯庸。
⑧ 揆（kuí）：揣度。
⑨ 初度：刚出生时。
⑩ 锡：赐。
⑪ 扈：披在身上。
⑫ 纫（rèn）：连缀。

Sorrow after Departure

Descendant of High Sunny King, oh!
My father's name shed sunny ray.
The Wooden Star appeared in spring, oh!
When I was born on Tiger's Day.

My father saw my birthday bright, oh!
He gave me an auspicious name.
My formal name was Divine Right, oh!
I was also called Divine Flame.

I have so much beauty inside, oh!
And add to it a style ornate.
I weave sweet grass by riverside, oh!
Into a belt with orchids late.

汨^①余若将弗及兮，　　　　　如水光阴难以追赶，
恐年岁之不吾与。　　　　　　　唯恐年岁会不等待我。
朝搴阰之木兰兮^②，　　　　清晨我折取土山上的木兰，
夕揽洲之宿莽。　　　　　　　　黄昏采摘水边上的青藻。

日月忽其不淹^③兮，　　　　日落月出周而复始，
春与秋其代序。　　　　　　　　春去秋来年复一年。
惟草木之零落兮，　　　　　　　想到草木一到秋天便凋零，
恐美人之迟暮。　　　　　　　　我便担心佳人青春的逝去。

不抚壮而弃秽兮，　　　　　　　为何不趁着年轻改变秽恶的行为，
何不改乎此度？　　　　　　　　为什么不改变现在的法度？
乘骐骥以驰骋兮，　　　　　　　驾着骏马我将要奔驰，
来吾道夫先路！　　　　　　　　你来吧，我要为你在前面引路！

昔三后之纯粹兮，　　　　　　　古时候的三王是多么公正无私，
固众芳之所在。　　　　　　　　在那时固然是群贤聚集如群芳聚会。
杂申椒与菌桂兮，　　　　　　　其中也夹杂着申椒和菌桂啊，
岂惟纫夫蕙茞^④？　　　　　不仅有白芷连缀蕙草。

彼尧、舜之耿介兮，　　　　　　想唐尧和虞舜真是光明正直，
既遵道而得路。　　　　　　　　沿着正路走上了正当轨道。
何桀纣之猖披^⑤兮，　　　　而夏桀和殷纣是怎样糊涂，
夫唯捷径以窘步。　　　　　　　总爱贪走捷径反而走投无路。

① 汨（gǔ）：水流急促，形容时光如水，一去不返。
② 搴（qiān）：拔取。阰（pí），小山坡。
③ 淹：长久地停留。
④ 蕙：香草名。茞（chǎi），白芷。
⑤ 猖披：穿着衣服不系腰带，形容放荡不检。

Like running water years will pass, oh!
I fear time and tide wait for none.
At dawn I gather mountain grass, oh!
At dusk I pick secluded one.

The sun and the moon will not stay, oh!
Spring will give place to autumn cold.
Grass will wither and trees decay, oh!
I fear that beauty will grow old.

Give up the foul while young and strong, oh!
Why won't you my lord, change your style and way?
Ride your fine steed, gallop along, oh!
I'll go before you lest you stray.

Three ancient kings were pure and true, oh!
Around them flocked all fragrant things.
Pepper and cassia also grew, oh!
Sweet orchids were formed into rings.

The first two monarchs were so bright, oh!
That they followed and gained the way.
The two last kings were in sad plight, oh!
They sought bypaths and came to bay.

惟夫党人①之偷乐兮，	结党营私的人们只知道苟且偷安，
路幽昧以险隘。	他们的道路黑暗而狭隘。
岂余身之惮殃兮，	难道我怕自己会遭殃吗？
恐皇舆②之败绩。	我只是怕君王的天下要覆亡。

忽奔走以先后兮，	我匆匆地在前在后奔走效力，
及前王之踵武。	希望能追赶上先王们的脚步。
荃③不察余之中情兮，	君王你既不肯明察我胸中的忠诚，
反信谗而齌怒④。	反而听信谗言对我勃然发怒。

余固知謇謇之为患兮，	我诚然知道耿直会招来祸害啊，
忍而不能舍也。	但我却忍耐着痛苦不能放弃。
指九天以为正兮，	我要请九重的上天做我的证人，
夫唯灵修之故也。	我忠于君王并无他意。

曰黄昏以为期兮，	既然有约在先，
羌中道而改路。	为何中途要改变心意？
初既与余成言兮，	当初既然已经和我有约，
后悔遁而有他。	后来为何反悔而改变主张。
余既不难夫离别兮，	我和你的分离也不怎么难堪，
伤灵修之数化。	只叹息你的为人太反复无常。

① 党人：结党营私的小人。
② 皇舆：君王所乘的车子，比喻国家。
③ 荃（quán）：一种香草，比喻君王。
④ 齌（jì）怒：怒火旺盛。

Your partisans love stolen pleasure, oh!
Their way is dark, with perils sown.
Do I dread my personal woe? oh!
I fear the royal cab o'erthrown.

I run before it and behind, oh!
I wish you would follow your sire.
To my loyalty you're unkind, oh!
You heed slander and burst in fire.

With frank advice you won't comply, oh!
I endure and cannot have done.
Be my witness, Ninth Heaven high, oh!
I've done all for you Sacred One.

The word you've given still remains, oh!
But you go back on it and stray.
Departure causes me no pains, oh!
Of your fickleness what to say?

余既滋^①兰之九畹^②兮，	我已经种下了九畹的春兰，
又树蕙之百亩。	又栽下上百亩的秋蕙。
畦留夷与揭车^③兮，	我曾把留夷和揭车种了一田，
杂杜衡^④与芳芷。	还夹杂着一些杜衡和芳芷之类。
冀枝叶之峻茂兮，	希望它们枝叶茂盛，
愿竢时乎吾将刈^⑤。	等待时机我便要收割。
虽萎绝其亦何伤兮，	即使它们萎谢了也不要紧，
哀众芳之芜秽。	可悲的是芳草的荒芜。
众皆竞进以贪婪兮，	大家都争着钻营而又贪婪，
凭不厌乎求索。	利欲熏心全然不知满足。
羌内恕己以量人兮，	放纵着自己而猜忌别人，
各兴心而嫉妒。	处心积虑而互相嫉妒。
忽驰骛以追逐兮，	忙忙碌碌争名夺利，
非余心之所急。	那些都不是我关心的。
老冉冉其将至兮，	衰老正在渐渐地来到，
恐修名之不立。	我担心好的声名难以确立。

① 滋：种植。
② 畹（wǎn）：古代计量单位，三十亩田为一畹。
③ 留夷：香草名。揭车：香草名。
④ 杜衡：香草名。
⑤ 刈（yì）：收割，收获。

I grow spring orchids in fields nine, oh!
And a hundred acres of clover.
I plant peonies line by line, oh!
Mixed with fragrant grass all over.

I'd see their leaves green and blooms red, oh!
And reap the fruit in season due.
I am not grieved they're withered, oh!
But they decay 'mid weeds in view.

All vie in avarice and greed, oh!
Their lust is never gratified.
Judging others by their own deed, oh!
They're jealous-minded and green-eyed.

I am not so eager as they, oh!
To run after wealth here and there.
Old age draws near from day to day, oh!
Have I a name lasting and fair?

朝饮木兰之坠露兮，	清晨我饮用着木兰花上的清露，
夕餐秋菊之落英。	傍晚以凋落的菊瓣充饥。
苟余情其信姱以练要兮，	只要我的情操坚贞不屈，
长颇颔①亦何伤！	即使长久地面黄肌瘦啊又有何妨！

揽木根以结茝兮，	用树木的细根来编织芷草，
贯薜荔之落蕊。	又穿上了薜荔花落下的花朵。
矫菌桂以纫蕙兮，	我把菌桂削直后连缀蕙英，
索胡绳之缅缅。	用胡绳草编成长长的绳索垂曳。

謇吾法夫前修兮，	我以古代的贤人为榜样，
非世俗之所服。	因此才不为世俗所喜欢；
虽不周于今之人兮，	虽然不能和今世的人志同道合，
愿依彭咸之遗则！	我宁愿遵从彭咸遗留下的法则。

长太息以掩涕兮，	我长长叹息不禁泪流满面，
哀民生之多艰。	可怜人生多么艰难。
余虽好修姱以鞿羁兮，	我虽然是爱好修洁并因此自我约束，
謇朝谇而夕替。	早上进谏晚上便被废弃。

既替余以蕙纕兮，	既然说我不该佩戴蕙草，
又申之以揽茝。	更因为重新系上芷草而加罪。
亦余心之所善兮，	这是我内心的爱好，
虽九死其犹未悔！	纵使是死上九回我也不会悔改啊！

---

① 颇颔（kǎn hàn）：面黄肌瘦的样子。

From magnolia I drink the dew, oh!
And feed on aster petals frail.
My spirit being pure and true, oh!
Do I care to grow lank and pale?

I string clover with gathered vine, oh!
And fallen stamens thereamong.
I plait cassia tendrils and twine, oh!
Some strands of ivy green and long.

I'll imitate the ancient sage, oh!
Not the vulgar world of today.
Though I displease the modern age, oh!
I will follow the ancient way.

I sigh and wipe away my tears, oh!
I'm grieved at a life full of woes.
Good and just, I hear only jeers, oh!
Morning and night I suffer blows.

I make a belt of grasses' sweet, oh!
And add to it clovers and thymes.
My heart tells me it's good and meet, oh!
I won't regret to die nine times.

怨灵修之浩荡兮,	只恨君王真是荒唐,
终不察夫民心。	始终不了解我的忠心。
众女嫉余之蛾眉兮,	美女们嫉妒我的丰姿,
谣诼谓余以善淫。	争相造谣说我是生性淫荡。
固时俗之工巧兮,	他们本是媚俗的人,
偭规矩而改错[①]。	违背规矩而改变法度。
背绳墨[②]以追曲兮,	抛弃了一定的准绳只图邪曲,
竞周容以为度。	争相以圆滑为处世法则。
忳[③]郁邑余侘傺兮,	真是忧郁、孤独、失望,
吾独穷困乎此时也。	我独独在这个时候如此困窘。
宁溘死以流亡兮,	我宁愿立刻死去而魂飞魄散,
余不忍为此态也!	也决不肯做出同流合污的丑态。
鸷鸟之不群兮,	鹰和隼不能够和凡鸟同群,
自前世而固然。	自古就是这样。
何方圜之能周兮,	哪有方和圆能够互相契合,
夫孰异道而相安?	政见不合哪能相安无事?
屈心而抑志兮,	我委屈着情怀,抑制着意气,
忍尤而攘诟。	忍受着谴责,排遣着羞耻。
伏清白以死直兮,	抱定清白的节操为正义而死,
固前圣之所厚。	本是前代的圣人之所称许。

① 偭(miǎn):违背。错,同"措",措施。
② 绳墨:画直线的工具。
③ 忳(tún):忧虑。

The Sacred One neglects his duty, oh!
He will not look into my heart.
The slanderers envy my beauty, oh!
They say I play licentious part.

The vulgar praise what is unfair, oh!
They reject common rules with pleasure
They like the crooked and not the square, oh!
Accommodation is their measure.

Downcast, depressed and sad am I, oh!
Alone I bear sufferings long.
I would rather in exile die, oh!
Than mingle with the vulgar throng.

The eagle cleaves alone the air, oh!
Since olden days it has been fleet.
The round cannot fit with the square, oh!
Who go different ways ne'er meet.

I curb my will and check my heart, oh!
Endure reproach as well as blame.
I'd die to play a righteous part, oh!
The ancient sages would bear no shame.

悔相道之不察兮,	后悔当初没有察看清楚我的道路,
延伫乎吾将反。	略为停顿我便要回头。
回朕车以复路兮,	把我的车马掉转走回老路,
及行迷之未远。	趁着迷途还不算远赶快罢休。

步余马于兰皋兮,	让我的马儿在长满兰草的水边徜徉,
驰椒丘且焉止息。	奔跑一阵后我们在椒丘上暂时休息。
进不入以离尤兮,	我不想再进谏以遭受祸殃,
退将复修吾初服。	我要退回故乡整理我的旧衣。

制芰荷以为衣兮,	我要把菱荷裁成上衣,
集芙蓉以为裳。	把荷花编织成下裳。
不吾知其亦已兮,	没人知道我也就算了吧,
苟余情其信芳。	只要我的内心是真正的芬芳。

高余冠之岌岌兮。	让头上的帽子耸起得高又高,
长余佩之陆离。	让项下的玉佩长长曳地,
芳与泽其杂糅兮,	芳香和污垢即使混在一起,
唯昭质其犹未亏。	清白的本质丝毫无损。

忽反顾以游目兮,	忽然又回过头四处张望,
将往观乎四荒。	打算往四方荒远之地观光。
佩缤纷其繁饰兮,	佩上五彩缤纷的装饰,
芳菲菲其弥章。	浓郁的花香向四方远扬。

Regretting I've gone a wrong way, oh!
I hesitate and will go back.
Before I go too far astray, oh!
I wheel my cab to former track.

I loose my horse by waterside, oh!
At Pepper Hill I take a rest.
I won't advance to turn the tide, oh!
I will retire to mend my vest.

I'll make a coat with lotus leaves, oh!
And patch my skirt with lilies white.
Unknown, I care not if it grieves, oh!
My heart will shed fragrance and light.

I raise my headdress towering high, oh!
And lengthen pendants sparkling long.
My fragrance 'mid the dirt won't die, oh!
My brilliancy ne'er wanes thereamong.

I look around and feast my sight, oh!
On scenes north and south, east and west.
My pendants seem all the more bright, oh!
My fragrance outshines all the rest.

民生各有所乐兮，	世上的人们各有所好，
余独好修以为常。	我独独爱好修洁习以为常。
虽体解吾犹未变兮，	即使粉身碎骨也不肯变更，
岂余心之可惩！	难道我的心还会怕受人威胁？

女嬃①之婵媛兮，	我的姐姐殷勤地替我操心，
申申其詈予曰：	她一再劝诫着我说：
鲧婞直以亡身兮，	鲧就是刚直而不顾性命，
终然夭乎羽之野。	终竟早夭在羽山下。

汝何博謇而好修兮，	你为什么总是要孤高而洁身自好，
纷独有此姱节？	偏偏一个人穿着这样的奇装？
薋菉葹②以盈室兮，	牡苞和臬耳堆满了屋子，
判独离而不服。	你却与众不同地远离它们。

众不可户说兮，	众人不能够一一地加以说服，
孰云察余之中情？	谁人能够看清我们的本心？
世并举而好朋兮，	世人都喜欢结党营私，
夫何茕独而不予听？	你为何宁愿孤独也不听我的劝？

依前圣以节中兮，	我按照先圣的言行节制性情，
喟凭心而历兹。	但遭遇这样的不公不禁悲愤填膺。
济沅湘以南征兮，	渡过了沅水和湘水走向南方，
就重华③而陈词：	我要到舜帝灵前诉说我的委屈。

---

① 女嬃（xū）：屈原的姐姐。一说，屈原的侍女。
② 薋（cí）：杂草堆积。菉（lù）、葹（shī）：都是普通的草。比喻小人之多充斥朝廷。
③ 重华：舜帝，相传死后葬在九嶷山。

All men delight in what they please, oh!
Alone I always love the beauty.
My body rent, my heart at ease, oh!
Can I change and neglect my duty?

My sister gently comes downcast, oh!
She warns me again and again:
The flood-fighter selfless, steadfast, oh!
By mountainside at last was slain.

Fond of beauty, why are you straight? oh!
Why hold alone your virtue high?
When thorns and weeds o'errun the State, oh!
Could you despise them and stand by?

You can't dissuade them one by one, oh!
Who would then understand your heart?
There're many cliques under the sun, oh!
Why hear me not and stand apart?

I follow sages of ancient day, oh!
I judge by heart from fall to spring.
I cross the streams and go south way, oh!
I state my case to ancient king:

启①《九辩》与《九歌》兮，　　夏启创作了《九辩》与《九歌》，
夏康娱以自纵。　　　　　　　太康便用它当作娱乐自行放纵。
不顾难以图后兮，　　　　　　毫无深远的谋虑以备后患，
五子用失乎家巷。　　　　　　因此五个儿子祸起萧墙。

羿淫游以佚畋兮，　　　　　　后羿沉溺于田猎，
又好射夫封狐②。　　　　　　喜欢射杀硕大的野狐。
固乱流其鲜终兮，　　　　　　淫乱之徒当没有好结果，
浞③又贪夫厥家。　　　　　　况臣子寒浞霸占了他的妻子。

浇④身被服强圉⑤兮，　　　　寒浞的儿子浇自恃武力，
纵欲而不忍。　　　　　　　　寻欢作乐放纵着自己，
日康娱而自忘兮，　　　　　　他每日里欢乐得忘乎其形，
厥首用夫颠陨。　　　　　　　终于失掉了他自己的脑袋。

夏桀之常违兮，　　　　　　　夏桀总是违背正道，
乃遂焉而逢殃。　　　　　　　到头来还是遭逢祸殃。
后辛⑥之菹醢⑦兮，　　　　　纣王把自己的忠良剁成肉酱，
殷宗用而不长。　　　　　　　殷朝的王位也因而不能久长。

---

① 启：夏启，大禹的儿子。
② 封狐：大狐狸。
③ 浞（zhuó）：寒浞，传说是后羿的臣子，指使家臣逢蒙杀死后羿，强占了后羿的妻子。
④ 浇（ào）：寒浇，寒浞的儿子。
⑤ 圉（yǔ）：防御。
⑥ 后辛：纣王。
⑦ 菹（zū）：酸菜。醢（hǎi）：肉酱。

The second king of Xia loved songs, oh!
He was indulged in his desire.
He heeded nor dangers nor wrongs, oh!
His five sons threw the land in fire.

The hunter loved each shot to tell, oh!"
Shooting fox, he led a wild life.
Such wantonness could not end well, oh!
His friend slew him and stole his wife.

The traitor's son with might and main, oh!
Did what he would without restraint.
All day long he sought pleasures vain, oh!
At last he lost his head blood-stained.

The last king of Xia's stormy age, oh!
Abused all laws and he lost his crown.
That of Shang burned alive his sage, oh!
His dynasty was overthrown.

汤、禹俨而祗①敬兮，	商汤和夏禹都很谨慎处世，
周论道而莫差。	周初的帝王也善于讲求理法，
举贤而授能兮，	他们都能在政治上举贤任能，
循绳墨而不颇。	遵守着法度规矩没有偏颇。

皇天无私阿兮，	上天真是公道无私，
览民德焉错辅。	看到了有德行就予以帮助。
夫维圣哲以茂行兮，	也正因为有德的圣人和贤士，
苟得用此下土。	才能让统治下的四海之滨成为乐土。

瞻前而顾后兮，	回顾过去展望未来，
相观民之计极。	我明白了人生的路径。
夫孰非义而可用兮？	不义的人不可以任用吗？
孰非善而可服？	不善的事不会为人服膺吗？

阽②余身而危死兮，	纵使是面临丧失性命的危险，
览余初其犹未悔。	我回顾过去也绝不反悔。
不量凿而正枘兮，	不度量凿孔就直接插楔子，
固前修以菹醢。	古代的贤人因此被剁成肉酱。

曾歔欷③余郁邑兮，	我是多么忧闷而呜咽哭泣，
哀朕时之不当。	哀怜自己生不逢时。
揽茹蕙以掩涕兮，	拿起柔软的蕙草擦干眼泪，
沾余襟之浪浪。	伤心的眼泪沾湿了衣襟。

① 祗：尊敬。
② 阽（diàn）：接近边缘即将堕落。
③ 歔欷（xū xī）：反复叹息。

Kings Tang and Yu full of respect, oh!
And that of Zhou went the right way.
The good and wise they did select, oh!
They followed the rule as kings may.

Heaven august was fair and square, oh!
It gave to ministers their due.
Only the sages were employed there, oh!
They might rule o'er the land in view.

Looking before and after then, oh!
I find the rules for livelihood.
None would employ those unjust men, oh!
Nor obey those who are not good.

I've risked my life and braved death, oh!
I don't regret I've held my ground.
The sage would lose his life and breath, oh!
Like square pegs unfit for holes round.

Melancholy and sad I stay, oh!
Why live I at a time that grieves?
With soft grass I wipe tears away, oh!
Which have streamed down and wetted my sleeves.

跪敷衽①以陈辞兮，　　　铺开前襟我跪下表述衷情，
耿吾既得此中正。　　　　心中耿耿心绪渐渐安宁。
驷玉虬以乘鹥②兮，　　　我要以玉虬为马驾车，
溘埃风余上征。　　　　　飘忽地离开尘世向那天上冉冉升去。

朝发轫③于苍梧兮，　　　清晨我从苍梧之野出发，
夕余至乎县圃。　　　　　晚上便落到昆仑山上的悬圃。
欲少留此灵琐兮，　　　　我想在这神灵门前逗留片刻，
日忽忽其将暮。　　　　　太阳匆匆地就要西下。

吾令羲和④弭节兮，　　　我便叫羲和把车慢慢地依节前行，
望崦嵫⑤而勿迫。　　　　不要让太阳迫近崦嵫。
路曼曼其修远兮，　　　　途程还十分长远，
吾将上下而求索。　　　　我要上天入地去寻索真理。

饮余马于咸池兮，　　　　姑且让我的马儿在咸池喝水，
总余辔⑥乎扶桑。　　　　让我的车子系上扶桑，
折若木以拂日兮，　　　　折取若木的丫枝遮蔽太阳，
聊逍遥以相羊⑦。　　　　姑且留在这儿逍遥徜徉。

---

① 敷衽（fū rèn）：跪下时把衣服的前襟铺在地面。
② 鹥（yī）：凤凰一类的鸟，有五彩羽毛。
③ 轫：放在车轮前的木头，以制止车轮滚动。
④ 羲和：神话传说中驾驭太阳的人，传说中他以六条龙为太阳驾车。
⑤ 崦嵫（yān zī）：传说中太阳落山之处。
⑥ 辔（pèi）：马缰绳。
⑦ 相羊：徜徉。

I kneel aground and plead my ease, oh!
My heart is glad to find the true.
Dragon and phoenix start my race, oh!
I rise on wind into the blue.

At dawn I leave the E'ergreen State, oh!
At dusk I reach the mountain's crest.
I halt before Celestial Gate, oh!
To see the sun sink in the west.

I bid the Driver of the Sun, oh!
To Holy Mountains slowly go.
My way ahead's a long, long one, oh!
I'll seek my Beauty high and low.

I drink my steeds in the Sun's Bath, oh!
I tie their reins to giant tree.
I break a branch to brush Sun's path, oh!
I wander for a while carefree.

前望舒使先驱兮，	想叫望舒替我做前驱，
后飞廉使奔属。	让风伯飞廉在后紧紧跟随。
鸾皇为余先戒兮，	鸾凰替我在前面警卫，
雷师告余以未具。	雷师走来告诉我还未准备就绪。
吾令凤鸟飞腾兮，	我便令凤凰展翅高飞，
继之以日夜。	日日夜夜不做停留。
飘风屯其相离兮，	旋风聚集着紧紧相连，
帅云霓而来御。	率领着云和霓对我表示欢迎。
纷总总其离合兮，	乱纷纷聚散不停，
斑陆离其上下。	或上或下光辉灿烂。
吾令帝阍①开关兮，	我命令天国的守卫把门打开，
倚阊阖②而望予。	他倚着天门对我不理不睬。
时暧暧其将罢兮，	时光匆匆天色已晚，
结幽兰而延伫。	我寄情幽兰而长久伫立。
世溷浊而不分兮，	世间是这样混浊而不辨贤愚，
好蔽美而嫉妒。	因为嫉妒而抹杀人的美德。
朝吾将济于白水兮，	等到天明时我渡过白水，
登阆风③而绁马。	我要登上那阆风山把马拴住。
忽反顾以流涕兮，	忽然回望我泪流满面，
哀高丘之无女。	可怜这天国再无神女可求。

① 阍（hūn）：守门人。帝阍，天宫的守门人。
② 阊阖（chāng hé）：天门。
③ 阆（làng）风：神话中的山名。

The Moon's Charioteer goes before, oh!
The curtain-rolling Wind runs after.
To clear the way the phoenixes soar, oh!
The Lord of Thunder bursts in laughter.

I order giant birds to fly, oh!
All day long, by night as by day.
The whirlwinds gather up on high, oh!
The rainbow greets me all the way.

They part and join in proper order, oh!
In various hues and up and down.
To open I bid Heaven's Porter, oh!
He looks at me with a deep frown.

The day grows dark, its end is night, oh!
Twining orchids, I linger there.
The beauty's oft viewed with green eye, oh!
The foul can't be told from the fair.

I tether steeds on Endless Peaks, oh!
After I crossed the Deathless Stream.
Gazing back, tears run down my cheeks, oh!
On high I find no beauty of my own.

溘吾游此春宫兮，　　　我飘忽地来到了春神的宫殿，
折琼枝以继佩。　　　　折下琼枝来点缀我的兰佩。
及荣华之未落兮，　　　趁着这琼枝上的瑶花还未飘零，
相下女之可诒。　　　　我要到下方寻找可以相赠的佳人。

吾令丰隆[①]乘云兮，　云师丰隆为我驾着云彩，
求宓[②]妃之所在。　　替我找寻宓妃的踪迹。
解佩纕以结言兮，　　　我把兰佩解下致意，
吾令蹇修以为理。　　　拜托了蹇修代表我去传情达意。

纷总总其离合兮，　　　开始总是忙碌奔波若即若离，
忽纬繣其难迁。　　　　忽然又执拗说难以说服对方。
夕归次于穷石兮，　　　她晚上回家在穷石过夜，
朝濯发乎洧盘。　　　　清晨在洧盘堆云梳头。

保厥美以骄傲兮，　　　她因为保存着美貌而骄傲，
日康娱以淫游。　　　　成天都欢乐着在外游玩。
虽信美而无礼兮，　　　面貌纵然娇艳但不守礼节，
来违弃而改求。　　　　我要丢弃她另做他求。

览相观于四极兮，　　　在天空中观遍了四极八荒，
周流乎天余乃下。　　　周游一番我又回到这下界。
望瑶台之偃蹇兮，　　　遥望巍峨的瑶台，
见有娀[③]之佚女。　　我看见了有娀氏的佳人。

① 丰隆：云神。
② 宓（fú）：神话中人名。
③ 有娀（sōng）：古代国名。

I visit Vernal Temple hall, oh!
Adorn my belt with jasper bough.
Before the jasper blossoms fall, oh!
I'll send them to my Beauty below.

I bid the Lord of Cloud above, oh!
To find a stream the Nymphean Queen.
I give my belt as pledge of love, oh!
To Lord of Dream as go-between.

She comes and goes, we meet and part, oh!
Irreconcilably, I deem.
She passes the night with her sweetheart, oh!
And washes her hair in the stream.

She's arrogant, though fair and bright, oh!
She is wanton beyond compare.
She's beautiful but impolite, oh!
I will seek a beauty elsewhere.

I look around from side to side, oh!
Go down after circling the sky,
And find the Swallow's beauteous bride, oh!
Alone in Jasper Tower high.

吾令鸩为媒兮，	我吩咐鸩鸟给我做媒，
鸩告余以不好。	鸩鸟告诉我说她不好。
雄鸠之鸣逝兮，	雄的斑鸠善于言辞远飞而去，
余犹恶其佻巧。	但我又嫌他实在轻薄佻巧。
心犹豫而狐疑兮，	我心里踌躇着而又狐疑，
欲自适而不可。	想要自己前去又觉得不妥。
凤皇既受诒兮，	凤凰已替我把礼物送她，
恐高辛之先我。	我怕高辛氏赶在我之前。
欲远集而无所止兮，	想去远方但又无可投靠，
聊浮游以逍遥。	我只能流浪着逍遥彷徨。
及少康之未家兮，	趁少康还没有结婚，
留有虞之二姚。	还留下有虞氏的两位姚姓美女。
理弱而媒拙兮，	但信使无能媒人又没有口才，
恐导言之不固。	我恐怕这次的求婚也是不成；
世溷浊而嫉贤兮，	人世间是混浊而嫉妒贤能，
好蔽美而称恶。	总喜欢隐人美德而说人过失。
闺中既以邃远兮，	这些美人的香闺既深邃而难于接近，
哲王又不寤。	英明的君王又始终不肯醒悟。
怀朕情而不发兮，	我满怀忠贞无处可诉，
余焉能忍与此终古！	我哪能够就这样忍耐着死去！

The falcon woos for me her love, oh!
He tells me that she is not good.
I bid the singing turtledove, oh!
He flies away with false birdhood.

I hesitate like fox in doubt, oh!
I'd go myself but that won't do.
With gifts the phoenix has set out, oh!
Lest before me my rival woo.

I take no rest and go misled, oh!
I rove and wander here and there.
If the young prince were not yet wed, oh!
I'd stay with his two ladies fair.

My clumsy match-maker, I fear, oh!
Cannot give convincing advice.
The foul, dark world will not revere, oh!
The fair and bright but praise the vice.

From inner hall kept far apart, oh!
The prince won't wake, though wise and fair.
To whom can I lay bare my heart? oh!
Can I go on like this fore'er?

索藑茅①以筳篿②兮，	我找来了灵草和细竹，
命灵氛③为余占之。	请求女巫灵氛为我占卜。
曰：两美其必合兮，	占辞道：男才女貌本是天配，
孰信修而慕之？	哪有真正的美人而没人爱他？

思九州之博大兮，	想想九州的广大，
岂唯是其有女？	难道只有这里有佳人？
曰：勉远逝而无狐疑兮，	又说：鼓励你去四方不要逡巡，
孰求美而释女？	又哪有寻求君子的佳人会把你丢下？

何所独无芳草兮？	天地间哪儿会没有香草呢？
尔何怀乎故宇？	你为什么一定要眷恋故乡？
世幽昧以眩曜兮，	这个世界是黑暗而又蒙昧，
孰云察余之善恶？	谁能够辨别出我的好坏？

民好恶其不同兮，	人们的好恶到底各不相同，
惟此党人其独异。	只有一帮小人特别怪异。
户服艾以盈要兮，	他们都拿些野蒿挂满腰间，
谓幽兰其不可佩。	偏要说芬芳的幽兰不可佩戴。

览察草木其犹未得兮，	连草木的好坏都还不能辨清，
岂珵④美之能当？	又怎么能评价美玉？
苏粪壤以充帏兮，	用粪土来充满香囊，
谓申椒其不芳。	偏要说申椒一点也不芳香。

① 藑（qióng）茅：一种仙草。
② 筳篿（tíng zhuān）：用来占卜的竹器。
③ 灵氛：古代占卜的人。
④ 珵（chéng）：美玉。

With magic herbs and slips of bamboo, oh!
I bid the witch for me to divine.
He says, Two beauties will meet, true, oh!
Who won't admire the fair and fine?

The Nine States are vast in and out, oh!
Can you find beauties only here?
Go far away and put off doubt, oh!
Beauty-lover will call you dear.

Where can you not find fragrant grass, oh!
Why linger in old neighborhood?
The world is dark, a dizzy mass, oh!
Who can tell evil from the good?

Likes and dislikes depend on taste, oh!
This gang appears strange and unfair.
They gird foul mugwort on their waist, oh!
And say orchids unfit to wear.

They cannot tell good plants from bad, oh!
How can they know the precious gem?
In filthy clothes they are clad, oh!
But pepper's fragrance they condemn.

欲从灵氛之吉占兮,	本打算听从这灵氛的吉言,
心犹豫而狐疑。	我心里踌躇着犹疑不决。
巫咸①将夕降兮,	听说巫咸将要在暮昏时降神,
怀椒糈②而要之。	我抱着香椒和精米前往接迎。

百神翳其备降兮,	众多神仙缥缈地降临,
九疑缤其并迎。	九嶷山的神仙纷纷前往迎接。
皇剡剡其扬灵兮,	神祇发出了无限的灵光显示真诚,
告余以吉故。	巫咸又告诉了我一些吉祥往事。

曰:勉升降以上下兮,	他说:你应该努力地上天下地索求,
求矩矱③之所同。	去追求意气相投的同道。
汤、禹严而求合兮,	商汤和夏禹都虔诚地寻求贤臣,
挚、咎繇④而能调。	终于得到了伊尹和皋陶。

苟中情其好修兮,	只要内心善良纯洁,
又何必用夫行媒?	没有媒介君臣也能遇合。
说操筑于傅岩兮,	傅说原本在傅岩筑墙,
武丁用而不疑。	武丁拜他为相毫不猜疑。

吕望之鼓刀兮,	姜子牙本是拿刀的屠夫,
遭周文而得举。	遇到周文王便得到举荐。
宁戚之讴歌兮,	宁戚一边唱歌一边敲击着牛角,
齐桓闻以该辅。	齐桓公听后便请他为宰相。

① 巫咸:古代神巫。
② 糈(xǔ):精米。
③ 矩矱(jǔ yuē):前面所说的规矩绳墨。
④ 咎繇(gāo yáo):皋陶,舜帝的贤臣。

I'd follow the witch's advice, oh!
But still I doubt and hesitate.
At dusk I prepare peppered rice, oh!
For the wizard to tell my fate.

All angels shade with wings the sky, oh!
Nine fairies come from Shady Peaks.
The wizard comes in splendor high, oh!
All lend their ear to what he speaks.

Go up and down, look high and low, oh!
For one who'd share your common fate!
As ancient kings share weal and woe, oh!
With ministers and magistrate.

If you love beauty above all, oh!
Why do you need a go-between?
A convict pounding earthen wall, oh!
Was employed by his sovereign.

A butcher brandished his knife, oh!
King Wen raised him to Master Great.
A cowherd sang and played his fife, oh!
Duke Huan made him Lord of the State.

及年岁之未晏兮，	趁着年岁还不老，
时亦犹其未央。	时光还很充裕。
恐鹈鴂①之先鸣兮，	只怕杜鹃早早鸣唱，
使夫百草为之不芳！	百草都为之枯萎。
何琼佩之偃蹇兮，	为何我的玉佩会黯然失色，
众薆然②而蔽之。	是因为小人们将它的光芒掩盖。
惟此党人之不谅兮，	这些结党营私的小人真不诚信，
恐嫉妒而折之。	恐怕是因为妒忌才会掩盖它的光芒。
时缤纷其变易兮，	世事纷乱变化无常，
又何可以淹留？	又怎么能长留此地？
兰芷变而不芳兮，	兰芷都已改变而失去芬芳，
荃蕙化而为茅。	荃蕙也都成了无用的茅草。
何昔日之芳草兮，	为何昔日的香草，
今直为此萧艾也。	现在都成了萧艾之流的贱草。
岂其有他故兮，	难道还有别的原因吗？
莫好修之害也！	都是它们不洁身自好啊！
余以兰为可恃兮，	我本以为香兰可以依靠，
羌无实而容长。	谁知它内无诚信虚有外表。
委厥美以从俗兮，	丢弃美好的品德追随媚俗，
苟得列乎众芳。	苟且排在众多芳草之列。

① 鹈鴂(tí jué)：杜鹃。
② 薆(ài)然：遮蔽的样子。

You're still in the prime of your years, oh!
Time has not yet run out, though fleet.
But autumn birds may cry in tears, oh!
And fragrant grass no longer sweet.

Your jasper branch gleams low and high, oh!
All try to darken it with shade.
On partisans you can't rely, oh!
Through envy they will make it fade.

The age disordered changes pell-mell, oh!
How can I linger here so long?
Sweet orchids have lost fragrant smell, oh!
Sweet grass turn to weeds stinking strong.

How can sweet plants of days gone by, oh!
Turn to weeds and wormwood unfair?
Is there another reason why? oh!
For beauty no one seems to care.

On orchids I thought to rely, oh!
They're not so good as they appear.
Beauty is spurned in vulgar eye, oh!
Weeds grow and rise in fragrant sphere.

椒专佞以慢慆兮，	香椒专横而傲慢，
樧①又欲充夫佩帏。	连茱萸也想填满香囊。
既干进而务入兮，	既然这么钻营求进，
又何芳之能祗？	又怎么能对芳华本有的品格抱有敬意？
固时俗之流从兮，	世人都会随波逐流，
又孰能无变化？	谁又能毫不动摇？
览椒兰其若兹兮，	看到香椒和兰草这样，
又况揭车与江离？	又何况揭车和江蓠呢？
惟兹佩之可贵兮，	只有我的玉佩值得尊敬，
委厥美而历兹。	经种种患难仍能坚持忠贞操守。
芳菲菲而难亏兮，	芬芳依旧丝毫不减，
芬至今犹未沬。	清香至今都还没有消失。
和调度以自娱兮，	我的格调与法度自相和谐，
聊浮游而求女。	姑且周游各地寻求佳人。
及余饰之方壮兮，	趁着我的服饰正华美繁艳，
周流观乎上下。	我要周游天上人间。
灵氛既告余以吉占兮，	灵氛既然把吉卦告诉了我，
历吉日乎吾将行。	选个吉日子我将上路。
折琼枝以为羞兮，	折下琼枝当作精美的佳肴，
精琼靡②以为粻③。	将美玉碾碎以当粮。

① 樧（shā）：茱萸。
② 靡（mí）：同"糜"，细屑。
③ 粻（zhāng）：粮食。

The pepper flatters and looks proud, oh!
It wants to fill a noble place.
It tries to climb upon the cloud, oh!
But it has nor fragrance nor grace.

All men do so on such a day, oh!
Who can remain unchanged at heart?
Orchid and pepper act this way, oh!
Let alone stream-sage and halt-cart.

I prize my jasper pendant rare, oh!
Despite what other people say.
It's flower-like, fragrant and fair, oh!
Its sweetness lingers still today.

To wear my pendant I take pleasure, oh!
In search of Beauty I will rove.
In an adorned dress which I treasure, oh!
I'll seek her below and above.

The witch foretold good luck for me, oh!
I choose to start on a day nice.
I eat the fruit on jasper tree, oh!
I grind fine jasper into rice.

为余驾飞龙兮，	请为我驾起飞龙，
杂瑶象以为车。	用美玉和象牙装饰我的车。
何离心之可同兮？	意见不合怎能共处，
吾将远逝以自疏。	我将独自踏上远游的征程。
邅①吾道夫昆仑兮，	我转道去往昆仑山，
路修远以周流。	路途遥远曲折回环。
扬云霓之晻蔼②兮，	车上的云旗遮蔽了太阳，
鸣玉鸾之啾啾。	玉制鸾铃的声音玎玎玲玲如凤鸣。
朝发轫于天津兮，	清晨我从天河出发，
夕余至乎西极。	傍晚我便来到了西方辽远之地。
凤皇翼其承旂③兮，	凤凰展翅接住我的旌旗，
高翱翔之翼翼。	飞得又高又整齐。
忽吾行此流沙兮，	忽然间我来到西北沙漠地带，
遵赤水而容与。	沿着赤水我一路徜徉。
麾蛟龙使梁津兮，	指挥蛟龙为我搭起桥梁，
诏西皇使涉予。	命令西皇将我送往对岸。
路修远以多艰兮，	路途遥远而艰辛，
腾众车使径待。	让众车行在小路等待我。
路不周④以左转兮，	经过不周山我向左转，
指西海以为期。	指定西海为相约地点。

① 邅（zhān）：转。
② 晻蔼（ǎn ǎi）：云气很旺盛的样子。
③ 旂（qí）：旗帜。
④ 不周：神话中的山名。

The flying dragons draw my cart, oh!
Bright with ivory on display.
The gang differs from me at heart, oh!
I'll leave them and go far away.

I turn to Kunlun Mountains high, oh!
The winding way is wide and long.
The rainbow banners veil the sky, oh!
The phoenix bells ring merry song.

At dawn I start from Heaven's Ford, oh!
At dusk I reach the Western End.
The phoenixes sing in accord, oh!
Their wings with rainbow banners blend.

I go across the Sandy Ridge, oh!
I rove along the River Red.
I bid a dragon serve as bridge, oh!
For me to cross and go ahead.

The way is perilous and long, oh!
I bid cars go another way.
I turn left round Mount Pillar Strong, oh!
"Let's meet at Western Sea," I say.

屯余车其千乘兮, 再把千乘车子集合起来,
齐玉轪而并驰。 玉轮并排一起向前。
驾八龙之婉婉兮, 驾车的八条龙蜿蜒游动,
载云旗之委蛇。 云霓般的旗帜随风飘荡。

抑志而弭节兮, 姑且压抑心志缓缓而行,
神高驰之邈邈。 但心神驰骋广阔遥远。
奏《九歌》而舞《韶》兮, 奏响《九歌》舞起《韶》,
聊假日以媮①乐。 姑且借着大好时光及时行乐。

陟升皇之赫戏兮, 皇祖的赫赫灵光升起光明一片,
忽临睨夫旧乡。 恍惚中猛然又看到了故乡。
仆夫悲余马怀兮, 仆人悲痛我的马也有所思,
蜷局顾而不行。 屈身犹豫着止步不前。

乱②曰:已矣哉! 尾声唱:算了吧!
国无人莫我知兮, 既然楚国没人理解我,
又何怀乎故都? 我又何必怀念故都?
既莫足与为美政兮, 既然不能和他们共同实施美政,
吾将从彭咸之所居! 我只好追随彭咸前去他的居所。

---

① 媮(yú):快乐。
② 乱:终篇的结语,尾声。

A thousand chariots in my train, oh!
On wheels of jade run side by side.
I drive eight dragon-steeds amain, oh!
Cloud banners spread like rising tide.

I slow down speed and curb my will, oh!
My spirit soars far, far away.
I sing nine songs and dance my fill, oh!
I steal the pleasure of a day.

I rise to see the splendid sky, oh!
I bow to find my home below.
My horses neigh and my glooms sigh, oh!
Looking back, they won't forward go.

Epilogue
Alas! none understands me in the State, oh!
Why regret me native village?
Since I can't rule my kingdom's fate, oh!
I'd drown myself like ancient sage.

九歌

东皇太一①

吉日兮辰良②，	吉日啊良辰，
穆③将愉兮上皇。	恭敬庄严悦上皇。
抚长剑兮玉珥④，	手抚镶玉环的剑柄，
璆⑤锵鸣兮琳琅。	身配宝玉玎玲响。
瑶席兮玉瑱，	瑶草席上以宝玉做着压席之物，
盍将把兮琼芳。	手捧馥郁芬芳的鲜花。
蕙肴蒸兮兰藉，	兰草垫着蕙草包裹的祭肉，
奠桂酒兮椒浆。	祭品里还有桂椒酿成的美酒。
扬枹兮拊鼓⑥，	扬起鼓槌敲起鼓，
疏缓节兮安歌，	节奏舒缓歌声安详。
陈竽瑟兮浩倡。	伴着竽瑟齐奏放声歌唱，
灵偃蹇兮姣服，	众巫身着华服舞翩跹，
芳菲菲兮满堂。	香气弥漫整座祭堂。
五音纷兮繁会，	音乐交织奏出动人旋律，
君欣欣兮乐康。	祝福上皇快乐安康。

① 东皇太一：楚国人心目中尊贵而至高无上的神灵，不仅主宰天地日月星辰，还是开天辟地的造化神。
② 辰良：良辰，为押韵而采用倒文。
③ 穆：恭敬。
④ 珥（ěr）：玉环，多装饰于剑柄。
⑤ 璆（qiú）：一种美玉。
⑥ 枹（fú）：也作"桴"，鼓槌。拊（fǔ）：击打。

The Nine Songs

The Almighty Lord of the East

Auspicious hour, oh! of lucky day!
With deep respect, oh! we worship our lord.
His jade pendants, oh! chime on display;
He holds the hilt, oh! of his long sword.

Jade weights fasten, oh! his mat divine
Adorned with gems, oh! and flowers sweet.
We pour pepper sauce, oh! and laurel wine
And serve in orchids, oh! the spiced meat.

We raise the rod, oh! to beat the drum;
The drumbeats rise, oh! into the cloud.
In slow rhythm, oh! we sing and hum;
To pipes and flutes, oh! we chant aloud.
In fair array, oh! our lord appears;
His fragrance fills, oh! the ritual hall.
Five sounds mingle, oh! and charm our ears;
Our lord is glad, oh! and gladdens all.

云中君[1]

浴兰汤[2]兮沐芳,　　　　用兰花水沐浴带来满身芬芳,
华采衣兮若英。　　　　美丽的衣裳如鲜花灿烂。
灵连蜷兮既留,　　　　神灵婉转啊流连不去,
烂昭昭兮未央。　　　　烂漫的神光照彻大地。

蹇[3]将憺兮寿宫,　　　　你将在天宫安住!
与日月兮齐光。　　　　和太阳月亮一同放射万丈光芒。
龙驾兮帝服,　　　　　驾着龙车啊穿着天帝般的衣服,
聊翱游兮周章。　　　　在天地之间遨游。

灵皇皇兮既降,　　　　伟大的云神已经降临,
猋[4]远举兮云中。　　　忽然又如旋风般远飞入云中。
览冀州兮有余,　　　　你的光芒岂止照临神州,
横四海兮焉穷。　　　　泽被四海永不穷尽。

思夫君兮太息,　　　　思念云神令我叹息,
极劳心兮忡忡。　　　　思来想去直忧心忡忡。

---

[1] 云中君:掌管雷雨的神仙。
[2] 兰汤:用兰花煎熬过的热水。
[3] 蹇(jiǎn):发语词。
[4] 猋(biāo):迅速。

To The God of Cloud

Bathed in orchid's, oh! sweet-scented dews
And dressed in robes, oh! of varied hues,
With fleecy hair, oh! you slowly rise
To beautify, oh! the morning skies.

In deathless hall, oh! you stay at noon;
Your whiteness rivals, oh! sun and moon.
The dragon is, oh! your charioteer;
You waft and wander, oh! far and near.

In silver drops, oh! you come with rain;
On wings of wind, oh! you rise again.
Upon the land, oh! you come with ease;
You float over, oh! and beyond four seas.

Longing for you, oh! I can't but sigh;
My yearning heart, oh! to you would fly.

湘君①

君不行兮夷犹②,	湘君啊！你为何犹豫不决,迟迟不去,
蹇谁留兮中洲?	你是为了谁在沙洲中逗留?
美要眇兮宜修③,	我把自己打扮得美丽动人,
沛④吾乘兮桂舟。	急忙划起我的桂木船儿去见你。
令沅湘兮无波,	沅水、湘水啊！不要起波澜,
使江水兮安流。	江水啊你缓缓地流淌。
望夫君兮未来,	翘首盼望的人儿不见踪影,
吹参差兮谁思?	吹起洞箫传递着谁的思愁?
驾飞龙兮北征,	划着飞龙船儿向北去,
邅⑤吾道兮洞庭。	百转千回啊我的船儿驶进了洞庭湖。
薜荔柏兮蕙绸,	用薜荔做帘子啊！蕙草做帐,
荪桡兮兰旌。	用荪草当桨啊！香兰为旌。
望涔阳兮极浦,	看那涔阳啊！在那遥远的水边,
横大江兮扬灵。	横越大江啊难挡心灵飞扬。
扬灵兮未极,	飞扬的心灵无处安放,
女婵媛兮为余太息!	连侍女都为我叹息。
横流涕兮潺湲⑥,	我的眼泪纵横流淌,
隐思君兮陫侧⑦!	对你的思念让我心痛神伤啊!

① 湘君：湘水的男神。
② 夷犹：犹豫不决。
③ 要眇（miǎo）：美丽，美好。宜修：修饰得恰到好处。
④ 沛：行动迅速。
⑤ 邅（zhān）：改变行程。
⑥ 潺湲（chán yuán）：水流的样子。
⑦ 陫侧：同"悱恻"，心神不宁。

To the Lord of River Xiang

Why don't you come, oh! still hesitating?
For whom on midway isle, oh! are you waiting?
Duly adorned, Oh! and fair, I float
On rapid stream, oh! my cassia boat.
I bid the waves, oh! more slowly go
And the river, oh! tranquilly flow.
I wait for you, oh! who have not come;
Playing my flute, oh! with grief I'm numb.

In dragon boat, oh! for north I make
And zigzag up, oh! to Dongting Lake,
Ivy behind, oh! lotus before,
Orchid for flag, oh! cedar for oar.
I gaze on the lake, oh! and its farthest side;
My soul can't cross, oh! the river wide.
Across the river, oh! I cannot fly;
For my distress, oh! my handmaids sigh.
My tears stream down, oh! and slowly flow;
Longing for you, oh! I hide my woe.

桂棹兮兰枻①，	桂树做桨啊！木兰为舵。
斲冰兮积雪。	斲碎冰块啊！冰屑如雪般纷飞。
采薜荔兮水中，	想到水中去采陆地生长的薜荔，
搴②芙蓉兮木末。	在树梢去采水里的荷花。
心不同兮媒劳，	心意不同，媒人也是徒劳；
恩不甚兮轻绝。	恩情不深，轻易便恩断义绝。
石濑兮浅浅，	石上的清泉，湍急地流淌；
飞龙兮翩翩。	飞龙船啊！翩翩掠过水面如飞鸟。
交不忠兮怨长，	交友不忠便长相怨恨，
期不信兮告余以不闲。	有约不守反而骗我说不得空闲。
朝骋骛兮江皋，	早上起来就往水边高地走，
夕弭节兮北渚。	到了黄昏还停留在北滩上。
鸟次兮屋上，	暮归的鸟儿栖息在屋檐上，
水周兮堂下。	流水在华堂前来回萦绕。
捐余玦③兮江中，	把我的玉玦抛入江水，
遗余佩兮澧浦。	将我的玉佩留在澧水畔。
采芳洲兮杜若，	我在香草丛生的洲上采摘杜若，
将以遗兮下女。	把它赠予陪侍女伴。
时不可兮再得，	时光一去不复返，
聊逍遥兮容与。	姑且逍遥地踱步盘桓。

① 棹（zhào）：船桨。枻（yì）：船舵。
② 搴（qiān）：手取。
③ 玦（jué）：玉玦。表示决断的意思。

With orchid rudder, oh! and cassia oar,
I break the ice, oh! and snow before,
As plucking ivy, oh! from the stream
Or lotus from trees, oh! in a dream.
The go-between, oh! cannot unite
Two divided hearts, oh! whose love is light,
As on a shallow stream, oh! a dragon boat,
Though its wings beat fast, oh! can't keep afloat.
Faithless as you're, oh! you deceive me;
Breaking our tryst, oh! you say you're not free.

At dawn I drive my cab, oh! by riverside;
At dusk on northern isle, oh! I stop my ride.
Under the eaves, oh! the birds reposed;
Around the house, oh! the river flows.
I throw in water, oh! my jasper rings
And cast away, oh! my offerings.
I pluck sweet flowers, oh! on the island
And give them to maids, oh! inferior hand.
For time once lost, oh! can't be found again;
From thinking of you, oh! I would refrain.

湘夫人[1]

帝子[2]降兮北渚，	公主降临在北边的沙滩上，
目眇眇兮愁予。	望而不见啊使我分外惆怅。
嫋嫋[3]兮秋风，	绵绵的秋风吹过，
洞庭波兮木叶下。	洞庭湖泛起波澜落叶飘旋。

白薠[4]兮骋望，	踏着白薠啊纵目期望，
与佳期兮夕张。	相约黄昏之时陈设帷帐。
鸟萃兮蘋中？	鸟儿啊为何集结水滨蘋草边，
罾[5]何为兮木上？	渔网啊又为什么挂在树梢上？

沅有茝兮澧有兰，	沅水里长有白芷啊！澧水里生着幽兰，
思公子兮未敢言。	我一心思念你啊却又不敢明言。
荒忽兮远望，	恍恍惚惚地向远处眺望，
观流水兮潺湲。	只见河水缓缓流淌。

麋何食兮庭中？	麋鹿觅食啊为何在庭院当中？
蛟何为兮水裔？	蛟龙戏水啊为什么竟在浅滩搁浅？
朝驰余马兮江皋，	清晨我驰骋在江边，
夕济兮西澨[6]。	傍晚渡河到西岸。

---

[1] 湘夫人：湘水的女神。
[2] 帝子：传说中尧的女儿，嫁给了舜，死后为湘水之神。
[3] 嫋嫋（niǎo niǎo）：风力细长的样子。
[4] 薠（fán）：一种秋天生长的水草。
[5] 罾（zēng）：渔网。
[6] 澨（shì）：水边。

To the Lady of River Xiang

Descend on northern isle, oh! my lady dear,
But I am grieved, oh! to see not clear.
The autumn breeze, oh! ceaselessly grieves
The Dongting waves, oh! with fallen leaves.

I gaze afar, oh! 'mid clovers white
And wait for our tryst, oh! in the twilight.
Among the reeds, oh! can birds be free?
What can a net do, oh! atop a tree?

White clover grows, oh! beside the creek;
I long for you, oh! but dare not speak.
I gaze afar, oh! my beloved one,
I only see, oh! rippling water run.

Could deer find food, oh! within the door?
What would a dragon do, oh! upon the shore?
At dawn by riverside, oh! I urge my steed;
Across the western stream, oh! at dusk I speed.

闻佳人兮召予，	似听见美人在向我召唤，
将腾驾兮偕逝。	想赶忙驾车和你相伴。
筑室兮水中，	把房子建在江水之间，
葺之兮荷盖。	用荷叶覆盖屋顶遮掩。
荪壁兮紫坛，	荪草装饰墙壁啊紫贝砌满庭院，
播芳椒兮成堂。	中堂里布满香椒的气息。
桂栋兮兰橑①，	用桂树做梁啊木兰为檐，
辛夷楣兮药房。	辛夷为门啊白芷铺满房间。
罔薜荔兮为帷，	编织薜荔啊作为帷帐，
擗蕙櫋兮既张。	用蕙草啊装饰帷帐。
白玉兮为镇，	洁白的美玉压在坐席上，
疏石兰兮为芳。	石兰散发出迷人的芬芳。
芷葺兮荷屋，	在荷叶的屋顶上再铺上芷草，
缭之兮杜衡。	房屋四周是杜衡的芳香。
合百草兮实庭，	庭院里摆满了花草啊，
建芳馨兮庑门。	花草的芳香啊在廊门缭绕。
九嶷缤兮并迎，	九嶷山上的诸神都来迎接，
灵之来兮如云。	神灵如行云般前来。
捐余袂②兮江中，	把我的夹袄抛入水中，
遗余褋③兮澧浦。	将我的外衣丢入澧水之源。

① 橑（liáo）：屋檐。
② 袂（mèi）：衣袖。
③ 褋（dié）：外衣。

For you bid me, oh! to come today;
Together we are, oh! to ride away.
A midstream palace, oh! shall soon be made;
Over its roof, oh! lotus weave a shade.

In purple court, oh! thyme decks the wall;
With fragrant pepper, oh! is spread the hall.
Pillars of cassia, oh! stand upright,
And rooms smell sweet, oh! with clover white.

We weave the ivy, oh! into a screen
And spread the ground, oh! with its leaves green.
The corner stones, oh! shall be white jade,
And fragrance of orchids, oh! shall never fade.

On lotus roof, oh! let vetch be found
And azaleas, oh! are fresh around.
The courtyard is filled, oh! with herbs so fair;
The corridor, oh! with perfume rare.

All gods will come, oh! from mountains high
Like rainbow clouds, oh! o'erspreading the sky.
I throw when I wake, oh! from my sweet dream,
My shirt with sleeves, oh! into the stream.

搴汀洲兮杜若，　　　　　　我在小洲上采摘杜若，
将以遗兮远者。　　　　　　用它送给远方的朋友。
时不可兮骤得，　　　　　　美好的时光总是难以立即得到，
聊逍遥兮容与。　　　　　　只能这般逍遥地松弛心灵。

大司命[1]

广开兮天门，　　　　　　　天官之门啊已然敞开，
纷吾乘兮玄云。　　　　　　我踏上了团团相接的乌云。
令飘风兮先驱，　　　　　　命令疾风为我先行开路，
使冻雨兮洒尘。　　　　　　暴雨啊为我清洗浮尘。

君迴翔兮以下，　　　　　　少司命如飞鸟般回环降临人间，
逾空桑兮从女。　　　　　　越过空桑山的时候我紧随在你身后。
纷总总兮九州，　　　　　　九州大地幅员广阔、人口众多，
何寿夭兮在予！　　　　　　人的寿命都掌握在我的手中。

高飞兮安翔，　　　　　　　飞翔得高而安闲，
乘清气兮御阴阳。　　　　　乘着清气啊掌握人间的生杀。
吾与君兮斋速，　　　　　　我和你齐头并进，
导帝之兮九坑。　　　　　　引导天帝你直达九州山冈。

灵衣兮被被，　　　　　　　云霞的衣服随风飘荡，
玉佩兮陆离[2]。　　　　　　玉佩散发出离奇的光芒。
壹阴兮壹阳，　　　　　　　世间万物阴阳生成之理，
众莫知兮余所为。　　　　　大家都猜不出我的行藏。

① 大司命：掌管人类寿夭之神。
② 陆离：形容很长。

I pluck sweet flowers, oh! upon the bay;
I'd give to strangers, oh! far, far away.
For time once lost, oh! can't be found again;
From thinking of you, oh! I would refrain.

The Great Lord of Fate

Open wide, wide, oh! the Heaven's door!
I will descend, oh! on cloud blue-black.
I bid whirlwind, oh! to go before
And icy rain, oh! to wash the track.

The lord in flight, oh! comes into view.
I'll cross mountains, oh! to follow you.
The young and old, oh! of the Nine Lands,
Your life or death, oh! is in my hands.

I soar up high, oh! serene in flight;
I ride on air, oh! on shade and light.
I will speed up, oh! with our lord divine;
I will lead him, oh! to holy peaks nine.

My cloudlike dress, oh! floats in the breeze;
My pendants hang, oh! in rainbow hue.
I control light, oh! and shade with ease.
The people know not, oh! what I will do.

折疏麻兮瑶华，	折取的神麻花啊如白玉般洁白无瑕，
将以遗兮离居。	我要将它送给远方的朋友。
老冉冉兮既极，	年华渐渐地老去，
不寖[1]近兮愈疏。	不再亲近就愈加疏远了。

乘龙兮辚辚，	坐上龙车啊车声辚辚，
高驰兮冲天。	驰骋高空冲入云霄。
结桂枝兮延伫[2]，	我手拈桂枝助力凝望，
羌愈思兮愁人。	为何思念让人更加心烦。

愁人兮奈何！	忧愁难耐却又无可奈何，
愿若今兮无亏。	但愿以后能像今天这样恩情圆满。
固人命兮有当，	人的寿命固然各有长有短，
孰离合兮可为？	人的聚散离合又有谁能预料？

少司命[3]

秋兰兮麋芜[4]，	秋日的兰草和细叶芎䓖，
罗生兮堂下。	遍生在神堂之下。
绿叶兮素枝，	绿色的叶啊白色的花，
芳菲菲兮袭予。	芳香扑鼻沁人心脾。
夫人自有兮美子，	世人自有美好的儿女，
荪[5]何以兮愁苦？	为何要替万民愁苦？

① 寖（jìn）：逐渐。
② 延伫：长久站立。
③ 少司命：掌管人间子嗣的神。
④ 麋芜：一种香草。
⑤ 荪（sūn）：指天帝。

Of Holy Hemp, oh! I pluck the flower
To give to our lord, oh! going away.
Old age draws nearer, oh! with each passing hour.
The farther he's, oh! the sadder I stay.

My dragon chariot, oh! rumbles loud.
I drive my steeds, oh! into the cloud.
Laurel in hand, oh! I wait and sigh;
The longer I wait, oh! the sadder am I.

With a broken heart, oh! what can I do?
Better keep fit, oh! in mind and heart!
Each man is fated, oh! to have his due;
It's not up to us, oh! to meet or part.

The Young Goddess of Fate

Autumn orchids, oh! and flowers sweet
Like silver stars, oh! grow at our feet.
Their leaves are green, oh! and blossoms white;
Fragrance assails us, oh! left and right.
All women have, oh! fair ones they love.
Why are you sad, oh! lonely above?

秋兰兮青青，	秋天的兰花繁茂青翠，
绿叶兮紫茎。	青青叶间掩映着花的紫茎。
满堂兮美人，	神堂上都是美人，
忽独与余兮目成。	忽然都向我投来多情的眼神。
入不言兮出不辞，	你来去都不言语一声，
乘回风兮载云旗①。	乘着回旋之风，以云霞为旌。
悲莫悲兮生别离，	人生最大的悲痛啊莫过于生生的别离，
乐莫乐兮新相知。	人生最大的欢喜啊莫过于遇到了新相识。
荷衣兮蕙带，	用荷做衣裳啊用蕙草做飘带，
倏而来兮忽而逝。	来也匆匆，去也匆匆。
夕宿兮帝郊，	暮昏时你停留在天帝的郊野，
君谁须兮云之际？	谁为你在云端守候？
与女沐兮咸池，	我和你一起在咸池里洗头发，
晞②女发兮阳之阿。	在旸谷晾干头发。
望美人兮未来，	盼望美人啊却没有到来，
临风怳③兮浩歌。	只好临风高歌抒发郁闷之情。
孔盖兮翠旌，	用孔雀翎做车盖啊翠鸟羽毛做旌旗，
登九天兮抚彗星。	登上九天把彗星抚持。
竦长剑兮拥幼艾，	你一手举长剑啊一手抱着孩童，
荪独宜兮为民正！	只有你才是万民的主宰。

① 云旗：以云为旗帜。
② 晞（xī）：晒干。
③ 怳（huǎng）：失意的样子。

Autumn orchids, oh! are lush with shoots;
Their leaves so green, oh! with purple roots.
The fair ones fill, oh! the hall with glee.
Why is amorous look, oh! but cast on me?

Wordless you come, oh! wordless you go
As cloud-flags spread, oh! and whirlwinds blow.
None is so sad, oh! as those who part;
Nor so happy, oh! as new sweetheart.

In lotus dress, oh! a belt at the waist,
Suddenly you come, oh! and you go in haste.
At dusk you lodge, oh! on Heaven's plain.
Why on the clouds, oh! should you remain?

I'd bathe with you, oh! in pools divine
And dry your hair, oh! in the sunshine.
But you won't come, oh! and I wait long;
Lost in the wind, oh! I sing a song.

With plumed banners, oh! and peacock canopy,
You grasp Broom Star, oh! to sweep the sky.
You wield long sword, oh! to grasp the young;
You are the one, oh! to right the wrong.

东君①

暾②将出兮东方,　　　　　　　一轮旭日将要升起在东方,
照吾槛兮扶桑。　　　　　　　照亮我的栏杆与神木扶桑。
抚余马兮安驱,　　　　　　　轻拍着我的车马啊缓缓前行,
夜皎皎兮既明。　　　　　　　自皎皎月夜直到黎明。

驾龙辀兮乘雷,　　　　　　　驾驶着龙车啊伴着隆隆雷声,
载云旗兮委蛇。　　　　　　　载着如旗的云朵舒卷飘拂。
长太息兮将上,　　　　　　　长叹一声啊向天空飞腾,
心低佪兮顾怀。　　　　　　　留恋家乡令我徘徊不定。

羌声色兮娱人,　　　　　　　歌舞声色让人快乐,
观者憺兮忘归。　　　　　　　入迷的观众几乎忘记了归路。
縆③瑟兮交鼓,　　　　　　　调紧瑟弦啊鼓声交错,
箫钟兮瑶簴;　　　　　　　　撞起大钟啊钟架不定。

鸣篪④兮吹竽,　　　　　　　鸣响竹篪来又吹笙,
思灵保兮贤姱。　　　　　　　想起神巫灵保是多么贤德。
翾飞兮翠⑤曾,　　　　　　　飘摇的舞姿啊赛过飞翔的翠鸟,
展诗兮会舞。　　　　　　　　吟诵诗歌吧我们一起舞蹈。

---

① 东君:日神,驾驭太阳之神。
② 暾(tūn):将出的太阳。
③ 縆(gēng):拉紧琴弦。
④ 篪(chí):一种竹制吹奏的乐器。
⑤ 翾(xuān):小飞轻扬的样子。翠:翠鸟。

The God of the Sun

Before my light, oh! dawns in the east,
I take a bath, oh! by Sacred Tree.
I stroke my steed, oh! with reins released;
The night brightens, oh! the day set free.

My dragon car, oh! is drawn by thunder;
My cloud-flags wave, oh! and undulate.
I sigh, go up, oh! and then look under,
My heart lingers, oh! I hesitate.

For ears and eyes, oh! what great delight!
Those who behold, oh! forget their land.
"Smite zither strings, oh! which are made tight,
And strike the bells, oh! till rocks their stand."

They play the flutes, oh! and the pipes blow.
The witch dances, oh! so bright and fair
As a green bird, oh! flies high and low.
All sing in glee, oh! and dance in pair.

应律兮合节,　　　　　　　和着旋律啊和着节拍真和谐,
灵之来兮蔽日。　　　　　神灵纷纭而至把太阳光都掩蔽。
青云衣兮白霓裳,　　　　用青色的浮云做衣啊白色的霓虹做裳,
举长矢兮射天狼[①]。　　举起长弓射向天狼星。

操余弧兮反沦降,　　　　抓起我的弯弓啊阻遏灾祸下降,
援北斗兮酌桂浆。　　　　拿起形如勺的北斗斟满桂花佳酿。
撰余辔兮高驰翔,　　　　拉着缰绳啊我要向高空飞翔,
杳[②]冥冥兮以东行。　　趁着夜色茫茫我又要去往东方。

河伯

与女游兮九河,　　　　　和你一起在黄河游玩,
冲风起兮横波。　　　　　旋风掀起巨大的波澜。
乘水车兮荷盖,　　　　　乘坐的水车荷叶为盖,
驾两龙兮骖螭。　　　　　驾驶着两条龙啊再配上两条螭。

登昆仑兮四望,　　　　　登上昆仑山四下张望,
心飞扬兮浩荡。　　　　　心情澎湃胸襟宽广。
日将暮兮怅忘归,　　　　天色将晚我竟忘记了归程,
惟极浦兮寤怀。　　　　　只有遥远的水尽头让我寤寐难安。

鱼鳞屋兮龙堂,　　　　　鱼鳞做房,蛟龙绕梁。
紫贝阙兮朱宫。　　　　　用紫贝砌宫门,朱丹饰墙。
灵何为兮水中?　　　　　神灵啊!你为什么孤独地住在水中央?

① 天狼:星宿的名称。
② 杳:深远幽暗。

All in accord, oh! to drums keep time;
The fairies come, oh! and shade the sun
In rainbow white, oh! and cloud sublime.
I shoot the Wolf, oh! it is undone.

I downward sink, oh! and grasp the Bow;
The Dipper's used, oh! to ladle wine.
I hold my reins, oh! by night I go,
For in the east, oh! at dawn I'll shine.

The God of the River

On rivers nine, oh! with you I roam
The whirlwinds rise, oh! and billows foam.
My water chariot, oh! lotus-canopied,
Two dragon-steeds, oh! run side by side.

On Mount Kunlun, oh! I look around;
My heart surges up, oh! beyond the bounds.
Homesick at dusk, oh! why not go back?
I gaze afar, oh! to find lost track.

You've fish-scaled house, oh! and dragon's hall,
Purple towers, oh! and pearly wall.
What would you do, oh! lord, after all?

乘白鼋①兮逐文鱼,	乘着白鼋鲤鱼追逐身旁。
与女游兮河之渚,	和你一起在河洲上游玩,
流澌纷兮将来下。	流水悠悠地从脚下流过。

子交手兮东行,	你拱手作别向东远行,
送美人兮南浦。	我默默地送你上南岸。
波滔滔兮来迎,	波涛汹涌将你迎接,
鱼鳞鳞兮媵②予。	列队成行的鱼儿伴着我为你张望。

山鬼③

若有人兮山之阿,	仿佛有人从那山隈经过,
被薜荔兮带女罗。	披着薜荔做的衣裳,系上女萝为腰带。
既含睇④兮又宜笑,	含情脉脉嫣然一笑,
子慕予兮善窈窕。	你将羡慕我窈窕婀娜。

乘赤豹⑤兮从文狸,	驾着赤色豹子文狸紧随其后,
辛夷车兮结桂旗。	用辛夷做车桂枝为旗。
被石兰兮带杜衡,	披着石兰杜衡为带,
折芳馨兮遗所思。	摘取香花打算送给情人。

---

① 鼋(yuán):大鳖。
② 媵(yìng):跟从,陪伴。
③ 山鬼:山神。
④ 含睇(dì):含情微视。
⑤ 赤豹:毛赤而纹黑的豹子。

I'd chase spotted fish, oh! on turtle white,
And roam with you, oh! on sands in delight,
while melted ice, oh! drifts left and right.

Let us go eastward, oh! hand in hand!
I'll see you off, oh! for southern land.
Waves on waves rise, oh! to welcome you;
Fish on fish leap, oh! to bid adieu.

The Goddess of the Mountain

In mountains deep, oh! looms a fair lass,
In ivy leaves, oh! girt with sweet grass.
Amorous looks, oh ! and smiling eyes,
For such a beauty, oh! there's none but sighs.

Laurel flags spread, oh! over fragrant cars
Drawn by leopards, oh! dotted with stars.
Orchids as belt, oh! and crown above,
She plucks sweet blooms, oh! for her dear love.

余处幽篁兮终不见天,	我住在竹林深处不见天日,
路险难兮独后来。	路途险阻而姗姗来迟。
表独立兮山之上,	我孤独地站在高山之巅,
云容容兮而在下。	浮云在我的脚下舒卷飘荡。
杳冥冥兮羌昼晦,	眼前白昼深沉黑暗不见阳光,
东风飘兮神灵雨。	东风忽然而至,点点雨滴降临。
留灵修兮憺忘归,	我为你在此停留忘了归程,
岁既晏兮孰华予?	年华老去有谁能唤回青春。
采三秀①兮於山间,	采摘巫山间的益寿芝草,
石磊磊兮葛蔓蔓。	山石和野葛四处缠蔓盘绕。
怨公子兮怅忘归,	我怨恨你啊怅然忘记归去,
君思我兮不得闲。	你也许思念我却没空赴约。
山中人兮芳杜若,	山中的女子如杜若的芳枝,
饮石泉兮荫松柏。	饮着山泉在松柏树底等候。
君思我兮然疑作。	对你的思念令我疑神疑鬼,
雷填填兮雨冥冥,	听那雷声鸣响苦雨飘零。
猿啾啾兮狖夜鸣。	猿声啾啾笼罩夜幕沉沉,
风飒飒兮木萧萧,	飒飒风声里草木萧萧作响,
思公子兮徒离忧②。	为了思念女神徒然横生忧愁。

① 三秀:灵芝草。
② 离忧:遭受忧愁。

The bamboo grove, oh! obscures the day;
I come too late, oh! hard is the way.
Standing alone, oh! on mountain proud,
I see below, oh! a sea of cloud.

The day is dark, oh! as dark as night;
The east wind blows, oh! rain blurs the sight.
Waiting for you, oh! I forget hours.
Late in the year, oh! who'd give me flowers?

Amid the mountains, oh! I seek herbs divine,
Here rock on rock, oh! there vine on vine.
Longing for you, oh! I forget to return.
Are you too busy, oh! for me to yearn?

Amid the mountains, oh! I feel not at ease;
I drink from springs, oh! beneath pine trees.
From missing you, oh! I am not free;
I doubt if you, oh! are missing me.
Thunder rumbles, oh! rain blurs the eye;
At night apes wail, oh! and monkeys cry.
Winds sigh and sough, oh! leaves fall in showers.
Longing for you, oh! how to pass lonely hours!

国殇[1]

操吴戈[2]兮披犀甲,	手持吴戈身披犀甲,
车错毂[3]兮短兵接。	战车交错短兵相接。
旌蔽日兮敌若云,	旌旗蔽日敌兵如云,
矢交坠兮士争先。	箭如雨下战士骁勇。
凌余阵兮躐[4]余行,	侵我阵地乱我阵列,
左骖殪[5]兮右刃伤。	左骖毙命右骖受刀伤。
霾[6]两轮兮絷[7]四马,	两轮深陷绊住四马,
援玉枹兮击鸣鼓。	主帅举槌猛敲战鼓。
天时怼兮威灵怒,	杀声震天鬼神震怒,
严杀尽兮弃原野。	全军覆没尸横遍野。
出不入兮往不反,	壮士一去永不回头,
平原忽兮路超远。	平原之路遥遥无边。
带长剑兮挟秦弓,	佩剑持弓横行沙场,
首身离兮心不惩[8]。	身首异处壮心不已。
诚既勇兮又以武,	顽强勇敢英武过人,
终刚强兮不可凌。	刚强坚毅不可凌辱。
身既死兮神以灵,	人虽死去精神长存,
魂魄毅兮为鬼雄!	魂魄当为鬼中雄杰。

[1] 国殇:祭祀为国捐躯的将士的祭歌。殇,未成年而死或死于野外。
[2] 吴戈:吴国生产的戈矛,比较锋利。
[3] 毂(gǔ):车轮和轴的连接处。
[4] 躐(liè):践踏。
[5] 殪(yì):死亡。
[6] 霾(mái):埋的假借词。
[7] 絷(zhí):绊住。
[8] 惩:悔恨。

For Those Fallen for the Country

We take our southern spears, oh! and don our coats of mail;
When chariot axes clash, oh! with daggers we assail.
Banners obscure the sun, oh! the foe roll up like cloud;
Arrows shower crisscross, oh! forward press our men proud.
Our line is broken through, oh! our position overrun;
My left-hand horse is killed, oh! and wounded my right-hand one.
The corpses block my wheels, oh! my chariot is stayed;
I beat the sounding drum, oh! in vain with rods of jade.
By angry Power's order, oh! our warriors are slain;
Their corpses and horses strew, oh! here and there on the plain.

They came out not to return, oh! to where they belong;
The battlefield's so vast, oh! their homeward way so long.
With their long sword in hand, oh! and bows captured from the west,
Though head and body sever, oh! their heart's not repressed,
They were indeed courageous, oh! and ready to fight,
And steadfast to the end, oh! undaunted by armed might.
Their spirit is deathless, oh! although their blood was shed;
Captains among the ghosts, oh! heroes among the dead!

礼魂

成礼兮会鼓,	礼仪圆满击鼓庆祝,
传芭①兮代舞。	传花嬉戏啊轮番舞蹈。
姱②女倡兮容与。	美女歌声从容安详,
春兰兮秋菊,	春有兰花啊秋有菊花,
长无绝兮终古。	千秋万代永不断绝。

---

① 芭:同"葩",初开的鲜花。
② 姱(kuā):美好。

The Last Sacrifice

The rites performed, oh! all beat the drum;
Flowers passed round, oh! fair dancers come,
With drums keep pace, oh! and sing with grace.
From spring to fall, oh! flowers will blow;
From age to age, oh! the rites will go.

天问[1]

曰：遂古之初，	请问：远古开始的情形，
谁传道之？	究竟是谁传播下来的？
上下未形，	那时天地尚未形成，
何由考之？	从何处得以成形？

冥昭[2]瞢暗，	天地之间昼夜不分，
谁能极之？	又有谁能将它辨认清楚？
冯翼[3]惟像，	混沌空蒙的模样，
何以识之？	到底根据什么来辨别？

明明暗暗，	宇宙间昼夜交替时暗时明，
惟时何为？	究竟又是怎样产生？
阴阳三合，	阴阳和元气三者结合产生万物，
何本何化？	它们又以谁为其本源呢？

圆则九重，	天为圆形高达九层，
孰营度之？	是谁在设计规划？
惟兹何功？	这项工程是如此伟大，
孰初作之？	到底是谁开始最初的创建？

---

[1] 天问：问天。
[2] 冥昭：黑夜和白昼。
[3] 冯（píng）翼：充盛。

Asking Heaven

Who could tell us at last
When did begin the past?
How could anyone know
The formless high and low?

Who knows where darkness did end
When light and shade did blend?
How to imagine things
In air but not on wings?

How could darkness turn bright
When was day divided from night?
How did light and shade strange
Originate and change?

Who did take measure of
The Ninth Heaven above?
Who built the firmament
Of such boundless extent?

斡维①焉系?	天体旋转的枢纽到底在哪儿?
天极焉加?	天之边际又在何方?
八柱②何当?	八柱撑天立于何处?
东南何亏?	地的东南角为什么会倾倒?
九天之际,	九重天的边际,
安放安属?	究竟怎样连接又如何安放?
隅隈③多有,	天边有多少角落,
谁知其数?	有谁知道它的数量吗?
天何所沓④?	天体运行在何处与地重合?
十二焉分⑤?	十二个时辰又是怎么划分?
日月安属?	太阳月亮是怎样挂在天上?
列星安陈?	灿烂星辰又为何布置成这样?
出自汤谷,	太阳每天在汤谷升起,
次于蒙汜。	晚上停留在蒙汜。
自明及晦,	一天自明而暗,
所行几里?	究竟运行多少里?

① 斡(wò):旋转的枢纽,古人认为天是可以旋转的。维:绳子,古人认为地是不动的。
② 八柱:支撑天的八根柱子,古人认为天是由八根柱子撑起来的。
③ 隈(yú):与"隅"字同义,指角落。
④ 沓:重合。
⑤ 十二焉分:古人将天分为十二部分,即子、丑、寅、卯、辰、巳、午、未、申、酉、戌、亥。

What string could bind the sky?
How was the Pole raised high?
Where did Eight Pillars stand?
Why lowered southeast land?

How did Nine Spheres divide
And join up side by side?
How many ins and outs
Of Heaven's whereabouts?

On what rests Heaven wide?
How did twelve hours divide?
And sun and moon shed rays
And stars in fine arrays?

Rising from Vale of Beam
And setting by Dark Stream,
How many leagues had run
From dawn till dusk the sun?

夜光何德,	月亮具有怎样的品德,
死则又育?	月圆月缺竟死而复生。
厥利维何,	月中黑影那是何物,
而顾菟在腹?	是否兔子腹中藏身?

女岐①无合,	女岐没有丈夫,
夫焉取九子?	又为何能生出九个儿子?
伯强何处?	伯强究竟住在什么地方啊?
惠气安在?	祥瑞之气又在何方?

何阖而晦?	什么关闭了便天黑?
何开而明?	什么开启了便天明?
角宿②未旦,	东方没有明亮之前,
曜灵③安藏?	太阳在哪里躲藏?

不任汩④鸿,	既然鲧不懂得治理洪水,
师何以尚之?	众人为何要推举他?
佥⑤曰"何忧",	人人都说这有何可忧,
何不课而行之?	为什么不让他去试试呢?

① 女岐:神女,传说没有婚配便生下九个儿子。
② 角宿(xiù):二十八星宿之一,晚上出现在东方。
③ 曜(yào)灵:太阳。
④ 汩(gǔ):治理。
⑤ 佥(qiān):都。

How could the moon be bright
And wax and wane by night?
What advantage was there
To keep in it a hare?

Unwed was Star Divine.
How could she have sons nine?
Where is Wind Star who frees
The freshening warm breeze?

What door, when closed, made night
And, when opened, gave light?
Where behind the closed gate
Did the sun hide and wait?

To stem the flood Kun was unfit.
Why was he ordered to do it?
"No one cares for the worst.
Why not let Kun try first?"

鸱①龟曳衔，	鸱龟或曳或衔而相助，
鲧②何听焉？	鲧具有何神圣德行？
顺欲成功，	他也想把洪水治理好，
帝何刑焉？	尧又为何非将他惩罚呢？
永遏在羽山，	把他永久囚禁在羽山上，
夫何三年不施？	为何过了三年仍不放他？
伯禹腹鲧，	大禹从鲧的腹中生出来，
夫何以变化？	治水之法如何变化？
纂就前绪，	大禹集成了鲧的事业，
遂成考功。	并终于完成了乃父的功业。
何续初继业，	他为何继承鲧的事业，
而厥谋不同？	又采取了什么不同的治水方法呢？
洪泉极深，	洪水如渊异常深邃，
何以窴之？	大禹又怎么能堵住呢？
地方九则，	神州土地沃瘠九等，
何以坟之？	这有什么依据呢？
河海应龙③，	应龙是怎么样规划的呢？
何尽何历？	江河究竟流过哪些地方呢？

① 鸱（chī）：猫头鹰一类的鸟。
② 鲧（gǔn）：大禹的父亲。
③ 应（yìng）龙：一种有翅膀的龙。

Bird-turtles made a sign.
How could Gun think it divine?
He would not sink but swim.
Why should the Lord punish him?

For three years cast away,
Why did his corpse not decay?
How was his son Yu born
Out of his belly torn?

How did his son succeed
In accomplishing his deed?
How did the plan begun
Become a different one?

How did Yu try to fill
Up the deep flood at will?
To build riverbanks and
To protect land on land?
How did the Dragon's tail
Braze on the earth a trail?
How did the rivers flow
And towards oceans go?

鲧何所营？	鲧治水的时候究竟做了什么？
禹何所成？	大禹又是怎样成功的呢？
康回①冯怒，	共工怒触不周山，
地何故以东南倾？	东南方大地为什么倾斜？
九州安错？	大地依据什么划分为九州？
川谷何洿②？	江河水道如何疏浚？
东流不溢，	百川东入海永不溢出，
孰知其故？	谁知道其中的道理呢？
东西南北，	东西南北之间的距离，
其修孰多？	究竟哪个更长呢？
南北顺椭，	南北方的地形狭长，
其衍几何？	它比东西方的地形长多少？
昆仑县圃，	昆仑山山顶县圃胜境，
其尻安在？	其山脊的末尾在何处？
增城九重，	昆仑山上增加的九层增城，
其高几里？	究竟有多高？
四方之门，	昆仑山上的四面大门，
其谁从焉？	有谁从此进进出出？
西北辟启，	打开昆仑山的西北门，
何气通焉？	什么风从此门通过？

---

① 康回：共工，传说共工和颛顼（zhuān xū）争夺帝位，怒而触不周之山。
② 洿（wū）：低洼地方掘挖成水池。

How could Yu well succeed
In Gun's miscarried deed?
And the Fury o'ergrown
Knock the southeast Peak down?

Why are the nine lands dry
And wet the valleys lie?
Who knows why streams east go
And seas never overflow?

How far is east to west
Or north to southern crest?
Is it longer than wide
From north to southern side?

The Hanging Garden's high.
But where did its base lie?
Kunlun walls were ninefold.
How high were they, all told?

Who went with rapid strides
Through the gates in four sides?
And what wind passed before
The open northwest door?

日安不到?	世上没有太阳照不到的地方,
烛龙①何照?	那么烛龙又怎样有光照耀?
羲和之未扬,	羲和还没有扬起驾驭太阳的皮鞭,
若华何光?	若木的花又怎么发光?
何所冬暖?	什么地方的冬天温暖?
何所夏寒?	什么地方的夏天寒冷?
焉有石林?	哪里的石头像树林一样?
何兽能言?	什么野兽能够说话?
焉有虬②龙,	什么地方有无角的虬龙,
负熊以游?	背着熊遨游?
雄虺③九首,	雄性虺蛇有九个头颅,
倏忽焉在?	飞速地窜来窜去在什么地方?
何所不死?	什么地方是不死之国?
长人何守?	长寿的人有何神术?
靡蓱九衢,	神异的萍草无数分叉盘错,
枲④华安居?	什么地方能生长出奇特的枲花?
一蛇吞象,	一条巨蛇能把大象吞下,
厥大何如?	它究竟该有多大啊?

① 烛龙:传说中的神龙。
② 虬:没有角的龙。
③ 虺(huǐ):凶恶的毒蛇。
④ 枲(xǐ):麻的别名。

Could Torch Dragon shed light
When the sun was not bright?
How could flowers divine
Before the sun's chariot shine?

Where's winter warm and old?
Where's summer young and cold?
Where could be found stone trees?
Where could beasts talk with ease?

Where's Dragon without horn
Swimming with bears airborne?
Where's the nine-headed Snake
Moving without a break?
Where would man never die?
Where lived giants on high?

Where's the nine-branched weed
And the hemp's blooming seed?
What serpent could devour
An elephant beyond its power?

黑水玄趾,	黑水在何处,
三危安在?	三危山又在何方?
延年不死,	玄趾和三危的人延年益寿长生不老,
寿何所止?	他们到底能活多久?

鲮鱼何所?	人面鱼身的鲮鱼生活在什么地方?
魖堆①焉处?	怪鸟魖堆住在何处?
羿焉彃②日?	后羿为何能射落九个太阳?
乌焉解羽?	太阳里的金乌羽毛落向何方?

禹之力献功,	大禹治理洪水献功,
降省下土四方。	还深入百姓中考察。
焉得彼涂山女③,	他怎么遇到了涂山国的姑娘?
而通之于台桑?	在台桑和她结合。

闵妃匹合,	涂山国的姑娘和他结合,
厥身是继,	是因为传宗接代的缘故。
胡为嗜不同味,	他与涂山姑娘并非同一族群,
而快朝饱?	为何要贪恋一时的快乐?

① 魖(qí)堆：神话传说中的魖雀，见《山海经·东山经》。
② 彃(bì)：古代神话传说中太阳里的三足乌。
③ 涂山女：传说大禹娶涂山女为妻子。

Where's Mount Perils and goes
Black Stream dyeing one's toes?
How could a deathless man
Live as long as he can?

Where lived man-fish unheard
Of and white-headed giant bird?
How did the Archer shoot down
Nine suns with golden crown
And the Raven in the sun
With its feathers undone?

Yu made flood-water flow
Through nine channels below.
How with a Southern lass could
He make love in the wood?

If he loved the fair one,
He should have loved their son.
Why did he make up his mind
To leave their son behind?

启代益作后，	夏启取代益成为君王，
卒然离蠚①。	没想到自己突然遭殃。
何启惟忧，	为什么夏启遭遇此种忧患，
而能拘是达？	却又能从牢狱逃亡？
皆归射鞠，	那是因为勤谨而鞠躬尽瘁，
而无害厥躬。	因而夏启毫发未伤。
何后益作革，	为何益不能成功接受禅让，
而禹播降？	而大禹的后嗣却能久长？
启棘宾商，	夏启梦为天帝之客，
《九辩》《九歌》。	把《九辩》和《九歌》带回地上。
何勤子屠母，	夏启为什么出生后便杀死生母，
而死分竟地？	并将她尸骨分离弃地？
帝降夷羿，	天帝派来了夷羿，
革孽夏民。	消除夏朝忧患以慰百姓。
胡射夫河伯，	羿为什么要将河伯射瞎，
而妻彼雒嫔？	又娶了洛水的女神？
冯珧利决，	夷羿持着手中的弓箭套着扳指，
封豨是射。	专门射杀大野猪。
何献蒸肉之膏，	夷羿用蒸肉祭祀天帝，
而后帝不若？	天帝为什么还不适意？

① 蠚（niè）：忧，难。

How did Qi take Yi's place
After he met disgrace?
Put in prison by Yi,
How could Qi be set free?

All shot at Qi with bows;
He was not hurt by blows.
How was Yi overthrown?
How did Qi win the crown?

Qi sought favor divine
And got melodies nine.
How could his stony breath
Entail his mother's death?

The Lord sent Archer down
That Xia's evils be mown.
Why did he shoot the Lord of Stream
And wive his Lady Dream?

He bent to the full his bow
And killed the big swine below.
Why was his sacrifice
Not accepted as nice?

浞娶纯狐,	寒浞想娶羿的妻子纯狐,
眩妻爰谋。	纯狐与他合谋害死夷羿。
何羿之射革,	羿的力气足够射穿甲胄,
而交吞揆之?	而遭其妻与浞暗算?

阻穷西征,	向西的道路险峻受阻,
岩何越焉?	重重山岩怎样越过?
化为黄熊,	鲧变成了黄熊,
巫何活焉?	西方的神仙怎样让他复活?

咸播秬黍①,	鲧教会大家种黍,
莆雚②是营。	还把田里的水草铲除。
何由并投,	为什么鲧还遭受放逐,
而鲧疾修盈?	难道他恶贯满盈?

白蜺婴茀,	身披白霓为衣饰,
胡为此堂?	为何常仪如此堂皇?
安得夫良药,	从哪儿得来的不死之药,
不能固臧?	又不能好好保藏?

天式纵横,	天地间的法则是经纬纵横,
阳离爰死。	如果阳气消失了人就会死亡。
大鸟何鸣,	大鸟为什么还在鸣叫,
夫焉丧厥体?	它本来的躯体怎样消亡?

① 秬（jù）黍：黑小米。
② 莆：通"蒲"，水草。雚（huán）：芦苇类植物。

The traitor wed his wife
And plotted against his life.
How was he boiled and slain,
Piercing seven shields in vain?

Barred from returning west,
Could Gun cross Mount Crest?
Turned into a yellow fish,
Could he revive at wish?

Gun had black millet sown
And weeds and grasses mown.
Why should he bear the blame
And have ever a bad name?

Adorned with rainbow white,
Why should the Belle take flight
With herbs divine to hide
Herself at the moon's side?

Heaven rules left and right;
Death comes when there's no light.
Should not the Golden Raven cry
When shot down from the sky?

蓱号起雨，	雨师屏翳呼号掌管云雨，
何以兴之？	那云雨又是怎样兴起？
撰体协胁，	体质柔顺驯良，
鹿何膺之？	鹿身风神又是怎样响应？
鳌戴山抃[①]，	巨鳌承载着大山游舞，
何以安之？	大山怎么能稳固不移？
释舟陵行，	弃舟舍船在陆地上行走，
何以迁之？	又怎么能走得动呢？
惟浇在户，	寒浇到他嫂子家中，
何求于嫂？	他对嫂子有何企图？
何少康逐犬，	为什么少康田猎的时候驱使猎犬，
而颠陨厥首？	就能砍掉寒浇的头？
女歧缝裳，	寒浇的嫂子女歧给寒浇缝补衣服，
而馆同爰止。	晚上两人便同屋同住。
何颠易厥首，	少康为什么错砍了女歧的头，
而亲以逢殆？	而使自己遭遇危险？
汤谋易旅，	少康整顿部下，
何以厚之？	又是通过什么方法使部队壮大？
覆舟斟寻，	他讨伐了斟寻覆其船，
何道取之？	到底是怎样取得的胜利？

① 抃（biàn）：拍手。

How did the Lord of Rain shout
And showers fall all about?
How did the wings of Deer
Raise the wind far and near?

How could the Turtles great
Bear the five Islands' weight?
Without the giant boat,
How could the island float?

What did Strong Ao ask for
At his brother's widow's door?
Was Strong Ao's head cut down
By the Hunter wearing crown?

The sewing widow kept
Ao at home and they slept.
How did she lose her head
By mistake while in bed?

How was Ao's armor planned
The stoutest of the land?
Boats overturned, by what way
Was the foe brought to bay?

桀伐蒙山，　　　　　　　　夏桀起兵讨伐蒙山国，
何所得焉？　　　　　　　　在那里得到了什么？
妹嬉①何肆，　　　　　　　妹嬉到底有什么过错，
汤何殛②焉？　　　　　　　商汤非要惩罚她？

舜闵在家，　　　　　　　　舜在家里十分仁孝，
父何以鳏③？　　　　　　　他父亲为什么不让他成家？
尧不姚告，　　　　　　　　尧事先并没有告诉舜的父亲，
二女何亲？　　　　　　　　两个女儿如何嫁给了舜？

厥萌在初，　　　　　　　　生命最初的情形，
何所亿焉？　　　　　　　　我们怎么推断它？
璜台十成，　　　　　　　　用玉石做成十层高台，
谁所极焉？　　　　　　　　是谁能建成这样之美的建筑？

登立为帝，　　　　　　　　上古时候的帝王登位，
孰道尚之？　　　　　　　　是根据什么来推举的？
女娲有体，　　　　　　　　女娲特殊的人面蛇身，
孰制匠之？　　　　　　　　到底是谁赐予她这样的躯体？

舜服厥弟，　　　　　　　　舜对他的弟弟那么顺从，
终然为害。　　　　　　　　还是被他弟弟算计，
何肆犬体，　　　　　　　　为什么舜的弟弟如狗般放肆，
而厥身不危败？　　　　　　而舜却没有受到伤害？

① 妹嬉（mò xī）：末喜氏。
② 殛（jí）：杀死，处罚而死。
③ 鳏（guān）：同"鳏"。

King Jie attacked Meng State.
How did this change his fate?
His queen with charm was filled.
How by Tang was she killed?

How did Shun's father blind
Leave unwed his son kind?
And Yao give him princess,
Telling not the sightless?

Who did at the first sign
Foretell the Shang's decline?
By whom was built and made
The ten-floored tower of jade?

When Snake-Queen mounted the throne,
Who said it was well done?
Who made her body change
Into seventy shapes strange?

Shun yielded to his brother,
Still he was harmed by the other.
How could the dog prevail
And his tricks never fail?

吴获迄古,	吴国能够长久存在,
南岳是止。	江南山川百姓安栖。
孰期去斯,	谁能预料到这种情况,
得两男子?	是因为两个贤人的缘故?
缘鹄饰玉,	伊尹用天鹅和玉饰的容具,
后帝是飨。	进献美味给商汤。
何承谋夏桀,	承用伊尹的计谋,
终以灭丧?	最终使夏桀灭亡?
帝乃降观,	商汤来到民间视察,
下逢伊挚。	在民间碰到了伊尹。
何条放致罚,	商汤把夏桀放逐到鸣条,
而黎服大说?	诸侯和民众为什么都皆大欢喜?
简狄在台,	简狄住在九层瑶台之上,
喾何宜?	为什么帝喾要迎娶她?
玄鸟①致贻,	燕子给简狄带来了聘礼,
女何喜?	她为什么这么高兴?
该②秉季德,	王亥秉承了其父王季的德行,
厥父是臧。	以父亲的品德为善。
胡终弊于有扈,	为什么他最终困于有易国,
牧夫牛羊?	为有易国放牧牛羊呢?

① 玄鸟:燕子。
② 该:通"亥",即王亥。

Old Wu State extended far
Southward up to Mount Bar.
How did two princes great
Come to rule over the State?

In cauldron decked with swan of jade
The sacrifice was made.
King Jie of Xia received the crown.
Why was he overthrown?

How did Lord Tang advise
Yi his minister wise
To have King Jie destroyed
And people overjoyed?

How did King Kuts favor shower
On fair Janedy in the tower?
How did the Swallow's egg
Make her conceived, I beg?

Hai was **Qi**'s worthy son;
He did as **Qi** had done.
Why did he go and keep
In Youyi ox and sheep?

干协时舞,	王亥手持盾牌起舞,
何以怀之?	有易国的少女为何要思恋他?
平胁曼肤,	这位姑娘体态丰满肌肤润泽,
何以肥之?	为何长得如此丰满美丽呢?
有扈牧竖,	有易国人发现王亥淫乱,
云何而逢?	他们是怎样碰上这件事的呢?
击床先出,	有易国派人在床上袭击王亥,
其命何从?	他的性命如何得以保存?
恒秉季德,	王恒继承了其父的美德,
焉得夫朴牛?	从哪儿得到了这些大牛满栏?
何往营班禄,	王恒还得到了有易国的俸禄赏赐,
不但还来?	不仅仅是徒手而来。
昏微遵迹,	昏庸的上甲微遵循其父王亥的德行,
有狄不宁。	使得有易国的人民不得不宁。
何繁鸟萃棘,	为什么群鸟聚集在荆棘丛中,
负子肆情?	与其子妇在野地里放纵淫荡?
眩弟并淫,	坏兄弟想奸淫他的嫂子,
危害厥兄。	因此要谋害他的兄长。
何变化以作诈,	这些变化无常行为奸诈的小人,
而后嗣逢长?	为什么后代兴盛不衰?

How was the Youyi queen entranced
When shield in hand Hai danced?
How could the oxherd win
The queen with lovely skin?

How did a herdsman find
Them making love and from behind
Strike and miss them in bed
And they lost not their head?

How could Heng tend his flocks
And get back his fat ox?
Why did he, gifts in hand,
Not come back to his land?

Wei followed up Hai's trace
And put Youyi out of place.
Why should he risk his life
To make love with his son's wife?

His brother full of lust
Did him harm, so unjust.
How could one doing wrong
Have descendants in throng?

成汤①东巡,	成汤到东部巡察,
有莘爰极。	一直到了莘这个地方。
何乞彼小臣,	为什么他只索取伊尹这个小臣,
而吉妃是得?	因此还得到了贤淑的妃子?
水滨之木,	在那水边的空心桑树中,
得彼小子。	有莘氏得到了伊尹。
夫何恶之,	为什么国君讨厌伊尹,
媵有莘之妇?	把伊尹作为陪嫁送给成汤呢?
汤出重泉,	成汤从重泉被释放出来,
夫何罪尤?	是因为什么罪过而被囚禁呢?
不胜心伐帝,	成汤本没有下决心攻伐帝桀,
夫谁使挑之?	是什么人挑唆他呢?
会朝争盟,	诸侯会盟誓师,
何践吾期?	他们如何履行武王的约定呢?
苍鸟群飞,	武王的将帅勇猛若鹰,
孰使萃之?	是谁使它们聚集在一起?
列击纣躬,	整顿队伍攻伐商纣,
叔旦不嘉。	周公旦非常不赞同。
何亲揆发足,	为什么周公帮武王伐纣,
周之命以咨嗟?	完成天命后又要叹息呢?

① 成汤:商汤。

Lord Tang the victor great
Went east to Youshen State.
How could he need a cook
And win a princess of good look?

In a riverside tree
Was found a baby free.
How did the minister mean
Come with Youshen's fair queen?

Jailed in the Double Spring,
What wrong did Tang do the king?
Who provoked him to overthrow
The Xia by blow on blow?

How did lords in array
Arrive on battle day?
Who made grey eagles fly
And flock up in the sky?

Fa beat the corpse of Yin's king bad.
Why was Fa's brother sad?
When Fa ruled the Zhou State,
Why did his brother sigh over Yin's fate?

授殷天下，	上帝把天下授予殷王朝，
其位安施？	这种王位施舍的根据是什么？
反成乃亡，	等到殷朝建立后又要灭亡它，
其罪伊何？	殷朝的罪过究竟是什么？
争遣伐器，	八百诸侯争先恐后派部队讨伐纣王，
何以行之？	这些部队如何调集起来？
并驱击翼，	周军并驾齐驱攻击商军的两翼，
何以将之？	是谁指挥这些士兵出击？
昭[①]后成游，	周昭王完成了游历天下的志愿，
南土爰底。	他来到了楚国的土地才停止。
厥利惟何？	最终有什么贪求？
逢彼白雉？	难道是为了遇见白色野鸡？
穆王巧梅，	周穆王善于驰骋，
夫何为周流？	为什么要周行天下？
环理天下，	周穆王的足迹遍布天下，
夫何索求？	他到底在寻找什么？
妖夫曳衒，	妖人携带货物在街上叫卖，
何号于市？	在市场叫卖的是什么东西？
周幽谁诛？	周幽王到底是被谁杀死？
焉得夫褒姒？	他是怎样得到美女褒姒的？

① 昭：周昭王。

When Yin had divine grace,
What had they done in place?
Thriving and then overthrown,
What crimes committed the crown?

Who made Zhou's ranks proceed
With weapons at full speed,
Keep pace and forward go
And smite the wings of the foe?

How was King Zhao's tour planned
As far as the Southern land?
How was he drowned at sight
Of a great pheasant white?

King Mu was fond of steed.
How did he tour with speed
The western land all o'er?
What was he searching for?

What did a man and his wife base
Cry in the market place?
Did King You kill the pair
To get Bao Si the fair?

天命反侧，	天命是如此地反复无常，
何罚何佑？	究竟保佑谁惩罚谁？
齐桓九会，	齐桓公举行了九次诸侯会盟，
卒然身杀？	最后为什么会被人残杀？
彼王纣之躬，	商纣王的性情为人，
孰使乱惑？	是谁令他昏庸狂暴？
何恶辅弼，	为什么会厌恶身边贤良的臣子，
谗谄是服？	而重用谄媚的小人？
比干何逆，	比干到底有何大逆不道之处，
而抑沉之？	为何不受重用反受处罚？
雷开阿顺，	雷开对待纣王是何等顺从，
而赐封之。	因此受到了赏赐和拜封。
何圣人之一德，	为什么圣人的德行都那么相似，
卒其异方？	处事方法却大不相同？
梅伯受醢，	梅伯被剁成肉酱，
箕子详狂。	箕子假装疯狂。
稷维元子，	后稷是帝喾的嫡长子，
帝何竺之？	帝喾对他为何这样狠毒？
投之于冰上，	在他出生后即抛弃在冰上，
鸟何燠之？	群鸟覆羽其上给他保护？

Capricious is the Fate
To punish and to compensate.
How was Duke Huan denied
To be buried long after he died?

How could King Zhou's crowned head
Into folly be led?
How did he hate advice,
And not flattery and vice?

What wrong did Bi Gan do
That his heart was pierced through?
What good did Yesman Kai
To be raised to rank high?

Why did men excellent
Have a fate different?
Mei Bo was minced, so sad;
Ji Zi pretended mad!

Ji was King Ku's first-born.
How was he made Lord Corn?
Why, left out on the ice,
Was he warmed by birds nice?

何冯弓挟矢，	为何后来后稷能持弓善射，
殊能将之？	具有将帅的领导才能？
既惊帝切激，	他的出生既然惊了帝营，
何逢长之？	为什么还让他兴盛不衰？
伯昌号衰，	周文王施行号令在商朝衰亡之际，
秉鞭作牧。	掌握大权成为诸侯之长。
何令彻彼岐社，	为什么让他丢弃西岐的社稷，
命有殷国？	顺应天命享有殷商之国？
迁藏就岐，	人们带着财物迁居西岐，
何能依？	他们为什么要归顺周国？
殷有惑妇，	纣王被妲己迷惑，
何所讥？	劝谏的言语又有何用？
受赐兹醢①，	纣王把人肉酱赐给文王，
西伯上告。	文王便向上天控诉。
何亲就上帝罚，	为何纣王亲受上天的惩罚，
殷之命以不救？	殷商的命运无法挽救？
师望在肆，	军师吕望在都城朝歌的店铺里，
昌何识？	周文王是怎样了解他的呢？
鼓刀扬声，	吕望舞刀发出声音，
后何喜？	文王听后为何高兴起来？

① 醢（hǎi）：肉酱。

How did he bend his bow
And special talent show?
His birth surprised the king.
Could he teem with offspring?

Lord Chang at Yin's decline
Became a herdsman fine.
How did he move his altar great
From Qi to replace the Yin State?

How did the people free
Bring their wealth and move to Mount Qi?
How much did the jeered king care
For the bewitching fair?

Given the minced flesh of his son,
Lord Chang denounced the deed done.
Should not God punish the Yin State
If its last king cursed its own fate?

How could Lord Chang recognize
The butcher as master wise?
Hearing the butcher's knife ring,
How glad was the future king?

武发杀殷,	周武王砍下纣王的头,
何所悒?	他为什么会有难抑的怒火?
载尸集战,	用车装载文王的灵位会战,
何所急?	周武王为何如此焦虑?
伯林雉经,	纣王燃薪上吊自焚,
维其何故?	到底是什么原因?
何感天抑地,	为何他的死感动了天地?
夫谁畏惧?	而又有谁为此恐惧?
皇天集命,	上天既降天命于王者,
惟何戒之?	又怎样告诫那些受命的人?
受礼天下,	既然让他治理天下,
又使至代之?	为何还要派人取而代之?
初汤臣挚,	伊尹起初只是商汤的小官,
后兹承辅。	后来才做到了辅政宰相。
何卒官汤,	为何最后上追成汤,
尊食宗绪?	死后还享祭商汤的宗庙?
勋阖梦生,	有功的阖庐是寿梦的子孙,
少离散亡。	少年时曾遭受过流亡之苦。
何壮武厉,	为何到了壮年便英武刚强,
能流厥严?	威名赫赫震慑四方?

When Yin's last king was killed,
Why was Wu with sorrow filled?
Carrying the corpse of the knight,
Why was he so eager to fight?

Why should Yin's last king be
Hanged on a cypress tree?
What on earth did he tread?
Who would tremble in dread?

Heaven ruled royal fate.
How did it warn Yin State?
Yin's kings ruled over the land.
Why were they replaced by the grand?

At first Yi Yin was Tang's slave,
Then he became a lord brave.
How did he share Tang's nice
Ancestral sacrifice?

He Lu was Meng's grandson;
While young, he was a vagrant one.
Grown up, strong he became.
How did he spread his fame?

彭铿斟雉,	彭祖献上野鸡做的羹,
帝何飨?	帝尧为何乐于品尝?
受寿永多,	彭祖有着很长的寿命,
夫何久长?	为什么他能活那么长时间?
中央共牧,	诸侯共同管理天下,
后何怒?	周厉王为何要发怒?
蠭^①蛾微命,	蜂蚁虽然微小,
力何固?	它们的力量是多么顽强?
惊女采薇,	夷齐在首阳山采薇被女人讥讽,
鹿何祐?	为什么神鹿反而护佑他们?
北至回水,	他们向北到了首阳山,
萃何喜?	为何欢喜地留在这里?
兄有噬犬,	兄长秦景公有一条恶狗,
弟何欲?	弟弟为何非要把它弄到手?
易之以百两,	他要用一百辆车来换取,
卒无禄?	怎么最后连官禄也丢了?
薄暮雷电,	天色将晚雷电交加,
归何忧?	回到家中的我为何还如此忧愁?
厥严不奉,	楚王已然不像一个国君般威严,
帝何求?	我又去求得什么呢?

① 蠭(fēng): "蜂"的异体字。

How did God like to eat
Peng-cooked pheasant's meat?
Peng lived eight hundred years.
Why should he still shed tears?

Lords ruled the Central State.
Why was the king in anger great?
How could the ant-like throng
Be powerful and strong?

The two brothers ate no fern.
How did the doe show its concern?
In northern waterside retreat,
Why were they glad to meet?

Why should the duke's younger brother
About the duke's dog bother?
He would for it give gold,
But of his rank lost hold.

At dusk a tempest roared.
Why, on backward way feel bored
And without dignity
Appeal to His Majesty?

伏匿穴处,	遭受放逐隐居山林,
爰何云?	还有什么可说的呢?
荆勋作师,	楚王追求功绩兴师动众,
夫何长?	国运怎能长久?

悟过改更,	如果楚王能悔过并改正所犯错误,
我又何言?	我又何必多说?
吴光争国,	吴国与楚国交战,
久余是胜?	为何吴国总能获胜?
何环穿自闾社丘陵,	环绕穿越闾里丘陵,
爰出子文?	淫乱之后还能生出子文?

吾告堵敖以不长,	我曾告诉贤者堵敖,
何试上自予,	楚国将衰时间不会长久,
忠名弥彰?	为何成王杀了国君自立,
	忠贞的名声更加显著彰扬?

When hidden in a cave,
For what could one still crave?
Repent and mend your way!
What more have I to say?
Why raise an army vast
And how could it long last?

How beaten ever since
He fought against Wu prince?
Why go by winding way
To the hill far away,
Where to make love in mirth
And to Zi Wen give birth?

Why say the king did wrong
And his State would not last long?
Why kill him and replace
Him and win divine grace?

九章

惜诵①

惜诵以致愍②兮，	讽谏君王而招来不幸，
发愤以抒情。	发泄愤懑来抒写衷情。
所作忠而言之兮，	我所说的都是对君王的忠言，
指苍天以为正。	苍天可以为我做证。
令五帝③以折中兮，	请五帝辨析刑书条文，
戒六神④与向服。	告六神对证控罪之词。
俾山川⑤以备御兮，	使山川之神当我的陪审，
命咎繇⑥使听直。	让皋陶裁决我的是非曲直。
竭忠诚以事君兮，	我竭尽忠心侍奉楚王，
反离群而赘肬。	反而被斥责为朝廷的毒瘤。
忘儇⑦媚以背众兮，	我没有巧言令色的本领得罪了小人，
待明君其知之。	只能等待明君能够了解真相。

---

① 惜：哀痛。诵，谏议。
② 愍（mǐn）：忧苦，同"悯"。
③ 五帝：指少皋、颛顼、帝喾、帝尧、帝舜。
④ 六神：指日、月、星、水旱、四时、寒暑之神。
⑤ 山川：指代山川之神。
⑥ 咎繇（gāo yáo）：皋陶，舜时的法官。
⑦ 儇（xuān）：轻佻，奸诈。

The Nine Elegies

I Make my Plaint

I make my plaint and tell my grief, oh!
I vent my wrath to seek relief.
If what I say is not in honesty, oh!
I ask Heaven my witness be.

I bid the Five and Six Lords to, oh!
Judge if I am guilty or true.
I call on streams and mountains here and there, oh!
To be magistrates fair and square.

I serve my prince with soul and heart, oh!
Unwanted, I am set apart.
I nor flatter nor please the mass, oh!
My prince should know me from an ass.

言与行其可迹兮,	我言行一致有迹可寻,
情与貌其不变。	我表里如一不会变化。
故相臣莫若君兮,	没有人能比君王更了解臣子,
所以证之不远。	因为在日常生活中就能验证。

吾谊先君而后身兮,	我遵从的道义是为人臣者要先君后己,
羌众人之所仇。	结果遭到了众人的反对。
专惟君而无他兮,	我一心侍奉君王,
又众兆之所雠。	又成为小人们的仇雠。

壹心而不豫兮,	我专心国事毫不迟疑,
羌不可保也。	谁曾想竟不能自保。
疾亲君而无他兮,	我急切地亲近君王毫无私念,
有招祸之道也。	又成为招致祸害的根源。

思君其莫我忠兮,	我想君王对我还是非常信任的,
忽忘身之贱贫。	因而忘记了我的身份是多么贫贱。
事君而不贰兮,	侍奉君王我忠心不贰,
迷不知宠之门。	哪里知道怎样得到君王的宠信。

忠何罪以遇罚兮,	忠诚有何罪过乃至招来惩罚,
亦非余心之所志。	这我完全意料不到。
行不群以巅越兮,	我因为不肯合作才遭受挫折,
又众兆之所咍[①]。	还为小人们耻笑。

[①] 咍(hāi): 嘲笑。

My word can find in deeds its trace, oh!
I've changed nor feeling nor face.
No judge is better than my king, oh!
Proofs are not far to seek or bring.

It's right to put before myself my prince, oh!
But I have earned the crowd's enmity since.
I care for none but my prince dear, oh!
But this has caused hatred and fear.

Whole-hearted, I don't hesitate, oh!
But I cannot secure my state.
My devotion will only to him go, oh!
But it's the way to bring me woe.

None's truer to the prince than me, oh!
But I forget my poverty.
I serve him and ask for nothing more, oh!
But to win his favor I ignore.

I ask myself from time to time, oh!
Why I am punished without crime.
Peerless. I am turned upside down, oh!
The crowd jeers at the overthrown.

纷逢尤以离谤兮,　　　　　　　　　我多次遭受毁谤责难,
謇不可释。　　　　　　　　　　　　忧愁集结在心无法释然。
情沉抑而不达兮,　　　　　　　　　压抑之心不能表白,
又蔽而莫之白。　　　　　　　　　　君王被蒙蔽有口难辩。

心郁邑余侘傺①兮,　　　　　　　　我心情郁郁苦闷至极,
又莫察余之中情。　　　　　　　　　又无人能体察我的忠心。
固烦言不可结诒兮,　　　　　　　　要说的太多以致无法用书信表达啊!
愿陈志而无路。　　　　　　　　　　即便写出来也无路投递。

退静默而莫余知兮,　　　　　　　　寂寞隐退没人能理解我啊!
进号呼又莫吾闻。　　　　　　　　　大声呼号又没有回音。
申侘傺之烦惑兮,　　　　　　　　　多次的烦闷令我迷惑啊!
中闷瞀②之忳忳③。　　　　　　　　心绪烦乱真是伤心。

昔余梦登天兮,　　　　　　　　　　我曾经梦想登上天庭,
魂中道而无杭。　　　　　　　　　　魂魄升到半路却失去了上天的航船。
吾使厉神占之兮,　　　　　　　　　我请厉神为我占卜,
曰:有志极而无旁。　　　　　　　　他说:志向很高,但无辅佐之人。

终危独以离异兮?　　　　　　　　　我最终会被孤立遭受放逐吗?
曰:君可思而不可恃。　　　　　　　他说:"君王可以思念却不可以依仗。
故众口其铄金兮,　　　　　　　　　众口一词的谗言能把金属熔化,
初若是而逢殆。　　　　　　　　　　刚想尽忠就被小人迫害。

① 侘傺(chà chì):失意的样子。
② 闷瞀(mào):烦闷,愤懑。
③ 忳忳(tún tún):忧伤的样子。

Slanders and blames are laid on me, oh!
So many that from them I can't be free.
My feelings stifled, I'm set apart, oh!
Screened from my lord, I can't open my heart.

Heavy with sorrow and despair, oh!
To whom can I lay my feelings bare?
My disordered words find no vent, oh!
My thought has no way to present.

If I'm retired and silent, who will know, oh!
Who will hear if I cry and onward go?
My mind feels troubled and suppressed, oh!
How can my sorrow be expressed?

Once I dreamed to ascend the sky, oh!
Halfway I could not go more high.
I bade the Dream Lord to divine!
He said, None'd help your aspiration fine.

At last a stranger should face peril alone, oh!
The prince might be thought of, not relied on.
Many tongues could even melt gold, oh!
Good men risk failure as of old.

惩于羹者而吹齑①兮，	被烫的人吃冷食也要吹气，
何不变此志也？	你为什么不改变你的志向？
欲释阶而登天兮，	如果你想丢弃梯子而登天，
犹有曩②之态也。	就会和从前一样遭殃。

众骇遽以离心兮，	众人都惊骇你所为而心志不一，
又何以为此伴也？	你又何必与这些人为同伴？
同极而异路兮，	事君的目的相同但观念不同，
又何以为此援也？	你又怎么能从他们那里得到帮助？

晋申生之孝子兮，	晋太子申生本是一个孝子，
父信谗而不好。	他父亲听信谗言逼他自杀。
行婞③直而不豫兮，	鲧的行为刚直而不可动摇，
鲧功用而不就。	功夫用到了却没能使洪水平定。

吾闻作忠以造怨兮，	我听说尽忠能引起旁人的怨恨，
忽谓之过言。	以前一直以为这是夸大的言论。
九折臂而成医兮，	九次折臂而成良医，
吾至今而知其信然。	我到现在才明白这个道理。

矰弋④机而在上兮，	蓄势待发的箭对着天空，
罻罗⑤张而在下。	地面上布满了罗网。
设张辟以娱君兮，	小人们设下重重圈套算计君王，
愿侧身而无所。	想要侧身远避而无可投。

① 齑（jī）：切碎的冷菜。
② 曩（nǎng）：往昔，以前。
③ 婞（xìng）：正直。
④ 矰弋（zēng yì）：带有丝绳的短箭。
⑤ 罻（wèi）罗：捕鸟的网。

Burnt by broth, you blow on cold food, oh!
Why don't you change your attitude?
Ladders cast down, skyward you'd go, oh!
Such were your ways long, long ago.

Frightened, all turn their hearts against you, oh!
How can you find companions new?
Different ways lead to the same end, oh!
Who would help you as your old friend?

Prince Shen Sheng was a filial son, oh!
Slandered, not loved, he was undone.
Gun would not change, so stiff and straight, oh!
He failed in work at any rate."

They said that loyalty might lead to hate, oh!
I thought they did exaggerate.
Wounds would make a physician good, oh!
At last I know it's not falsehood.

The cross-bow is set overhead, oh!
And the bird-nets below are spread.
Traps are laid to mislead His Grace, oh!
Where by his side can I find a place?

欲儃佪①以干傺兮，	我本想寻找一个好的时机，
恐重患而离尤。	又怕遭受更大的灾难。
欲高飞而远集兮，	我曾想远离楚国，
君罔谓女何之？	只怕君王问我为何去向他处。

欲横奔而失路兮，	我想抛弃正道同流合污，
坚志而不忍。	但是我意志坚强不忍背离初衷。
背膺牉②以交痛兮，	我的胸背撕裂般隐隐作痛，
心郁结而纡轸③。	心思郁结痛苦缠身。

捣木兰以矫蕙兮，	我捣碎木兰揉碎蕙草，
糳④申椒以为粮。	舂碎申椒用作我的粮食。
播江离与滋菊兮，	播种上江离培植些菊花，
愿春日以为糗⑤芳。	希望来年的春天就能品尝。

恐情质之不信兮，	我怕内心的真情不能申诉，
故重著以自明。	因此一再说清申明的缘故。
矫兹媚以私处兮，	我拥有如此多美德却不被人了解，
愿曾思而远身。	愿反复思量而远去。

---

① 儃佪（chán huái）：徘徊，留恋不去的样子。
② 牉（pàn）：分裂。
③ 纡（yū）：缠绕。轸（zhěn）：疼痛。
④ 糳（zuò）：舂米。
⑤ 糗（qiǔ）：炒米，干粮。

If I tarry in such a state, oh!
I fear there would fall a heavier fate.
If I fly and perch far away, oh!
Won't my prince ask, "Where will you stay?"

If I a winding path pursue, oh!
Would my strong will allow me to?
My back and breast are split with pain, oh!
My heart is torn and aches again.

Magnolia and orchid I pound, oh!
And pepper flowers for food are ground.
I sow and plant asters to bring, oh!
Savors for provender in spring.

I fear none would believe my heart, oh!
So I say again and again my part.
I will retire to think and stay, oh!
With these sweet flowers far away.

涉江

余幼好此奇服兮，	我从小就喜爱这样奇特的服饰，
年既老而不衰。	即使年老也不曾改变。
带长铗①之陆离兮，	身配长长的剑，
冠切云②之崔嵬③，	头戴巍巍耸立的切云冠，
被明月兮珮宝璐。	系上明月般的宝石啊配上宝贵的珍珠。
世溷浊④而莫余知兮，	这个世界太混浊没人了解我，
吾方高驰而不顾。	我将要奔向远方再不回头。
驾青虬⑤兮骖白螭，	青龙驾车啊白螭在旁边辅佐。
吾与重华游兮瑶之圃。	我要和舜同在种满玉树的园圃里游玩，
登昆仑兮食玉英，	登上昆仑山以玉树花为食。
与天地兮同寿，	和天地一样长寿，
与日月兮同光。	同日月一样永放光芒。
哀南夷之莫吾知兮，	可怜南方的人都不了解我，
旦余济乎江湘。	清晨我就要渡过湘水和长江。

---

① 铗（jiá）：剑。
② 切云：一种很高的帽子。
③ 崔嵬（cuī wéi）：高耸的样子。
④ 溷（hùn）浊：污浊。
⑤ 虬（qiú）：有角的龙。

Crossing the River

While young, I loved rare brilliant dress; oh!
When old, my love grows none the less.
My long sword dazzles far and nigh; oh!
My cloud-cleaving crown towers high.
My robe adorned with pearls moon-bright, oh!

My belt with gems shedding rare light.
The world is foul and knows not me; oh!
I won't look down when up I flee.
I'd ride on dragons blue, oh! and white snakes as I please,
I would tour with King Shun, oh! the Garden of Jade Trees.
I would ascend, oh! the Kunlun Mountains,
Eat jade flowers, oh! and drink from fountains.
I'd live as long, oh! as earth and sky,
I would outshine, oh! sun and moon on high.

Misunderstood, oh! my heart will ache.
I'll cross the river, oh! at daybreak.

乘鄂渚而反顾兮，	登上鄂水岸上回头张望来路，
欸①秋冬之绪风。	唉！秋冬的寒风使人哀愁。
步余马兮山皋，	在山边让我的马信步，
邸余车兮方林。	让我的车在山林里安放。
乘舲②船余上沅兮，	坐上船上溯沅水，
齐吴榜以击汰③。	众人划桨冲锋破浪。
船容与而不进兮，	船儿徘徊着不能前进，
淹回水而凝滞。	在漩涡中荡漾。
朝发枉渚兮，	早晨从枉渚出发，
夕宿辰阳。	晚上在辰阳住下。
苟余心其端直兮，	只要我的心志还端直，
虽僻远之何伤！	即便放逐远方又有何悲伤！
入溆浦余僮佪④兮，	进入溆浦我犹豫不前，
迷不知吾所如。	突然之间迷失了方向。
深林杳以冥冥兮，	深山老林阴暗异常，
乃猿狖⑤之所居。	这里是猿猴栖息的地方。

---

① 欸（āi）：叹息。
② 舲：有窗户的船。
③ 汰：水波。
④ 僮（chán）佪：徘徊。
⑤ 狖（yòu）：古书上所说的一种猴。

I look back, coming to the Beach, oh!
Where autumn or winter winds screech.
By mountainside pace my steeds good, oh!
I stop my chariot near the wood.

I take a boat and upstream go, oh!
We beat the waves with oars and row.
Slowly it makes little headway, oh!
The whirling waves cause its delay.

At dawn I leave for farther west; oh!
At night in Southern Star I rest.
But since my heart is true and straight, oh!
What if I'm in a distant state?

By poolside I pace to and fro, oh!
Perplexed, I know not where to go.
Amid deep woods in twilight gloom, oh!
There are the haunts where monkeys loom.

山峻高以蔽日兮，	山峰高耸遮云蔽日，
下幽晦以多雨。	山谷毕竟阴湿多雨。
霰雪纷其无垠兮，	小雪下得纷纷扬扬无边无际，
云霏霏而承宇。	云雾缠绕在屋檐之下。
哀吾生之无乐兮，	可怜我一生不得快乐，
幽独处乎山中。	只能孤独地在此山中。
吾不能变心而从俗兮，	但我不能改变心志随波逐流，
固将愁苦而终穷。	因此宁肯愁苦而终身失意。
接舆①髡首兮，	狂者接舆剃掉头发，
桑扈②臝行。	隐士桑扈裸身出行。
忠不必用兮，	忠诚的人不一定被重用，
贤不必以。	贤良的人也难得出人头地。
伍子③逢殃兮，	伍子胥遭受了祸害，
比干菹醢。	比干被剁成了肉酱。
与前世而皆然兮，	前代的贤良之臣都是这样，
吾又何怨乎今之人！	我又为何要埋怨当世的人啊！
余将董道而不豫兮，	我将坚持正道毫不犹豫，
固将重昏而终身！	注定一辈子处在重重黑暗之中。

① 接舆：楚国狂人。
② 桑扈：古代一名隐士。
③ 伍子：伍子胥。

The sun is screened by mountains steep; oh!
It's clark with rain in valleys deep.
Sleet and snow fall without an end; oh!
The heavy clouds with roof-tops blend.

About my joyless life I groan, oh!
Living in the mountains alone.
To please the crowd I cannot change my heart; oh!
I'd live a poor, sad life apart.
His head shaved, Jie Yu was called mad; oh!
The recluse ran about, unclad.

A loyal man may not be used; oh!
A wise man is often refused.
General Wu suffered his last defeat; oh!
Lord Bi Gan was cut into minced meat.

Of former times this was the way, oh!
Why should I complain of today?
I will go straight and do no wrong; oh!
I'll live in the dark all my life long.

乱曰：鸾鸟凤皇，	尾声唱道：鸾鸟和凤凰，
日以远兮。	越飞越远。
燕雀乌鹊，	燕雀和乌鸦，
巢堂坛兮。	筑巢在庙堂坛前。
露申辛夷，	瑞香和辛夷，
死林薄兮。	枯死林下杂草间。
腥臊并御，	腥臊之物一起进用，
芳不得薄兮。	芳香不到眼前。
阴阳易位，	阴阳倒置，
时不当兮。	时序不当。
怀信侘傺，	胸怀忠心却落得失意惆怅，
忽乎吾将行兮。	飘忽间我将行向远方。

哀郢[①]

皇天之不纯命兮，	这真是天降厄运，
何百姓之震愆？	为何要让百姓迁徙流离？
民离散而相失兮，	人民流落他乡亲人失散，
方仲春而东迁。	正值二月就要向东逃难。

---

① 郢（yǐng）：楚国都城。

Epilogue

The phoenixes from day to day
Fly farther and farther away, oh!
Swallows and sparrows, crows and pies all
Build their nests o'er the temple hall, oh!

Daphnes and lily-magnolias die
On the verge of the woods nearby, oh!
Stinking weeds overrun the place;
Fragrant flowers, cannot gain grace, oh!

Darkness replaces light;
The time is far from right, oh!
Faithfulness becomes doubt;
How can I not set out? oh!

Lament for the Chu Capital

Inconstant is Heaven on high. oh!
How people tremble far and nigh!
Scattered, all men are lost in woe; oh!
Just in mid-spring eastward I go.

去故乡而就远兮，	背井离乡迁徙到远方去，
遵江夏以流亡。	沿着长江和夏水流亡。
出国门而轸怀①兮，	走出国门那一刻我内心悲伤，
甲之朝吾以行。	记得那正是甲日的早上。

发郢都而去闾兮，	从郢都出发我告别了家乡，
荒忽其焉极？	心思恍惚几乎辨不清方向。
楫齐扬以容与兮，	齐划桨缓缓地前进，
哀见君而不再得。	伤心的是再也见不到君王。

望长楸②而太息兮，	望着故都高大的梓树叹息，
涕淫淫其若霰。	泪水滚落就像雪珠涟涟。
过夏首而西浮兮，	经过夏口我们继续向西行，
顾龙门而不见。	再回首时龙门已经看不见了。

心婵媛③而伤怀兮，	思绪绵绵让人心碎，
眇不知其所蹠④。	前途渺茫不知道落脚何方。
顺风波以从流兮，	任船儿随波逐流，
焉洋洋而为客。	我们飘飘摇摇客居他乡。

---

① 轸（zhěn）怀：沉痛地思念。
② 楸（qiū）：树名，落叶乔木。
③ 婵媛（chán yuán）：牵挂的意思。
④ 蹠（zhí）：踏。

I leave my home for far-off place; oh!
Exiled, along the stream I pace.
I pass through city gate with heavy heart, oh!
On the first day at dawn I part.

Leaving the capital of Chu, oh!
I am at a loss what to do.
In time we dip slowly the oar; oh!
My prince is not seen, I deplore.

Gazing on high trees, I heave sighs; oh!
Like sleet sad tears fall from my eyes.
Passing Summer Head, westward we float, oh!
The Dragon Gate can't be seen from my boat.

Hurt by an invisible wound, oh!
I know not where to stand aground.
I follow the waves and the breeze, oh!
As if I traveled at my ease.

凌阳侯之泛滥兮，	乘着大波之神的滚滚波涛，
忽翱翔之焉薄？	我们像迷途的鸟儿去哪里栖息？
心絓结^①而不解兮，	心中的死结无法解开，
思蹇产而不释。	内心忧郁不能释怀。

将运舟而下浮兮，　　　撑着船继续往东漂流，
上洞庭而下江。　　　　经过洞庭湖继续东入大江。
去终古之所居兮，　　　离开了我们世代繁衍的家乡，
今逍遥而来东。　　　　现在流浪到了东方。

羌灵魂之欲归兮，　　　我的灵魂是多么地眷恋故土，
何须臾而忘反？　　　　怎么有一时一刻忘记回返？
背夏浦而西思兮，　　　背对着夏水，我思念西方，
哀故都之日远。　　　　悲哀的是故乡已是越来越远。

登大坟[②]以远望兮，　　登上高处向远方眺望，
聊以舒吾忧心。　　　　暂且疏散一点内心的忧伤。
哀州土之平乐兮，　　　这一带原是多么地平静祥和，
悲江介之遗风。　　　　可叹沿江何处还保留着古老的风俗。

当陵阳之焉至兮，　　　面向着陵阳山还能去向哪里，
淼南渡之焉如？　　　　渡过浩渺的江水又将到什么地方呢？
曾不知夏之为丘兮，　　真没想到华屋宗庙竟成废墟，
孰两东门之可芜？　　　古都的两座东门就任其慢慢荒芜？

---

① 絓（guà）结：心有牵挂郁结于心。
② 坟：水边的高地。

I ride on waves which overflow, oh!
Like birds in flight knowing not where to go.
My heart is in unresolved doubt, oh!
My thought in a maze can find no way out.

I let my boat float downstream through, oh!
The Dongting Lake and River Blue.
I've left the home where I lived since old days, oh!
At random I go eastward way.

Not for a moment does my soul not yearn, oh!
To the old capital to return.
Gazing westward on Summer Bay, oh!
I'm grieved each day to be farther away.

I climb the bank to look afar, oh!
To ease the sorrow of my heart.
I'm sad to see the land so wide, oh!
And the old ways of the riverside.

Where will the waves in the south flow? oh!
Crossing the river, where shall I go?
Who could foresee the ruined palace great, oh!
With its two ruined eastern gates?

心不怡之长久兮，	我情绪低落已经很久了，
忧与愁其相接。	忧郁哀愁远远没有尽头。
惟郢路之辽远兮，	再回郢都已经路途遥远，
江与夏之不可涉。	长江和夏水是那么难以渡过。

忽若不信兮，	突然被迫离开是因为我不被信任，
至今九年而不复。	到今天已经九年了还不能回返。
惨郁郁而不通兮，	内心悲伤愤懑理不清头绪，
蹇侘傺①而含戚。	失意之人只能默默悲戚。

外承欢之汋约兮，	有人表面装出一副媚态，
谌荏弱而难持。	实际懦弱胆小无法承担救国大任。
忠湛湛而愿进兮，	我忠心耿耿期望获得重用，
妒被离而鄣之。	可惜嫉妒者总是阻挡着我。

尧、舜之抗行兮，	尧舜的行为是多么崇高，
瞭杳杳而薄天。	眼光远大似乎直逼青天。
众谗人之嫉妒兮，	但嫉妒他们的人还是生出许多谗言，
被以不慈之伪名。	让他们背负不仁的虚假罪名。

憎愠怆②之修美兮，	国君憎恨着忠厚高尚的人，
好夫人之慷慨。	却偏爱伪君子的慷慨谗言。
众踥蹀③而日进兮，	小人们一天天靠近君王，
美超远而逾迈。	君子被排挤远远地站在一边。

① 侘傺（chà chì）：困顿失意的样子。
② 愠怆（yùn lǔn）：诚实而不善言辞。
③ 踥蹀（qiè dié）：轻狂的步伐。

My heart feels unhappy for long, oh!
And grief and sorrow come in throng.
The capital in mist is lost, oh!
The Summer River can't be crossed.

Unbelievably olden time disappears; oh!
I have not been back for nine years.
My sadness cannot be expressed; oh!
In despair my grief is compressed.

By outward flattery you're charmed, oh!
How could the weak not be disarmed?
Loyal, I tried to come near you; oh!
Jealousy cut me off from your view.

Kings Yao and Shun's deeds spread far and nigh; oh!
Their glory reaches to the sky.
The backbiters envious of their fame, oh!
Give them a false and unkind name.

You dislike the straightforward beauty, oh!
And say the braggarts doing their duty.
They press forward and win each day more grace; oh!
True beauty's forced to far-off place.

乱曰：曼余目以流观兮，	尾声：我放眼四方，
冀壹反之何时？	期待着何时能够回归故都？
鸟飞反故乡兮，	鸟儿都要飞回故乡，
狐死必首丘。	狐狸死去头要朝向出生的山冈。
信非吾罪而弃逐兮，	被放逐确实不是我的过错
何日夜而忘之！	这些忧愁思念我日日夜夜都不会忘记！

抽思[①]

心郁郁之忧思兮，	心绪郁结，愁苦不能自已。
独永叹乎增伤。	独自叹息，愁绪没有终点。
思蹇产[②]之不释兮，	思绪绵绵，不知如何解忧。
曼遭夜之方长。	长夜漫漫，何时才是尽头？

悲秋风之动容兮，	秋风一吹万物飘零，
何回极之浮浮！	跌落尘埃为何回旋不定？
数惟荪之多怒兮，	你为何那样多怒，
伤余心之忧忧。	着实令我忧心忡忡。

愿摇起而横奔兮，	我本该离开故乡，
览民尤以自镇。	看见人民的苦难而作罢。
结微情以陈辞兮，	我把菲薄真情写成诗篇，
矫以遗夫美人。	诚挚地献给君王。

---

① 抽思：一一陈述志向。
② 蹇（jiǎn）产：曲折缠绕。

Epilogue

Gazing with longing eyes, I stand; oh!
When may I come back to my homeland?
A bird flies nowhere but home-bound; oh!
A dying fox turns its head to its mound.
Guiltless but banished, I take flight; oh!
How can I forget you day and night?

Sad Thoughts Outpoured

Of gloomy thoughts my heart not eased, oh!
Alone I sigh, my grief increased.
My mental knot can't be untied; oh!
The night is long; the world is wide.

I'm grieved the autumn wind's changed the world's face; oh!
There're whirls and ebbs from place to place.
My gracious lord is moved to ire; oh!
My heart is drowned in sorrow dire.

I would rise up and elsewhere go; oh!
I refrain when I see people in woe.
I put my feelings into word, oh!
In homage to my gracious lord.

昔君与我成言兮，	你早先已经跟我约好，
曰"黄昏以为期"。	说黄昏时候见面。
羌中道而回畔兮，	但你在半途又改变主意，
反既有此他志。	另有新欢缠绵。

憍吾以其美好兮，	你把他们好处向我夸耀，
览余以其修姱。	你把你的长处向我矜示。
与余言而不信兮，	你对我说的话全不守信用，
盖为余而造怒。	为何还无由地对我生气。

愿承闲而自察兮，	本想趁着你空闲向你表白，
心震悼而不敢。	心里害怕又不敢这样做。
悲夷犹而冀进兮，	我犹豫，但我总想见你，
心怛伤之憺憺①。	可怜我忧心如焚六神无主。

兹历情以陈辞兮，	我把我的真情编织成歌词，
荪详聋而不闻。	但你假装耳聋不肯倾听。
固切人之不媚兮，	正直诚实的人不会谄媚，
众果以我为患。	小人们也真的当我成眼中钉。

初吾所陈之耿著兮，	当初我所陈述的有凭有据，
岂至今其庸亡？	难道现在你已忘怀？
何独乐斯之謇謇②兮	我为什么总喜欢忠言直谏，
愿荪美之可光。	是希望你的美德更加辉耀。

① 怛(dá)：伤痛。憺(dàn)憺：动荡不安。
② 謇(jiǎn)謇：正直。

My lord made once a tryst with me, oh!
Saying the dusk our time should be.
Half-way he went back on what he said, oh!
And turned his mind upon another head.

Proud of his beauty on display, oh!
He showed me all his fine array.
From keeping his words he was free; oh!
Why should he vent his ire on me?

I'd take my chance to tell my part; oh!
I did not dare with trembling heart.
Hesitating, I'd still go near, oh!
But my heart was wounded with fear.

I put in words my feelings true; oh!
Feigning deafness, he'd not listen to.
An honest man pleased not his master; oh!
The crowd said I would bring disaster.

What I said first in a plain way, oh!
Can it be forgotten today?
How could my advice give me delight? oh!
But I wish my lord's beauty shine bright.

望三五以为像兮,	愿以三王五伯作为你的楷模,
指彭咸以为仪。	愿以彭咸作为我自己的准则。
夫何极而不至兮?	还有什么没有尽善尽美,
故远闻而难亏。	我要普天下都传遍我们的名声。
善不由外来兮,	善行要靠自己努力,不从外来,
名不可以虚作。	名声要与实际相符,不要虚假。
孰无施而有报兮?	哪有不给予的而能得到酬报?
孰不实而有获?	哪有不播种便有收获的?
少歌曰:与美人抽怨兮,	少歌:我向你表达我的忠心,
并日夜而无正。	日日夜夜都无人佐证。
憍吾以其美好兮,	将他的美好向我夸耀,
敖朕辞而不听。	把我的歌词当作耳边风。
倡曰:有鸟自南兮,	唱道:一只鸟儿从南方飞来,
来集汉北。	停留在汉水之北。
好姱佳丽兮,	浑身的毛羽十分绚丽,
胖①独处此异域。	孤孤单单漂泊在异乡做客。
既茕独而不群兮,	举目无亲茕茕独立,
又无良媒在其侧。	也没有好的媒人帮忙介绍。
道卓远而日忘兮,	路途遥远而渐渐被人忘怀,
愿自申而不得。	想要自荐苦于没有途经。

① 胖(pàn):分离。

He might imitate the three and five kings, oh!
And I might learn from Peng to do good things.
Is there an end that cannot be attained? oh!
Could a world-wide renown be stained?

Good virtue comes not from outside, oh!
Nor can good name be falsified.
If you don't give, what reward can you keep? oh!
If you don't sow, what can you reap?

Intermezzo

I pour out thoughts to my prince fair and bright; oh!
There is no witness day and night.
He showed his beauty in high glee; oh!
He's too proud to listen to me.

A bird comes with the southern breeze, oh!
And perches on northern riverside trees.
How fair and bright alone he stands, oh!
Forsaken in these foreign lands.

Alone and cast off from the mass am I, oh!
None would recommend me near by.
My home's forgotten day by day, oh!
I would explain but find no way.

望北山而流涕兮，	望着北山而流眼泪，
临流水而太息。	对着流水而叹息哀伤。
望孟夏之短夜兮，	初夏的夜晚本来很短，
何晦明之若岁！	为什么长起来就像一年？

惟郢路之辽远兮，	郢都的路途确是遥远，
魂一夕而九逝。	但我的梦魂一夜要走九遍。
曾不知路之曲直兮，	我不管是弯路还是捷径，
南指月与列星。	只顾向南行披星戴月。
愿径逝而未得兮，	想直走但又未能，
魂识路之营营。	梦魂往来多么劳顿。

何灵魂之信直兮，	为什么我的性情这样端直，
人之心不与吾心同！	可别人的看法却和我不同。
理弱而媒不通兮，	替我传媒的人都很软弱，
尚不知余之从容。	可能还不知道我现在的强颜欢笑。

乱曰：长濑湍流，	尾声：浅水漫长激流浩荡，
溯江潭兮。	我溯江而上。
狂顾南行，	频频回望南方，
聊以娱心兮。	聊以宽慰愁肠。

轸石崴嵬，	山路怪石崎岖，
蹇吾愿兮。	阻断了我前行的脚步。
超回志度，	迂回曲折，
行隐进兮。	使我进退两难。

I gaze on hills with tearful eyes, oh!
By riverside I heave long sighs.
Though summer nights so short appear, oh!
They seem to me as long as a year.

The capital's so far away, oh!
My soul haunts it nine times a day.
know not the road's twists and turns, oh!
For southern moon and stars my soul yearns.
In vain I dream to go there straight, oh!
My soul is busy early and late.

Why should my soul be true and fine? oh!
Other hearts are not the same as mine.
My recommender is so weak; oh!
None knows I am so hard to seek.

Epilogue
Water runs fast in shallow long;
I go against the current strong, oh!
With wild glances southwards I go
To ease my heart of grief and woe, oh!

Before me stands a craggy hill,
Barring me from doing what I will, oh!
Shall I go back or forward through?
I am at a loss what to do.

143

低徊夷犹, 迟疑不进,
宿北姑兮。 只好在北姑山暂住。
烦冤瞀容, 心烦意乱,
实沛徂兮。 万事颠沛糊涂。

愁叹苦神, 叹息悲伤,
灵遥思兮。 神魂飞向远方。
路远处幽, 地偏路远,
又无行媒兮。 没人代为诉苦肠。

道思作颂, 调整思路,
聊以自救兮。 作歌聊以自娱。
忧心不遂, 忧愁难解,
斯言谁告兮? 这些话有谁可以倾诉?

怀沙

滔滔孟夏兮, 初夏的天气真是悠长,
草木莽莽。 草木茂密遍布莽原。
伤怀永哀兮, 我心思重重独自悲伤,
汨徂南土。 毅然决定远去南方。

I bend my head and hesitate;
I pass the night at Northern Gate, oh!
With troubled looks I'm tired and weary;
On my long journey I feel dreary, oh!

With knitted brows I heave long sighs;
High up and far away my soul flies, oh!
The way is long, the place obscure,
I have no recommender sure, oh!

I pour my thoughts out in this verse
To save myself from getting worse, oh!
My sorrow can find no way out.
To whom can I complain about? oh?

Longing for Changsha

Early summer runs like a stream, oh!
The blooming trees and grasses teem.
Laden with endless grief, my heart, oh!
For far-off southern land should part.

眴① 兮杳杳, 　　　　　前方的道路充满了迷茫,
孔静幽默。 　　　　　一路上悄然无声响。
郁结纡轸②兮, 　　　　重重委屈压抑在我心头,
离慜而长鞠③。 　　　　遭受困厄何时才能安康。

抚情效志兮, 　　　　　扪心自问我一贯的志向,
冤屈而自抑。 　　　　　遭受委屈也要强行压抑。
刓方以为圜兮④, 　　　方的东西可以削成圆形,
常度未替。 　　　　　　但正确的法度不能改变。

易初本迪兮, 　　　　　如果把最初的本真抛弃,
君子所鄙。 　　　　　　正直的人们会认为可鄙。
章画志墨兮, 　　　　　就像工匠遵守绳墨规画,
前图未改。 　　　　　　我们从前的法度也不变。

内厚质正兮, 　　　　　内心敦厚正直,
大人所盛。 　　　　　　君子常常赞美。
巧倕⑤不斫兮, 　　　　如果巧匠不动斧头,
孰察其拨正？ 　　　　　有谁知他合乎正轨？

---

① 眴(shùn)：同"瞬",看的意思。
② 纡轸：委曲而痛苦。
③ 离慜(mǐn)：忧患。鞠：困穷。
④ 刓(wán)方以为圜(yuán)兮：把方的削成圆的。刓,削。圜,同"圆"。
⑤ 倕(chuí)：人名,传说是尧时的巧匠。斫(zhuó)：砍,削。

Into the hazy gloom my eyes strain,
Where silence and quietude reign.
Tormented and tortured, I go, oh!
I've suffered long in grief and woe.

Over my feelings and thoughts I brood, oh!
I restrain myself though misunderstood.
You may fit the square into the round, oh!
I will stand on my proper ground.

To change my course and first intent, oh!
Is what good men disdain and resent.
Making with ink a picture clear, oh!
From former path I do not veer.

Outwardly straight and inwardly sound, oh!
Great men extol you all around.
If the carpenter cuts no line, oh!
Who could tell if it's curved or fine?

玄文处幽兮，	五彩被放置在黑暗的地方，
矇瞍①谓之不章②。	盲人说它不漂亮。
离娄微睇兮③，	明察秋毫的离娄微闭着眼睛，
瞽④以为无明。	盲者说他和自己一样。

变白以为黑兮，	把白的说成黑的，
倒上以为下。	又把上下颠倒。
凤皇在笯⑤兮，	美丽的凤凰关进笼罩，
鸡鹜翔舞。	鸡和鸭得意地翱翔。

同糅玉石兮，	玉与石混合在一起，
一概而相量。	不分彼此地衡量。
夫惟党人鄙固兮，	只有那些结党营私的人卑劣，
羌不知余之所臧。	他们都不知道我的喜好。

任重载盛兮，	我的责任大担子重，
陷滞而不济。	使我身陷其中不能承担。
怀瑾握瑜兮，	我怀抱着珍珠美玉，
穷不知所示。	穷困的时候不知向谁展示。

---

① 矇瞍（méng sǒu）：瞎子。
② 章：文采。
③ 离娄：传说中的人名，眼力很好，善于看东西。睇（dì）：微视。
④ 瞽（gǔ）：盲人。
⑤ 笯（nú）：竹笼。

The sightless old man could, not mark, oh!
Out colored brocade in the dark.
The keen-eyed peered in broad daylight; oh!
The dim-eyed thought him dim in sight.

The black is changed into the white, oh!
The low is put onto the height.
The phoenix shut up in a cage, oh!
The hens and ducks gambol with rage.

Jewels are mixed up with stone, oh!
Into the same measure they're thrown.
The partisans whom I despise, oh!
Do not know what in me I prize.

When laden with a heavy load, oh!
I sink in the mire on the road.
I hide within me jade and gem, oh!
But do not know how to show them.

邑犬之群吠兮，　　　　　　村里的狗成群吠叫，
吠所怪也。　　　　　　　　是因为见到了不熟悉的形象。
非俊疑杰兮，　　　　　　　把英雄俊杰说成是怪物，
固庸态也。　　　　　　　　这是庸人们一贯的伎俩。

文质疏内兮，　　　　　　　我文质彬彬表里通达，
众不知余之异采。　　　　　谁都看不出我才华出众。
材朴委积兮，　　　　　　　粗大的木头堆积在一起，
莫知余之所有。　　　　　　没人知道它们能成栋梁。

重仁袭义兮，　　　　　　　我非常重视仁和义，
谨厚以为丰。　　　　　　　再用忠诚充实自己。
重华不可遌①兮，　　　　　舜帝不可能再遇上，
孰知余之从容！　　　　　　谁还能了解我雍容的气度。

古固有不并兮，　　　　　　自古以来圣贤就不同时而生，
岂知其何故？　　　　　　　这到底是什么缘故？
汤、禹久远兮，　　　　　　大禹和商汤离我们太远，
邈而不可慕。　　　　　　　以至于我们无法追慕。

惩连改忿兮，　　　　　　　抑制着心中的愤恨，
抑心而自强。　　　　　　　我必须学会自己坚强。
离愍而不迁兮，　　　　　　即使遭殃也不悔改，
愿志之有像。　　　　　　　希望为后人树立榜样。

① 遌（è）：遇见。

The dogs of the village bark, oh!
At what they see not in the dark.
It is the vulgar attitude, oh!
To condemn the wise and the good.

Within and without fair and square, oh!
The crowd know not my talent rare.
I store material to excess, oh!
But no one knows what I possess.

I multiply what's good and right, oh!
Generous, careful, fair and bright.
I have not met Shun, the sage king, oh!
Who knows my ease when I take wing?

Few kings and lords meet as of old, oh!
The reason why cannot be told.
Kings Yu and Tang lived long before, oh!
Too remote for me to adore.

I'll curt my pride and check my ire, oh!
Restrain my heart and my desire.
I will not change my mind in woe, oh!
To give an example I'll go.

进路北次兮,	顺着北边的方向前进,
日昧昧其将暮。	已近日落黄昏时候。
舒忧娱哀兮,	姑且吐出我的悲哀,
限之以大故。	生命已经走到了尽头。

乱曰：浩浩沅、湘,	尾声：那浩荡的沅水、湘水呵,
分流汩兮。	日夜不停汩汩流淌。
修路幽蔽,	经过多少艰难险阻,
道远忽兮。	前途还那么渺茫。

怀质抱情,	我怀着一颗忠诚的心,
独无匹兮。	独独没有同道之人。
伯乐既没,	伯乐已经死去,
骥焉程兮？	千里马有谁品评？

万民之生,	各人的生命有所凭,
各有所错兮。	他们都有自己的位置。
定心广志,	我要坚定我的志向,
余何畏惧兮！	我决不畏死贪生。

曾伤爰哀[①],	那些无休无止的悲哀,
永叹喟兮。	令人深沉叹息。
世溷浊莫吾知,	世间混浊无人了解我,
人心不可谓兮。	人心叵测无话可说。

① 曾：同"增"。爰（yuán）哀：悲哀无休无止。

I will halt on my northward way, oh!
At sunset dusky turns the day.
I'll give out a sorrowful breath, oh!
Lest it should blow after my death.

Epilogue
The mighty rivers roll along,
Singing a gurgling song, oh!
The long, long road looks dim and grey,
Stretching far, far away, oh!

I cherish feelings pure
I have no witness sure, oh!
The connoisseur is dead,
Who knows the steed well-bred? oh!

All mortals live and die,
Ordained by Heaven high, oh!
My heart is calm and broad my mind.
Of what am I afraid behind? oh!

Long grieved, I vent my discontent;
Sighing, I oft lament, oh!
To me the world is foul and cold;
The heart of man cannot be told, oh!

知死不可让,	我也知道死亡不可避免,
愿勿爱兮。	何必爱惜自己的身体。
明告君子:	光明磊落的先贤,
吾将以为类兮!	你们就是我学习的楷模!

思美人

思美人兮,	思念你啊我心爱的人,
揽涕而伫眙①。	擦干眼泪伫立久久凝望。
媒绝路阻兮,	媒介之路已经断绝道路变得险阻,
言不可结而诒。	我满腹忠言想写却又无法成章。
蹇蹇②之烦冤兮,	我至诚一片忠言直谏却遭受冤屈,
陷滞而不发。	心情忧郁却又无处发泄。
申旦③以舒中情兮,	愿每日倾诉我的心思,
志沉菀④而莫达。	心情沉重而难以表达。
愿寄言于浮云兮,	愿浮云能为我捎信,
遇丰隆而不将。	云神丰隆却不肯讲情。
因归鸟而致辞兮,	托归鸿为我传书,
羌宿高而难当。	无奈鸟高飞难以寻觅。

① 伫眙（zhù chì）：立视。伫，立。眙，视。
② 蹇（jiǎn）蹇：同"謇謇"，忠信正直之貌。
③ 申旦：表明心意。
④ 沉菀（yù）：沉闷而郁结。

I know that none can avoid death.
Why should I grudge my breath? oh!
I declare to those I revere,
I will take you as my compeer, oh!

Thinking of the Fair One

Thinking of the Beauty on high, oh!
I wipe my tears and gaze with longing eye.
The way is blocked, there's no go-between, oh!
How to send word to the unseen?

Laden with wrong on wrong, my cart, oh!
Sunken and stayed, I cannot start.
Pouring forth my feelings all day, oh!
Could a sinking heart express what I'll say?

I'd trust my word to floating cloud, oh!
But Feng Long says I'm not allowed.
I'd confide it to homing birds, oh!
But they're too high and fast to hear my words.

高辛之灵盛兮，	高辛的品行是多么高尚，
遭玄鸟而致诒。	能遇玄鸟而得到馈赠。
欲变节以从俗兮，	我本想要变节而随流俗，
愧易初而屈志。	可违背理想我又不愿做。

独历年而离愍兮，	多年来我遭受摧残，
羌冯心[①]犹未化。	心中的愤懑至今未消减。
宁隐闵而寿考兮，	我宁可忍受痛苦直到死去，
何变易之可为？	一生的志向怎能随便改变？

知前辙之不遂兮，	我明知前面的路很艰难，
未改此度。	但我绝不会改变我的初衷。
车既覆而马颠兮，	即便是车翻马倒，
蹇独怀此异路。	我依旧坚持这与众不同的路。

勒骐骥而更驾兮，	我再把好马缰上，
造父[②]为我操之。	请造父为我执鞭。
迁逡次而勿驱兮，	让马儿慢慢地走不必驱驰，
聊假日以须时。	趁着这时候等待时机。
指嶓冢之西隈[③]兮，	指着嶓冢山的西边，
与纁黄[④]以为期。	夕阳西下我们在那里约会。

① 冯（píng）心：愤懑的心情。冯，通"凭"。
② 造父：周穆王时人，以善于驾车闻名。
③ 西隈：西面的山边。
④ 纁（xūn）黄：黄昏之时。纁，一作"曛"。

When King Ku sought for a fair queen, oh!
The swallow served as go-between.
If I should follow vulgar ways, oh!
How could I change my mind of former days?

I passed through woes from year to year, oh!
I would nor shift my ground nor veer.
I'd rather endure to end my life, oh!
Than alter my course in the strife.

I know the road is rugged before, oh!
But I won't change my way of yore.
Though my chariot's turned upside-down, oh!
Alone, I'll pursue the way of my own.

I harness my steed for a trip, oh!
The best charioteer flips my whip.
My steed falters and won't run fast, oh!
I take time and let it go past.
I point to western mountainside, oh!
Let dusk be the end of my ride!

开春发岁兮，	春天开启了新的一年，
白日出之悠悠。	白日冉冉升起怡然自得。
吾将荡志而愉乐兮，	我要舒展心情放怀地歌唱，
遵江夏以娱忧。	逍遥在江水、夏水之滨。
揽大薄之芳茝兮，	我攀摘灌木中的香芷，
搴长洲之宿莽。	我采集沙滩上的卷施。
惜吾不及古人兮，	可惜不能和古人同时，
吾谁与玩此芳草？	摘来香草啊同谁共赏识。
解萹薄与杂菜兮，	采取萹蓄与同杂菜，
备以为交佩。	把它们编织成环佩。
佩缤纷以缭转兮，	密密麻麻互相缠绕绚丽一时，
遂萎绝而离异。	香草日益枯萎而遭毁败。
吾且儃佪[①]以娱忧兮，	我姑且快乐逍遥，
观南人之变态。	静观朝中小人的丑态。
窃快在中心兮，	我暗暗取得心灵的快乐，
扬厥凭而不俟。	把愤懑之情置诸度外。
芳与泽其杂糅兮，	芳香与污秽杂混一起，
羌芳华自中出。	浓郁的花香还是辨别得出来的。
纷郁郁其远承兮，	馥郁芬芳自然远扬，
满内而外扬。	内在充实才能传播更远。
情与质信可保兮，	只要真诚的素质长保不亡，
羌居蔽而闻章。	虽然居住隐蔽也能名声在外。

[①] 儃佪（chán huái）：徘徊。

When spring ushers in the new year, oh!
The bright sun shines long far and near.
I'll go along the stream carefree, oh!
And feast my eyes on scenes with glee.

I cull in woodland clovers white, oh!
And on the isle herbs of the night.
I have not seen the sages of yore, oh!
Who will enjoy beauties before?

I gather herbs of various hue, oh!
To twine a garland girdle new.
The girdle's wreathed with flowers around, oh!
Withered, they're rejected on the ground.

I roam to pass sorrowful days, oh!
And see southerners' varied ways.
I find joy hidden in my heart, oh!
And I put my sorrow apart.

With the foul is mingled the fair, oh!
But fragrance will emerge from there.
The fragrance reaches far and wide, oh!
Full within, it will waft outside.
Its form and matter safe and sound, oh!
Unseen, it will spread all around.

令薜荔以为理兮，	我想请薜荔替我说合，
惮举趾而缘木。	又怕走路去攀上树干。
因芙蓉以为媒兮，	想依靠荷花为我媒介，
惮褰裳而濡①足。	又怕下水打湿了裤腿。

登高吾不说兮，	登高我不高兴，
入下吾不能。	下水我也不能。
固朕形之不服兮，	固然是因为我手足不惯，
然容与而狐疑。	更是我心犹豫而不能定。

广遂前画兮，	完全依照旧日的主张，
未改此度也。	至死我也始终不肯改变。
命则处幽吾将罢兮，	命里注定住在荒野我也不管，
愿及白日之未暮也。	趁着这日子还未过完快快赶路。
独茕茕②而南行兮，	一个人孤单地走向南边，
思彭咸之故也。	只想追求彭咸的典范。

惜往日

惜往日之曾信兮，	回想过往也曾被君王信任，
受命诏以昭时。	接受君王的诏命整饬时政。
奉先功以照下兮，	守着先人的功绩光照下民，
明法度之嫌疑。	法度更显明以消除疑惑是非。

① 濡（rú）：湿。
② 茕茕（qióng qióng）：孤独的样子。

I'd ask the fig to plead for me, oh!
I fear to climb into the tree.
I'd bid lotus as go-between, oh!
I fear my skirts wet with water unclean.

I do not like to climb up high, oh!
And I cannot go down and lie.
My body will not yield, I wait, oh!
Undecided, I hesitate.

I will pursue my former plan, oh!
And will not change the course I ran.
In the gloaming I find no outlet, oh!
Still I will go before sunset.
Alone, I go my lonely southward way, oh!
Can I not think of the ancient sage's day?

The Bygone Days Regretted

In the past the king trusted me, oh!
I published the royal decree.
The ancestors' deeds shone about, oh!
I made laws plain to those in doubt.

国富强而法立兮,	国家富强好法度才能建立,
属贞臣而日娭①。	君上将国家大事委托忠臣。
秘密事之载心兮,	我全心全意为了国事操劳,
虽过失犹弗治。	即便有过失也不会胡治理。
心纯厖②而不泄兮,	我纵然心地纯厚绝不泄密,
遭谗人而嫉之。	却也遭到奸人的毁谤妒忌。
君含怒而待臣兮,	君主愤怒而不公地对待我,
不清澈其然否。	也不明察事情的是非曲直。
蔽晦君之聪明兮,	君王被小人蒙蔽聪明,
虚惑误又以欺。	花言巧语使其一次次被骗。
弗参验以考实兮,	不去比较验证事情真相,
远迁臣而弗思。	将我远远放逐不考虑周全。
信谗谀之溷浊兮,	偏偏听信小人污浊谗言,
盛气志而过之。	竟然怒气冲冲将忠臣责难。
何贞臣之无罪兮。	忠贞的臣子我有什么过错,
被离谤而见尤③。	为何遭受诽谤而受到放逐。
惭光景之诚信兮,	惭愧我像日月那样的忠诚,
身幽隐而备之。	即便身被远远放逐仍满怀忠诚。

① 娭(xī): 同"嬉"。
② 纯厖(máng): 纯厚朴实。
③ 离谤: 遭毁谤。尤: 责备。

The law on rich, strong land held sway, oh!
The king confided in me each day.
The secret locked in my heart, oh!
Casual misdeeds were put apart.

My heart was pure and free from wrong, oh!
But slanders' jealousy was strong.
Angry with me the king became, oh!
And cared not if I'm free from blame,

The king's eyes and ears were deceived, oh!
What was wrong and false was believed.
Unjustified, I met disgrace, oh!
And was removed to far-off place.
To trust traducers he was free, oh!
Angry, he would find fault in me.

Though, loyal, I have done no wrong, oh!
I suffer from slanders in throng.
Ashamed before the sunny scene, oh!
I hide myself behind the screen.

临沅湘之玄渊兮,	面对着沅水、湘水的万丈深渊,
遂自忍而沉流。	我怎么能够忍心葬身江中。
卒没身而绝名兮,	那样的结果只能身死名灭,
惜壅①君之不昭。	可惜君王被蒙蔽仍不明察。
君无度而弗察兮,	君王未立准则难察民情,
使芳草为薮幽②。	将芳草弃在幽深的大泽中,
焉舒情而抽信兮?	怎么能抒发衷情展示诚信?
恬死亡而不聊。	我宁愿死去也不苟且偷生。
独障壅③而蔽隐兮,	只因为前途壅塞掩蔽阻隔,
使贞臣为无由。	更使得忠臣个个无所适从。
闻百里④之为虏兮,	我听说百里奚曾身为俘虏,
伊尹⑤烹于庖厨。	伊尹早先也曾经做过厨师。
吕望⑥屠于朝歌兮,	姜子牙曾在朝歌屠杀牲畜,
宁戚⑦歌而饭牛。	宁戚一面唱歌还一边喂牛。
不逢汤武与桓缪兮,	若不遇商汤周武齐桓秦缪,
世孰云而知之?	世间有谁知道他们的才能?

① 壅:蒙蔽。
② 薮(sǒu)幽:大泽的深幽处。
③ 障壅:与"蔽隐"同义。
④ 百里:百里奚,春秋时虞国大夫。
⑤ 伊尹:原来是有莘氏的陪嫁奴隶,曾经当过厨师。后来任商汤的相。
⑥ 吕望:本姓姜,即姜尚。传说他本来在朝歌当屠夫,老年钓于渭水之滨,周文王认出他是个贤人,便重用了他。
⑦ 宁戚:春秋时人,他在喂牛时唱歌,齐桓公认出他是个贤人。

Of the dark river on the brink, oh!
Could I bear to plunge in and sink?
I'd drown myself and leave my name behind, oh!
But to the light my lord's still blind.
Without measure to judge man's deeds, oh!
He let sweet herb hidden in weeds.
Could I express my feelings fine? oh!
I would rather die than repine.
Screened from my lord and hidden in the shade , oh!
How could loyal request be made?

Bai Li was once a prisoner, oh!
A cook became Shang minister.
Master Jiang was a butcher strong, oh!
Ning Qi fed ox while singing a song.
If they had not met connoisseurs, oh!
Could they have become counselors?

吴信谗而弗味兮,	吴王听信谗言不仔细判别,
子胥死而后忧。	伍子胥被赐死后国家患忧。
介子①忠而立枯兮,	介子推忠贞被焚死而骨枯,
文君寤而追求。	晋文公一旦醒悟即刻访求。
封介山而为之禁兮,	于是下令封山而严禁砍柴,
报大德之优游。	这是报答子推的大恩大德。
思久故之亲身兮,	想起子推往日的割股献食,
因缟素而哭之。	晋文公身穿丧服痛哭泪流。
或忠信而死节兮,	有人忠贞诚信为节操而死,
或訑谩②而不疑。	有人阴险欺诈反而被重用。
弗省察而按实兮,	既不去认真调查也不核实,
听谗人之虚辞。	只听信小人们的虚妄之词。
芳与泽其杂糅兮,	芳香的与腥臭的混杂一处,
孰申旦而别之?	又有谁能夜以继日认真辨识呢?

何芳草之早殀兮,	为什么芳草会过早地枯萎,
微霜降而下戒。	因为微霜初降时没有防备。
谅聪不明而蔽壅兮,	确是君主不明受人蒙蔽,
使谗谀而日得!	才使进谗献谀者得意扬扬。

---

① 介子:介子推,春秋时晋文公的臣子。
② 訑(dàn)谩:欺诈。訑,通"诞"。

Wu trusted in slanderers' words, oh!
Killed his general and rued afterwards.
Loyal Jie would rather be burned, oh!
When his forgetful Duke Wen for him yearned.
The Duke made Mount Jie a holy place, oh!
To requite his service with grace.
The Duke thought of his old compeer, oh!
Clad in white, he shed tear on tear.
As martyrs loyal friends may die, oh!
Those are not doubted, who cheat and lie.
Acting nor with care nor on truth, oh!
One would believe slanders, forsooth.
The foul is mixed up with the fair, oh!
Who could discern between them anywhere?

Why are sweet herbs withered and lost, oh!
Before descends the hoary frost?
The unwise are more deaf each day, oh!
When flattery and slander hold sway.

自前世之嫉贤兮，	自古以来的贤才都被嫉妒，
谓蕙若其不可佩。	都说蕙草杜若不能佩戴身上。
妒佳冶之芬芳兮，	嫉妒那佳人的芬芳的香气，
嫫母①姣而自好。	丑陋的嫫母却自以为美丽妩媚。
虽有西施之美容兮，	纵然有西施般的绝顶美貌，
谗妒入以自代。	丑恶之人也会将你来取代。
愿陈情以白行兮，	我愿意陈述真情表白所为，
得罪过之不意。	反而出人意料地获罪过。
情冤见之日明兮，	挚情与冤屈显明于光天化日，
如列宿之错置。	有如天上的星宿各有陈列。
乘骐骥而驰骋兮，	跨上骏马在草原长途奔驰，
无辔衔而自载。	没有辔缰全凭自己的控制。
乘泛泭②以下流兮，	乘坐浮筏向下游行驶，
无舟楫而自备。	没有船桨全靠自己的掌握。
背法度而心治兮，	君王背弃法度凭私心治国，
辟与此其无异。	和上面所说的这些毫无差异。
宁溘死而流亡兮，	我宁肯忽然死亡魂飞魄散，
恐祸殃之有再。	唯恐灾难再一次祸害国家。
不毕辞而赴渊兮，	不等把话说完便投水自尽，
惜壅君之不识。	可惜蒙昧的君主仍不觉醒。

---

① 嫫母：传说是黄帝的妃子，貌极丑。
② 泭（fú）：同"桴"，筏子。

As of old, jealous of the fair, oh!
They say orchids unfit to wear.
Jealous of fragrant beauty sweet, oh!
The ugly queen thought herself neat.
The Western Lady had a lovely face, oh!
Jealous women would take her place.
I would explain what I have done, oh!
They say I am a guilty one.
The wrong done me becomes each day more clear, oh!
Like stars in the celestial sphere.

I'd ride my steed and gallop to and fro, oh!
Without bit and rein, how could I go?
I'd mount a raft and downstream float, oh!
Where could I find oars for my boat?
A lawless heart can never rule, oh!
Nor can a boat go without tool.

I would rather unburied die, oh!
Lest disasters come by and by.
Should I plunge in the stream with much unsaid, oh!
Could I clear my lord's muddled head?

橘颂

后皇^①嘉树,	皇天后土孕育的橘树,
橘徕^②服兮。	生而适应南国水土。
受命不迁,	秉承着不再迁离的使命,
生南国兮。	便永久生长在南楚。
深固难徙,	你根深蒂固,再难移徙,
更壹志兮。	立志无比专一。
绿叶素荣,	绿叶白花,
纷其可喜兮。	多么缤纷可爱。
曾枝剡^③棘,	重重枝蔓虽有尖锐的刺,
圆果抟^④兮。	却结有圆满的果子。
青黄杂糅,	青黄交错相映,
文章^⑤烂兮。	色彩灿若云霞。
精色内白,	你外色鲜明,内在一片洁白,
类可任兮。	类似仁人志士。
纷缊^⑥宜修,	芬芳无以伦比,
姱而不丑兮。	赋性坚贞,何其脱俗。

① 后:后土。皇:皇天。
② 徕(lái):同"来"。
③ 剡(yǎn):尖锐。
④ 抟(tuán):圆的样子。
⑤ 文章:文采。
⑥ 纷缊:同"氛氲",香气盛貌。

Hymn to the Orange Tree

Fair tree on earth without a peer,
Laden with oranges, you grow here, oh!
You are destined not to be moved
In the southern land you are loved, oh!

Your root's too deep from us to part;
What's more, you have a single heart, oh!
You have green leaves and flowers white.
What an exuberant delight! oh!

Your branches thick armed with sharp pine
Are laden with fruit round and fine, oh!
A riot of yellow and green,
What a dazzling splendid scene! oh!

Within you're pure; without you're bright,
Like a man virtuous and right, oh!
Luxuriant and trimmed, you thrive;
No blemish but charm's kept alive, oh!

嗟尔幼志，	啊，南国的橘树，
有以异兮。	你自幼即与众不同。
独立不迁，	你独立于世，不肯迁移，
岂不可喜兮？	此志节怎不令人欣喜？
深固难徙，	你根深蒂固，再难移徙，
廓其无求兮。	气度那么从容开阔无所欲求。
苏世独立，	你远出俗世，卓尔不群，
横而不流兮。	横立世上而不随从流俗。
闭心自慎，	你谨慎存心，清心自重，
终不过失兮。	不曾有任何过错罪愆。
秉德无私，	你至诚一片，
参天地兮。	期与天地合无私之德。
愿岁并谢，	我愿于百花凋零的岁暮，
与长友兮。	与你永做个坚贞的朋友。
淑离不淫，	你美善而从不放纵，
梗其有理兮。	挺直的枝干纹理纯明。
年岁虽少，	你年纪虽小，
可师长兮。	可以为世楷模。
行比伯夷，	足比古代的伯夷，
置以为像兮。	将永是我立身的榜样。

While young, you aspire as you please,
Quite different from other trees, oh!
Grown up, independent you stand.
How you're admired in southern land! oh!

You're too deep-rooted to transplant;
Seeking nothing, you're so exuberant, oh!
You stand alone in this world wide,
Unyielding to the vulgar tide, oh!

You seal your heart and act with care;
You've done nothing wrong anywhere, oh!
So selfless, you have virtues high,
And become one with earth and sky, oh!

All the trees fade by the year's end;
I will forever be your friend, oh!
You're free from sin, so pure and bright,
And your trunk is ever upright, oh!

Although you appear young in view,
Even the old may learn from you, oh!
You're an example and inspirer,
And I am your humble admirer, oh!

悲回风

悲回风之摇蕙[①]兮，	可怜蕙草被回旋之风摇落，
心冤结而内伤。	我心中冤屈郁结内心感伤。
物有微而陨性兮，	美好的蕙草本性微弱凋谢，
声有隐而先倡。	回旋之风来时悄无声息。
夫何彭咸之造思兮，	为什么彭咸产生出的思想，
暨志介而不忘！	与其心志相联系始终不忘。
万变其情岂可盖兮，	遭遇万变其真心不曾掩盖，
孰虚伪之可长！	虚伪做作又怎能保持久长。
鸟兽鸣以号群兮，	鸟兽吵嚷呼唤着同类，
草苴比[②]而不芳。	鲜花混杂枯草就没有芬芳。
鱼葺鳞以自别兮，	鱼儿鼓起鳞片来炫耀自己，
蛟龙隐其文章。	蛟龙反把自己的光彩隐藏。
故荼荠[③]不同亩兮，	苦荼甜荠不能种在一块田里，
兰茝幽而独芳。	兰芷在幽深之处独含清香。

---

① 回风：旋转之风。摇：撼动。蕙：香草。
② 苴（jū）：已死之草。比：比合。
③ 荼（tú）：苦菜。荠（jì）：甜菜。

Grieving at the Whirlwind

The whirlwind shakes the orchids down, oh!
My heart is drowned in grief overgrown.
A little thing is easy to fall, oh!
The faintest sound may arouse all.

Why ancient sages do I admire? oh!
I can't forget to what they aspire.
Who can conceal his change of heart, oh!
And play for long a deceitful part?

Birds and beasts seek their kind and meet, oh!
Herbs amid weeds are no longer sweet.
Fish show their scale's flickering light, oh!
The dragon hides its patterns bright.
Sweet herbs don't share the same field with the dead, oh!
When alone, orchids' fragrance will spread.

惟佳人之永都①兮，	只有那佳人才能永久美丽，
更统世而自贶②。	历经数代能自祈多福。
眇远志之所及兮，	远大的志向所达到的高度，
怜浮云之相羊③。	怜爱白云在天空随风飘荡。
介眇志之所惑兮，	耿介地抱有远大志向无人知，
窃赋诗之所明。	只能私自赋诗来明白倾诉。
惟佳人之独怀兮，	想那佳人博大的胸襟坦荡，
折若椒以自处。	采来了杜若申椒自我装扮。
曾歔欷之嗟嗟兮，	我屡屡悲慨哽咽连声叹息，
独隐伏而思虑。	独自隐居偏僻处思绪满怀。
涕泣交而凄凄兮，	我涕泪交错话不尽的凄凉，
思不眠以至曙。	思前想后辗转反侧到天亮。
终长夜之曼曼兮，	长夜漫漫如悲伤没有尽头，
掩此哀而不去。	无限的哀伤总是停驻心头。
寤从容以周流兮，	醒来后我从容地周游四方，
聊逍遥以自恃。	姑且以逍遥自在宽慰自我。
伤太息之愍怜兮，	我伤感叹息实在是可怜，
气於邑而不可止。	心思郁结总不能停止。

---

① 都：优美，漂亮。
② 贶（kuàng）：赐。自贶，犹言自求多福。
③ 相羊：徜徉。

A beauty will always be fair, oh!
For the changing world I don't care.
Far away aspire my thoughts proud, oh!
Like the pitiable floating cloud.
Lest my thoughts should aspire in vain, oh!
I write songs to make myself plain.

Over beauties alone I brood, oh!
I pluck flowers from fragrant wood.
I heave deep sigh upon deep sigh, oh!
Alone and pondering, I lie.

Dreary tears stream from nose and eyes, oh!
Sleepless, I ponder till sunrise.
The pace of long, long night is slow, oh!
The grief I would suppress won't go.

I rise and slowly rove with ease, oh!
I try my sorrow to appease.
I utter a pitiable sigh, oh!
My stifling sorrow will not die.

纠①思心以为纕兮，　　愁思如佩带般缠绕着我，
编愁苦以为膺。　　　　苦闷编结为我身上的背心。
折若木以蔽光兮，　　　折下若木的枝条遮蔽日光，
随飘风之所仍。　　　　任由那狂风将我吹到何方。

存仿佛而不见兮，　　　万物迷迷糊糊分不清真相，
心踊跃其若汤。　　　　我的心跳跃着就好像沸汤。
抚珮衽以案志兮，　　　抚着玉佩和衣襟抑制激动，
超惘惘而遂行。　　　　怅惘失意中将要奔向前方。

岁忽忽其若颓兮，　　　岁月匆匆有如水流水将尽，
时亦冉冉而将至。　　　年华老去我的归期也来临。
薠蘅槁而节离兮，　　　白薠杜蘅枯萎而节节折断，
芳已歇而不比。　　　　芬芳的鲜花已经不再绽放。

怜思心之不可惩兮，　　可怜我的愁思还无法消除，
证此言之不可聊。　　　足以证明这些谎言不可信赖。
宁溘死而流亡兮，　　　我宁愿忽然死去魂飞魄散，
不忍为此之常愁。　　　也不愿忍受无休止的痛苦。

孤子吟而抆泪兮，　　　孤独的人悲叹着拭去泪水，
放子出而不还。　　　　被放逐的人再也不能返回。
孰能思而不隐兮？　　　谁能受此痛苦而不悲伤啊？
照彭咸之所闻。　　　　我愿听到彭咸的出世法则。

① 纠（jiū）：纠缠。

I twist my longing round my breast, oh!
And weave my grief into a vest.
I break a branch to shade from light, oh!
And follow the wind left and right.

The world seems something vague which sleeps, oh!
My heart like boiling water leaps.
I clutch my belt to calm my heart, oh!
Lost in sorrow, slowly I start.

Quickly, quickly elapsed a year, oh!
Slowly, slowly my time draws near.
Withered grasses break one and all, oh!
Unrivaled fragrant flowers fall.

My longing heart cannot be cured, oh!
My stinging words must be endured.
Exiled, I'd die to find relief, oh!
Rather than bear this endless grief.

The orphan sobs and rubs his tears, oh!
The exile goes and disappears.
Who could think of this without pain? oh!
Did ancient sages hear this in vain?

登石峦以远望兮，	登上石山向远方瞭望，
路眇眇之默默。	道路那么遥远又那么寂静。
入景响之无应兮，	进入这寂寞无声的空阔地，
闻省想而不可得。	想听闻省视思索一无所获。
愁郁郁之无快兮，	我愁思郁郁毫无一点快乐，
居戚戚而不可解。	总处在悲戚之中无法解脱。
心鞿羁①而不形兮，	心思被紧紧捆绑挣扎不开，
气缭转而自缔。	血气纠缠打结我难以释怀。
穆眇眇之无垠兮，	静穆的宇宙渺茫没有边际，
莽芒芒之无仪。	广阔无垠的大地不着痕迹。
声有隐而相感兮，	声音虽然隐蔽而能相互感应，
物有纯而不可为。	事物纯美却只能独自叹息。
邈蔓蔓之不可量兮，	前途渺渺漫漫啊不可量度，
缥绵绵之不可纡。	思绪悠悠长长不可收束。
愁悄悄之常悲兮，	我愁心深重常自感到悲痛，
翩冥冥之不可娱。	在幽暗中飞翔也并不快乐。
凌大波而流风兮，	不如乘着大波顺风而流，
托彭咸之所居。	魂灵寄托在彭咸所居之处。
上高岩之峭岸兮，	登上高高的陡峭岩石之巅，
处雌蜺之标颠。	伫立于绚丽的霓虹的顶点。
据青冥而攄虹兮，	占据着青天舒展一抹彩虹，
遂倏忽而扪天。	于是刹时间我便抚摸苍天。

① 鞿（jī）羁：马缰，此处指受拘束。

I climb a rock and look afar, oh!
How silent the far-flung roads are!
No echo of shivering shade, oh!
I strain my eyes and ears, but all fade.

Sad and dreary I cannot stay, oh!
My sorrow can't be put away.
My heart is tied with unloosed care, oh!
My breath is twisted into despair.

Immensity mute has no border, oh!
Vast wilderness can have no order.
Sound unseen can be felt and heard, oh!
Things uncreated can't be put in word.

The farthest can't be measured out, oh!
The endless can't be turned about.
Grief in silence is sadder plight, oh!
Flight in darkness affords no delight.
On wind and waves I'd find the road, oh!
Toward the ancient sage's abode.

I mount the steepest mountain height, oh!
And ride the upper rainbow bright.
I dance the lower one near by, oh!
And stroke with hand the azure sky.

吸湛露之浮源兮，	我要饱饮浓重团聚的露水，
漱凝霜之雰雰，	用那清凉凝结的寒霜漱口。
依风穴以自息兮，	背靠着风的穴口短暂休息，
忽倾寤以婵媛。	忽然了悟而思绪仍在悲忧。

冯昆仑以瞰雾兮，	我依靠着昆仑山看那云雾，
隐岷山以清江。	依傍着岷山观察长江气势。
惮涌湍之磕磕兮，	水石撞击之声真让人害怕，
听波声之汹汹。	涛声汹涌的怒吼刺穿耳鼓。

纷容容之无经兮，	心思纷纷乱乱没有规律，
罔芒芒之无纪。	精神迷迷惘惘毫无头绪。
轧洋洋之无从兮，	浩瀚的江水滔滔难趋从，
驰委移之焉止？	连绵起伏奔腾到哪儿停息？

漂翻翻其上下兮，	心如急流翻飞着忽上忽下，
翼遥遥其左右。	两翼的回流翻腾忽左忽右。
氾潏潏①其前后兮，	汹涌泛滥的波涛前后奔腾，
伴张弛之信期。	伴着江水涨落定时的汛期。

观炎气之相仍兮，	观看那火焰将潮水蒸腾，
窥烟液之所积。	窥察那云朵雨滴所以集结。
悲霜雪之俱下兮，	悲慨秋霜冬雪纷纷落下，
听潮水之相击。	倾听着潮水波浪撞击雷鸣。

① 氾（fàn）：由主流分出而又复合的河水。潏（yù）潏：水流转的样子。

I sip from floating source the dew, oh!
And rinse my mouth with frost in view.
I rest in the Cave of the Breeze, oh!
Awake, I rove again with ease.

Into the mist on Mount Kunlun I peer, oh!
From Mount Min flows the River clear.
Angry torrents dash on boulders before, oh!
I hear violent billows roar.

The River overwhelms its border, oh!
Its water runs and rolls in disorder.
It churns, I know not whence it flows, oh!
It winds its way, I know not where it goes.

Waves fall and rise and reach their height, oh!
They swirl and sway from left to right.
The waves before are pressed by those behind, oh!
As if flood and ebb were combined.

I watch the heated vapor rise, oh!
Condensed into dew in the skies.
I'm grieved it falls in frost and snow, oh!
And shocks with tidal bore below.

借光景以往来兮，	我借着光与影来往天地间，
施黄棘之枉策。	使用棘刺做成的弯鞭驾驭。
求介子之所存兮，	我要寻求介子推隐居之地，
见伯夷之放迹。	再拜谒一下伯夷放逐之处。
心调度而弗去兮，	心里思量绝不能离开故国，
刻著志之无适。	我意志坚决哪儿也不会去。

曰：吾怨往昔之所冀兮，	尾声：我怨恨往昔那些期望成空，
悼来者之悐悐[①]。	悲悼未来更令人提心吊胆。
浮江淮而入海兮，	浮长江过淮水向东入海，
从子胥而自适。	去追随伍子胥以自求适意。
望大河之洲渚兮，	我眺望大河中的沙洲水渚，
悲申徒之抗迹。	独自悲伤申徒的高尚事迹。
骤谏君而不听兮，	他屡劝君王而得不到采纳，
重任石之何益！	于是抱石自沉又有何益处。
心絓结而不解兮，	心绪纠结难以解脱啊，
思蹇产而不释。[②]	思理不畅无法释怀。

[①] 悐（tì）悐：同"惕惕"，机警忧惧的样子。
[②] 英译文中漏译了此句。为尊重许渊冲先生原译稿，漏译部分未作补充。

I'd borrow daylight to make a trip, oh!
And use a crooked yellow thorn for whip.
I seek the hermit's dwelling place, oh!
I see the royal brothers' trace.
My mind once made up won't depart, oh!
I'll be true to the measure of my heart.

Epilogue
I grieve for hopes of days gone by, oh!
And mourn for those that will come nigh.
I would float down the River Blue, oh!
To the sea ruled by General Wu.
On Yellow River's isles I gaze, oh!
And mourn over Shen Tu of olden days,
Who rebuked his lord in vain, oh!
What good to be drowned in the main?

远游

悲时俗之迫阨兮，　　　　　悲叹世俗嫉贤妒能限制我的自由，
愿轻举而远游。　　　　　　我真想轻身飞翔向远处周游。
质菲薄而无因兮，　　　　　我的本性菲薄又没有依靠，
焉托乘而上浮？　　　　　　以什么为寄托驾着清气上升？

遭沉浊而污秽兮，　　　　　周围世界是污浊黑暗，
独郁结其谁语！　　　　　　只独自苦闷不知向谁去倾诉！
夜耿耿而不寐兮，　　　　　漫长的黑夜里辗转反侧不能成眠，
魂茕茕而至曙。　　　　　　守着孤魂一缕凄迷直到天明。

惟天地之无穷兮，　　　　　联想到只有天地才能无穷无尽，
哀人生之长勤。　　　　　　哀叹人生劳碌终生坎坷辛苦。
往者余弗及兮，　　　　　　过去了的事情我已经无法赶上，
来者吾不闻。　　　　　　　将要到来的事情我又难以预见。

步徙倚而遥思兮，　　　　　我徘徊不定思绪遥远，
怊惝怳①而乖怀。　　　　　惆怅失意理想难以实现。
意荒忽而流荡兮，　　　　　我的神志恍惚如水波激荡，
心愁悽而增悲。　　　　　　心中愁苦悲伤无限。

---

① 怊惝怳（chāo chǎng huǎng）：惆怅失意。

The Far-off Journey

Hard pressed by the world's ways and woe, oh!
I'd become light and upwards go.
Weak within and helpless without, oh!
On what can I ride and float about?

Fallen in the mire far and wide, oh!
To whom can I my grief confide?
Sleepless throughout the endless night, oh!
My lonely soul roves till daylight.

Between the boundless earth and sky, oh!
Forever man must toil, I sigh.
Beyond my reach are bygone days, oh!
Can I hear what the future says?

I pace and ponder here and there, oh!
Frustrated, I'm lost in despair.
My mind is bewildered in cloud, oh!
My heart with grief is overflowed.

神倏忽而不反兮,　　　魂灵忽然间飞散一去不返,
形枯槁而独留。　　　　枯槁的肉体独自留存在人间。
内惟省以端操兮,　　　我反复思索以坚持操守,
求正气之所由。　　　　寻求天地间的浩然正气从何而生。

漠虚静以恬愉兮,　　　内心清静才能安适愉悦,
澹无为而自得。　　　　淡泊无为才能怡然自得。
闻赤松①之清尘兮,　　听闻赤松子清高绝俗的事迹,
愿承风乎遗则。　　　　愿继承他的遗风和法则。

贵真人之休德兮,　　　我崇尚他养真之人的美德,
美往世之登仙。　　　　羡慕古人能超越生死成为神仙。
与化去而不见兮,　　　他们的身体虽然消失不见,
名声著而日延。　　　　名声却显耀而流传千年。

奇傅说之托星辰兮,　　我惊叹傅说死后能化为星辰,
羡韩众②之得一。　　　也羡慕韩众能得道成仙。
形穆穆以浸远兮,　　　他们的形体渐渐地远去,
离人群而遁逸。　　　　逃避世俗隐身不见。

因气变而遂曾举兮,　　他们凭借精气的变化高飞,
忽神奔而鬼怪。　　　　如鬼神往来神秘莫测。
时仿佛以遥见兮,　　　有时候朦胧中似乎远远可见,
精皎皎以往来。　　　　神灵光芒闪烁往来于宇宙之间。

① 赤松:赤松子,传说神农时为雨师。
② 韩众:韩终,春秋齐人,为王采药,王不肯服,于是他自己服下成仙。

My spirit goes and won't return, oh!
My body withered must sojourn.
I look in to learn to do right, oh!
And seek to know from where comes light.

I'm glad my mind is abstinent, oh!
With inaction I feel content.
I've heard how Red Pine was carefree, oh!
I'd learn from what he had left me.

I know the Real Beings' ways, oh!
And Immortals of bygone days.
They're deified and disappear, oh!
Their names will last from year to year.

I marvel how Fu to a star could run, oh!
And how Han with the Way could become one.
Their bodies tranquil go afar, oh!
Their spirit leaves the world for the star.

Transformed in air, I upward rise, oh!
As swift as gods and spirits in surprise.
The world is hazy, viewed from far, oh!
Spirits come to and fro, bright as star.

绝氛埃而淑尤兮,	他们超越世俗居住在名山洞府,
终不反其故都。	再也不愿返回故国乡里。
免众患而不惧兮,	他们摆脱众人的忧患而无所畏惧,
世莫知其所如。	世人都不知道他们的踪迹。
恐天时之代序兮,	我担心岁月流逝季节更替,
耀灵晔而西征。	灿烂的太阳正在渐渐西下。
微霜降而下沦兮,	薄薄的秋霜开始降临大地,
悼芳草之先零。	我可怜那些香草会最先凋零。
聊仿佯而逍遥兮,	我姑且徘徊而逍遥自在,
永历年而无成!	只虚度年华一事无成啊!
谁可与玩斯遗芳兮?	谁能与我赏玩这些残留的芳草啊?
晨向风而舒情。	只好长久地迎风抒情。
高阳邈以远兮,	帝高阳的时代距我们实在太远,
余将焉所程?	我将怎么去效法他高洁的德行?
重曰:	又一支歌曲:
春秋忽其不淹兮,	春去秋来光阴流逝,
奚久留此故居?	我怎么能长久留在故居?
轩辕不可攀援兮,	轩辕黄帝高贵至极不能高攀,
吾将从王乔①而娱戏。	我将跟随王子乔娱乐游戏。

---

① 王乔:王子乔,传说中得道成仙者,据说他是周灵王之子。

Leaving the dust, carefree I stand, oh!
I won't go back to my native land.
I'm not troubled by the world's woe, oh!.
Nobody knows where I will go.

The seasons will change without rest, oh!
I fear the sun will ever go west.
Hoar frost will fall, I am afraid, oh!
And fragrant grass and flowers will fade.

I try to wander far and near, oh!
Nothing's achieved from year to year.
Who would enjoy with me fragrance at ease? oh!
At dawn I bare my heart to the breeze.
The wise king long ago was gone, oh!
Who can I model myself on?

Again I say:
Spring and autumn will pass away, oh!
How in old home can I long stay?
The Yellow Emperor lived long ago, oh!
I'd play with Prince Qiao high and low.

餐六气①而饮沉瀣兮，	我要吞食六气渴饮清露，
漱正阳②而含朝霞。	漱着正阳之气含着朝霞之光。
保神明之清澄兮，	我要保持精神清新心灵清明，
精气入而粗秽除。	吸入精气将体内的浊气扫荡。

顺凯风以从游兮，	我将随着和煦南风出游，
至南巢而壹息。	休息在南方神鸟的巢穴之旁。
见王子而宿之兮，	见了王子乔就在那里留宿，
审壹气之和德。	询问他"一气"怎样"和德"。

曰："道可受兮，不可传；	王子乔说："道可以心领不可言传；
其小无内兮，其大无垠；	它是可以无限小或无限大的；
无滑而魂兮，彼将自然；	只要你的神魂不乱它就自然会出现；
壹气孔神兮，	这一元之气十分神通，
于中夜存；	只有半夜寂静之时才能感受。
虚以待之兮，	"你要以虚静之心来对待它，
无为之先；	万事之前都不要想着自己占先。
庶类以成兮，	如果万事万物都是这样生成，
此德之门。"	这就是'和德'的门槛。"

---

① 六气：据道家之说，世上有天地四时六种精气，修炼者服食之即能成仙。
② 正阳：六气中夏时之气。

I'd eat six essences and drink dew, oh!
I'd rinse my mouth with cloud and sunbeams new.
I'd keep my spirit pure and divine, oh!
Exhale the foul and inhale the fine.

I'd ride south wind to southern nest, oh!
Enjoy my fill and take a rest.
I'd greet the prince in serenity, oh!
And ask him how to attain unity.

He says, "We may learn the Way, oh!
Which we can't to others convey.
Small, nothing within it is found; oh!
Great, there is no boundary around.
If to disorder not inclined, oh!
Naturally will work your mind.
If your spirit is unified, oh!
At midnight it's kept pure inside.
Empty-minded you may await, oh!
Do not strive to be first or great!
Let all things be formed as they may, oh!
Then you'll find the door to the Way."

闻至贵而遂徂兮，	领教了这些至理名言我便想远去，
忽乎吾将行。	迫不及待我就出发去施行。
仍羽人于丹丘兮，	我随着飞仙到达丹丘仙境，
留不死之旧乡。	留在这神仙的不死之乡。
朝濯发于汤谷兮，	晨起在汤谷洗洗头发，
夕晞余身兮九阳[①]。	傍晚让九阳晒干我的全身。
吸飞泉之微液兮，	我要吮吸飞泉里的泉水，
怀琬琰之华英。	把美玉当作我的食粮。
玉色頩以脕颜[②]兮，	我的脸庞变得洁白而光泽滋润，
精醇粹而始壮。	我的体魄健壮精力充沛。
质销铄以汋约兮，	我的凡胎脱尽体质轻盈，
神要眇以淫放。	神气幽远自然无拘无束。
嘉南州之炎德兮，	南方气候温暖真令人赞赏，
丽桂树之冬荣；	美丽的桂树冬天也吐播芬芳。
山萧条而无兽兮，	这里的山林空寂没有野兽，
野寂漠其无人。	原野一片寂静不见人影。
载营魄而登霞兮，	载着魂魄登上朝霞，
掩浮云而上征。	乘着浮云向天宫飞升。
命天阍其开关兮，	我叫天宫的守门人将门打开，
排阊阖而望予。	他推开大门望着我进来。

① 九阳：古时传说，旸谷有扶桑树，上有一个太阳，下有九个太阳，十个太阳轮流值班一天。
② 頩（pīng）：貌美。脕（wàn）颜：滋润颜面。

Having learned this secret, I part, oh!
In a twinkling I start.
I see at Red Hill the Spirits with wings, oh!
They stay in the land of eternal springs.

At dawn I wash my hair in Val Divine, oh!
At dusk I dry myself beneath suns nine.
I sip the foam of Flying Spring, oh!
My breast adorned with gems in ring.

My jade-like face looks fair and bright, oh!
My spirit pure grows strong and light.
My body languishes by and by, oh!
My carefree soul flies upward high.

I like the warmth of Southern State, oh!
And laurel blooms in winter late.
The mountains without beast look dreary, oh!
The wilds seem lonely with no man weary.

My soul on rainbow cloud looks bright, oh!
Veiled in floating cloud, I reach the height.
I bid the porter open the door, oh!
He does and looks me o'er.

召丰隆使先导兮，　　　我召来雷神丰隆做我的向导，
问太微之所居。　　　　叫他去询问太微官的所在。
集重阳入帝宫兮，　　　积聚九重之阳进入帝宫，
造旬始而观清都①。　　我要旬始星参观天帝清都。

朝发轫于太仪兮，　　　早上从太仪殿驾车出发，
夕始临乎於微闾②。　　傍晚到达微闾停留。
屯余车之万乘兮，　　　众多马车屯聚一起，
纷溶与而并驰。　　　　浩浩荡荡齐驰而行。
驾八龙之婉婉兮，　　　驾车的八条龙蜿蜒前进，
载云旗之逶蛇。　　　　车上的云旗逶迤随风摆动。

建雄虹之采旄兮，　　　又把霓虹作为彩色之旗，
五色杂而炫耀。　　　　五色斑斓且光照千里。
服偃蹇以低昂兮，　　　驾车的马匹婉转起伏不定，
骖连蜷以骄骜。　　　　两边的马匹蹄曲纵横恣意。

骑胶葛以杂乱兮，　　　车马众多交错杂乱，
斑漫衍而方行。　　　　队列绵绵不绝浩荡前行。
撰余辔而正策兮，　　　我已经抓紧缰绳放正马鞭，
吾将过乎句芒③。　　　我的车马将要经过东方木神。

---

① 旬始：星宿名。清都：天宫之名。
② 微闾：医巫闾山，古人认为神仙所居。
③ 句（gōu）芒：东方木神之名。

I bid the Lord of Cloud to lead the way, oh!
And ask where does Divinity stay.
I reach the ninth sphere's palace hall, oh!
From Morning Star I view the capital.

At dawn I leave Heaven's Arcade, oh!
At dusk I reach Mountain of Jade.
Ten thousand chariots smoothly ride, oh!
The steeds go forward side by side.
We drive eight dragons serpentine, oh!
Cloud banners undulate in a line.

I make a flag of rainbow bright, oh!
Five colors form a dazzling sight.
The york-steeds run with their heads bowed, oh!
The trace-steeds arch, curve and look proud.

We hear the din and bustle rise, oh!
Our colorful train dazzles the eyes.
I hold my reins and flip my whip, oh!
We'll pass by the wood in our trip.

历太皓以右转兮,	经过了东帝太皞车马向右转,
前飞廉以启路。	让风伯飞廉在前开路。
阳杲杲其未光兮,	灿烂的太阳还没有放出光芒,
凌天地以径度。	就在天地之上横越飞迁。

风伯为余先驱兮,	风伯是我车队的先驱,
氛埃辟而清凉。	我已经逃离俗世一身轻松。
凤凰翼其承旂①兮,	凤凰张开双翼支撑云旗,
遇蓐收乎西皇②。	在西帝那儿又遇见了金神蓐收。

揽彗星以为旍兮,	摘下彗星作为我的旗帜,
举斗柄以为麾。	举起北斗之柄做大旗舒卷。
叛陆离其上下兮,	我的旗帜五色缤纷上下翻飞,
游惊雾之流波。	在云海惊涛中漫游流连。

时暧曃其曭莽③兮,	天色渐渐昏暗四周朦胧一片,
召玄武④而奔属。	我命北方玄武紧紧跟随。
后文昌使掌行兮,	让文昌在后面掌管随从,
选署众神以并毂。	安排众神和我并驾向前。

路曼曼其修远兮,	前方的路程迢迢多么漫长,
徐弭节而高厉。	我扬鞭缓缓地驰向高天。
左雨师使径侍兮,	叫雨师相伴在左边道路上,
右雷公以为卫。	让雷公保驾扈从在右边。

① 旂(qí):画龙系铜铃的旗。
② 蓐(rù)收:金神之名,为西方上帝少昊之子。西皇:少昊。
③ 暧曃(ài dài):昏暗不明。曭(tǎng)莽:幽暗迷蒙。
④ 玄武:二十八宿中北方七宿的总称,为龟蛇合体之象。

We cross the eastern sky and turn right, oh!
The Wind Lord leads the way in flight.
Before sunrise the Heaven's cool, oh!
We fly across the Heaven's Pool.

The Lord of Wind leads the way on high, oh!
Dust cleared away, clean and cold is the sky.
Phoenixes spread their wings like flags unrolled, oh!
And in the west we meet the Lord of Gold.

For banner I seize the Broom Star, oh!
For baton the Dipper's Handle stretching far.
Up and down all look strange, oh!
Into fleeting mist the drifting waves change.

Obscured and dimmed the stars appear, oh!
I bid the Black Star to bring up the rear.
The Star of Letters leads my trains, oh!
All gods go abreast holding reins,

The endless road stretches afar, oh!
We slow down to the highest star.
Left and right the Master of Rain Hard, oh!
And of Thunder serve as my guard.

欲度世以忘归兮,	我想要超越世俗乐而忘返,
意恣睢以担挢。	随心所欲腾飞翩翩。
内欣欣而自美兮,	我内心欣悦感觉美好,
聊愉娱以自乐。	暂且尽情欢乐求得快乐安恬。
涉青云以泛滥游兮,	穿过青云漫游四面八方,
忽临睨夫旧乡。	忽然俯瞰到我的故乡。
仆夫怀余心悲兮,	车夫感怀我也心中悲痛,
边马顾而不行。	两边的马匹也回顾不尽充满眷恋。
思旧故以想像兮,	我真想念故乡的父老兄弟,
长太息而掩涕。	不禁长叹一声擦拭泪眼。
泛容与而遐举兮,	游荡徘徊还是要远去,
聊抑志而自弭。	暂且抑制情感硬起心肠。
指炎神而直驰兮,	向着南方火神径直驰去,
吾将往乎南疑。	我要去南方的九嶷山。
览方外之荒忽兮,	我看见世外的渺茫,
沛罔象而自浮。	就像在浩瀚的大海中独自浮行。
祝融戒而还衡①兮,	火神祝融劝我掉转车头,
腾告鸾鸟迎宓妃。	又告诉青鸾神鸟将宓妃远迎。
张《咸池》奏《承云》兮②,	安排《咸池》之乐演奏《承云》之曲,
二女③御《九韶》歌。	娥皇女英进献《九韶》之歌。

① 祝融：火神之名。衡：车辕头上的横木。
② 《咸池》《承云》：都是黄帝所作的乐曲名。
③ 二女：舜帝的两位妃子娥皇、女英，她们是尧帝的女儿。

I'll leave the world and forget home, oh!
Carefree, I'll enjoy my fill and roam.
My heart content will find delight, oh!
I'll make merry in my wild flight.

I cross the clouds and freely go, oh!
When suddenly I see my home below.
My groom homesick, my heart downcast,
My steeds look back and won't go past.

I picture in fancy my dears, oh!
With heavy sighs I brush away my tears.
I float with ease and go farther still, oh!
I must restrain my heart and my will.

To Fiery God I gallop straight, oh!
Then to Mount Mysteries of Southern State.
I see the wilds beyond the main, oh!
I float over the watery plain.

The Fiery God warns me not to go, oh!
I send for the Goddess of River Luo.
She plays music to Cloud and Lake, oh!
Two princesses sing The Nine Songs they make.

使湘灵鼓瑟兮，	我让湘水之神也来鼓瑟，
令海若舞冯夷①。	叫海神与河伯跳起舞蹈助兴。
玄螭虫象并出进兮，	众多的水神都一起出没，
形蟉虬而逶蛇。	他们体形屈曲宛转延伸。
雌蜺便娟以增挠兮，	彩虹轻盈把我层层环绕，
鸾鸟轩翥而翔飞。	青鸾神鸟在高处翱翔不停。
音乐博衍无终极兮，	旋律舒展的音乐绵绵不绝，
焉乃逝以徘徊。	于是我在四周徘徊寻找。
舒并节以驰骛兮，	放下马鞭让车队尽情奔驰，
逴绝垠乎寒门。	奔向天边遥远的北极寒门。
轶迅风于清源②兮，	穿过疾风抵达八风之府清源，
从颛顼乎增冰。	追随北帝颛顼来到冰雪之地。
历玄冥③以邪径兮，	经过北方水神遇到崎岖道路，
乘间维以反顾。	在天地两维之间一阵回望。
召黔嬴④而见之兮，	召呼造化之神前来询问缘故，
为余先乎平路。	让他为我先行把道路铺平。

① 冯（píng）夷：河神。
② 清源：传说中八风之府。
③ 玄冥：北方水神。
④ 黔嬴：黔雷，造化之神。

The Fairies of the Xiang on zither play, oh!
The Sea God and River God dance in spray.
The water monsters come in and out, oh!
Their bodies coil and whirl about.

The lower rainbow circles over, oh!
The phoenixes soar up and hover.
The music swells without end, oh!
I leave them and continue to ascend.

I give free rein to my steeds running forth, oh!
Till the Cold Gate of Extreme North.
I overtake the swift wind at Clear Spring, oh!
Over piled ice I follow the Northern King.

I meet the Water God on rugged way, oh!
I look back as night yearns for day.
I bid the Creator to appear, oh!
And pave the way as pioneer.

经营四荒兮,	我已经驾车游遍了四方荒漠,
周流六漠。	也遨游了六方广袤之境。
上至列缺兮,	向上我到达闪电之处,
降望大壑。	向下俯瞰大壑的深邃。

下峥嵘而无地兮,	下界茫茫全不见大地,
上寥廓而无天。	上方空空看不见高天。
视倏忽而无见兮,	瞬息万变什么也看不见,
听惝怳而无闻。	恍恍惚惚什么也听不明。
超无为以至清兮,	超越无为清静的境界,
与泰初而为邻。	我要和天地元气结伴为邻。

I tour north and south, east and west, oh!
Down to the depth and up to the crest,
Up to the heaven's crack, oh!
And then down to the abyss black.

Below it's bottomlessly deep, oh!
Above it's heavenlessly steep.
I look but see not what changes fast, oh!
I listen but hear nothing in space vast.
I transcend Inaction to Purity, oh!
Then I come near the Realm of Unity.

卜居

屈原既放,	屈原已经遭受放逐,
三年不得复见。	三年了不能和国君见面。
竭智尽忠而蔽障于谗,	他竭尽智慧为国尽忠却被谗言阻隔,
心烦虑乱不知所从。	心绪烦乱不知道何去何从。
乃往见太卜郑詹尹。	于是去拜见太卜郑詹尹,
曰:"余有所疑,	和他说:"我心中存有疑惑,
愿因先生决之。"	希望能向先生请教以助我决断。"
詹尹乃端策拂龟,	詹尹就摆正蓍草拂净龟壳,
曰:"君将何以教之?"	说:"您有什么赐教的啊?"
屈原曰:	屈原说:
"吾宁悃悃款款①朴以忠乎?	"我应该忠诚自守勤勤恳恳呢?
将送往劳来斯无穷乎?	还是敷衍塞责迎上送下呢?
宁诛锄草茅以力耕乎?	是应该凭力气除草耕作呢?
将游大人以成名乎?	还是花言巧语骗取成就名声?
宁正言不讳以危身乎?	是应该直言不讳来不顾安危呢?
将从俗富贵以偷生乎?	还是贪图世俗苟且偷生?
宁超然高举以保真乎?	是应该超然脱俗远走高飞呢?
将哫訾②栗斯,	还是阿谀逢迎委屈随俗,
喔咿儒儿以事妇人乎?	奴颜媚骨巴结妇人?

① 悃悃(kǔn)款款:诚实的样子。
② 哫訾(zú zǐ):徘徊不前。

Divination

Qu Yuan exiled from the capital
For three years obtains no recall.
He served his prince loyally as he may,
But slanderers have barred his way.
His troubled mind is full of woe;
He does not know which way to go.
He calls on the diviner great
And asks about his fate.
"In my mind, " he says, "I have doubt.
Will you please help me to work it out? "
The diviner sets out magic herb and tortoise shell
And says, "What would you have me tell? "
"Should I spare no effort to plough and hoe up weeds
Or make a name by singing the great men's deeds?
Should I risk my life to say frankly what is right
Or save my skin by pleasing the rich and the might?
Should I preserve my purity and lofty stand
Or flatter and curry favor with a woman grand?

宁廉洁正直以自清乎?	是应该廉洁正直公正无私呢?
将突梯滑稽如脂如韦,	还是敷衍塞责,
以洁楹乎?	圆滑随俗?
宁昂昂若千里之驹乎?	是应该昂然如同千里马呢?
将泛泛若水中之凫乎?	还是如鸭子一般呢?
与波上下,	随波逐流,
偷以全吾躯乎?	苟且偷生?
宁与骐骥亢轭[①]乎?	是应该和良马一起呢,
将随驽马之迹乎?	还是跟随驽马的足迹呢?
宁与黄鹄比翼乎?	是应该与天鹅比翼齐飞呢?
将与鸡鹜争食乎?	还是跟鸡鸭一起争食呢?
此孰吉孰凶?	到底哪种选择是好哪种是坏?
何去何从?	我应该何去何从?
世混浊而不清:	现实世界浑浊不清黑白不分:
蝉翼为重,	轻薄蝉翼被认为重,
千钧[②]为轻;	而千钧被认为轻;
黄钟[③]毁弃,	黄钟被毁,
瓦釜雷鸣;	瓦锅却被敲得震耳;
谗人高张,	坏人当道黑白颠倒,
贤士无名。	贤良被逐默默无闻。
吁嗟默默兮,	算了吧,默不作声,
谁知吾之廉贞?"	我的廉洁忠贞有谁知呢?"

① 亢轭:并驾齐驱。
② 钧:三十斤为一钧。
③ 黄钟:古代乐律十二律之一,音调最响亮最宏大。

Should I be honest, blameless, pure and hold my ground
Or be slippery as leather, lard or pillar round?
Should I hold high my head like a steed running free
Or drift in water up and down like ducks in glee?
Should I be with the swiftest stallion and keep pace
Or follow a broken hackney's trace?
Should I fly with the skylark wing to wing
Or dispute with barnyard fowls for trifling thing?
Which way will lead to weal and which to woe?
Which way should I dodge and which should I go?
The world is dire
In mud and mire.
They call heavy cicada's wings
And think metal weights are light things.
Bronze bells are destroyed without cause;
Earthen vessels win thunderous applause.
Slanderers have renown
While wise men are unknown.
Alas! silent, what can I do?
Who knows I am loyal and true?"

詹尹乃释策而谢，	詹尹便放下蓍草拱手辞谢，
曰："夫尺有所短，	说："所谓尺有嫌它不足的地方，
寸有所长；	寸有觉得它太长的时候；
物有所不足，	万事万物都有不足的地方，
智有所不明，	再聪明的人也有不能明白的地方；
数有所不逮，	你的问题是算卦算不出答案的，
神有所不通。	即使是请教神灵也束手无策。
用君之心，行君之意，	你还是按照自己的心意决定吧，
龟策诚不能知事。	龟壳蓍草实在无法知道这些事。"

The diviner then puts away
His magic herb and tortoise shell to say:
"A foot may be too short for something long;
For something weak an inch is strong.
Everything has its weak points;
Sometimes a wise man disappoints.
There's something which to fate we must resign,
And other things beyond the power divine.
So you may act according to your mind and heart;
My magic herb and tortoise shell can play no part."

渔父

屈原既放，	屈原被放逐以后，
游于江潭，	游走在沧浪江边，
行吟泽畔，	一边走一边行吟，
颜色憔悴，	看起来憔悴枯瘦，
形容枯槁。	满脸愁容很瘦削。
渔父见而问之曰：	一位渔夫看到了他，
"子非三闾大夫[①]欤？	问道："您不是三闾大夫吗？
何故至于斯？"	为什么会流落到这个地方来呢？"
屈原曰：	屈原回答说：
"举世皆浊我独清，	"全天下的人都污浊，只有我一人清白；
众人皆醉我独醒，	所有的人都昏醉了，只有我一人清醒。
是以见放！"	因此才会被放逐。"
渔父曰：	渔夫说：
"圣人不凝滞于物，	"圣人是不会拘泥于外物的，
而能与世推移。	而且能够配合时局转变作为。
世人皆浊，	全天下的人都污浊了，
何不淈[②]其泥而扬其波？	您为什么不使水更浑浊而随波逐流呢？
众人皆醉，	所有人都昏醉不醒，
何不铺其糟而歠[③]其醨？	您为什么不一起痛饮沉醉呢？
何故深思高举，	您为什么太深思远虑，不合群，
自令放为？"	而使自己遭到放逐呢？"

[①] 三闾大夫：掌管楚国王族屈、景、昭三姓的官，屈原曾担任过此官。
[②] 淈（gǔ）：扰乱的意思。
[③] 铺（bū）：吃。歠（chuò）：喝。

The Fisherman

Banished, Qu Yuan wanders by riverside,
Singing alone.
At the sight of his haggard face,
All skin and bone,
A fisherman asks,
"Are you not Lord of the Three Clans? Alas!
What has brought you to such a pass?"
Qu Yuan says,
"When all the world in mud has sunk,
Alone I'm clean;
When all the people are drunk,
Sober I'm seen.
How can I not get banished?"
The fisherman says,
"A wise man will not stick to any climes
But should adapt himself to the times.
If all others are dire,
Why not wallow with them in mud and mire?
If all the men are drunk,
Why should you from liquor have shrunk?
If you should above others rise,
Can you not get exiled? Can you think yourself wise?"

屈原曰："吾闻之，	屈原回答说："我听说过，
新沐者必弹冠，	刚洗过头的人一定要弹弹帽子上的尘灰，
新浴者必振衣。	刚洗过澡的人一定要抖抖衣服上的灰土。
安能以身之察察，	怎么可以用洁净的身体，
受物之汶汶者乎？	去沾染上污秽的东西呢？
宁赴湘流，	我宁愿投身到湘江的流水中，
葬于江鱼之腹中。	葬身在江中的鱼肚里。
安能以皓皓之白，	怎么能够用清白的人格，
而蒙世俗之尘埃乎！"	去蒙受尘世污秽的玷污呀！"
渔父莞尔而笑，	渔夫微微一笑，
鼓枻①而去。	一边敲打着船板离去，
乃歌曰：	一面唱着歌说：
"沧浪之水清兮，	"沧浪的水清又清，
可以濯吾缨。	可用来洗我的头巾，
沧浪之水浊兮，	沧浪的水一片浑浊，
可以濯吾足。"	可用来洗我的双脚。"
遂去，不复与言。	渔夫随后便远去了，再也没有和屈原说话。

---

① 枻（yì）：划水的短桨。

Qu Yuan replies,
"I've heard it said:
After you wash your hair,
You should keep your hat fair.
After a bath, none the less
You should keep clean your dress.
How could I darken my mind bright
And blacken my skin white?
In River Xiang I would rather wish
To bury myself in the belly of the fish
Than spoil my spotless purity
With dirt and dust of vulgarity."
The fisherman has nothing more to say;
He faintly smiles and sings while paddling away:
"When the river is clear, oh!
I'll wash my headdress here.
When water is not neat, oh!
I may wash here my feet."

九辩

悲哉秋之为气也!	真令人悲伤啊这秋天的萧杀之气!
萧瑟兮草木摇落而变衰。	秋风萧瑟啊草木枯萎凋零。
憭慄①兮若在远行;	凄凉地感觉自己好像要出远门,
登山临水兮送将归。	登山临水送别伤情。
泬②寥兮天高而气清;	晴空万里啊天高气爽;
寂寥③兮收潦而水清。	浊水消尽啊秋水清澈。
憯凄增欷兮,薄寒之中人。	微寒袭人啊让人备感伤情。
怆怳懭悢④兮,去故而就新;	我悲怆地离乡背井去往新居,
坎壈⑤兮贫士失职而志不平。	坎坷的遭遇啊让我心中不平。
廓落兮羁旅而无友生;	我孤独失落啊没有知心朋友,
惆怅兮而私自怜。	心绪惆怅啊只能自我怜悯。

① 憭慄(liáo lì):凄凉。
② 泬(xuè):空旷。
③ 寂:寂静。寥(liáo):水聚集而不泛滥。
④ 怆怳(huǎng):失意的样子。懭悢(kuǎng lǎng):惆怅,怨恨。
⑤ 坎壈(lǎn):坎坷。

Nine Apologies

Ah! sad as death
Is Autumn's breath.
What a bleak day, oh!
Leaves shiver, fade, fall and decay!
Forlorn and dreary, oh!
As on a journey weary,
Climbing the hill, oh!
To see a friend off across the rill.
Empty and bare, oh!
The sky is high with chilly air.
Silent and drear, oh!
The river sinks with water clear.
Grieved, I heave sigh on sigh, oh!
Penetrated with the cold drawing nigh.
Heart-broken at the view, oh!
I leave the old for the new.
Rugged the way, oh!
The jobless poor is discontent with the day.
Lost in space endless , oh!
I stay on my journey friendless.
So desolate, oh!
I secretly pity my fate.

燕翩翩其辞归兮，	燕子翩翩飞翔归去，
蝉寂漠而无声。	寒蝉在寂寞中也悄然无声。
雁雍雍而南游兮，	大雁鸣叫着向南远飞，
鹍鸡①啁哳②而悲鸣。	鹍鸡啾啾地发出凄凉的悲鸣。
独申旦而不寐兮，	独自通宵达旦难以成眠，
哀蟋蟀之宵征。	蟋蟀整夜的哀鸣触动幽情。
时亹亹③而过中兮，	时光匆匆啊我已经人到中年，
蹇淹留而无成。	仕途阻滞仍是一事无成。
悲忧穷戚兮独处廓，	悲愁困迫啊我独处在辽阔大地，
有美一人兮心不绎；	有一位美人啊悲凉满心；
去乡离家兮徕④远客，	离开家乡啊到远方做客，
超逍遥兮今焉薄？	漂泊不定啊到哪里才能安定？
专思君兮不可化，	一心思念君王啊我绝不改变，
君不知兮可奈何！	若王不理解我，我又有什么办法啊！
蓄怨兮积思，	积满哀怨啊我思虑重重，
心烦憺兮忘食事。	心烦意乱啊我茶饭不思。
愿一见兮道余意，	但愿能见君王一面啊诉说我的心意，
君之心兮与余异。	可是君王的心思却与我截然不同。
车既驾兮朅⑤而归，	驾起马车啊我要返回旧地，
不得见兮心伤悲。	见不到君王啊我实在伤心。
倚结軨⑥兮长太息，	倚靠着车厢啊我长长叹息，
涕潺湲兮下沾轼。	泪水涟涟啊沾满车轼。

① 鹍（kūn）鸡：一种鸟。
② 啁（zhāo）哳（zhā）：声音多而细微的样子。
③ 亹（wěi）：行进不停的样子。
④ 徕：作"来"。
⑤ 朅（qiè）：离开。
⑥ 结軨（líng）：古代的车厢前面、左面和右面用木条构成的方格，因为形状和窗棂一样，所以叫作结軨。

Swallows fly wing to wing home-bound, oh!
Forlorn cicadas make no sound.
The honking wild geese southward fly, oh!
Clattering partridges mournfully cry.
Waiting for dawn alone I cannot sleep, oh!
The crickets fighting at night makes one weep.
Fast, fast, half my days have passed, oh!
I have done nothing that could last.

Hard-pressed and grieved, oh! alone I dwell apart
Like a fair one, oh! so sad at heart.
I've left my homeland, oh! and go far away;
I rove here and there, oh! where to go today?
I love my lord, oh! all my life through;
My lord knows not, oh! what can I do?
I complain, oh! and repeat;
My mind troubled, oh! I forget to eat.
I'd see him once, oh! and tell for what I pine,
But his heart is, oh! different from mine.
My chariot ready, oh! I come back again;
I can't see him, oh! my heart feels grief and pain.
I sigh and lean, oh! on the board of my car;
A stream of tears, oh! wet the chariot-bar.

忼慨绝兮不得,	愤愤不平和他断交啊实在不能,
中瞀乱①兮迷惑。	内心纷乱啊令我心惑神迷。
私自怜兮何极?	我独自伤悲啊哪里是个尽头?
心怦怦兮谅直。	内心的激动只因为忠诚和耿直。

皇天平分四时兮,	上天将一年分成四个季节,
窃独悲此凛秋。	我却独自悲叹寒冷凄凉的秋季。
白露既下百草兮,	白露已经沾湿了枯萎的百草,
奄离披此梧楸。	衰黄的树叶匆匆地飘离了梧桐枝头。
去白日之昭昭兮,	离开灿烂的白日昭昭,
袭长夜之悠悠。	我又进入黑暗的漫漫长夜。
离芳蔼之方壮兮,	百花盛开的时季已过,
余萎约而悲愁。	只剩下枯木衰草令人哀愁。

秋既先戒以白露兮,	白露降临带来秋天的信息,
冬又申之以严霜。	预报冬天又用严霜侵扰大地。
收恢台之孟夏兮,	初夏的勃勃生机都消失不见,
然欿②傺而沉藏。	生长培养的气机也全收。
叶菸邑③而无色兮,	叶子黯淡毫无光彩,
枝烦挐而交横;	枝条散乱纵横缠蔓。
颜淫溢而将罢兮,	草木改变颜色行将衰谢,
柯彷佛而萎黄;	树木枯萎露出暗黄的颜色。

---

① 瞀(mào)乱:昏迷错乱。
② 欿(kǎn):同"坎",陷落。
③ 菸(yū)邑:黯淡的样子。

I can't cut off, oh! and leave him behind;
I'm at a loss, oh! with a disordered mind.
I grieve without end, oh! for what I can't do;
My heart still beats, oh! honest and true.

High Heaven divides the four seasons, oh!
I grieve at autumn for no reasons.
Dew drops on grasses in the breeze, oh!
Withered leaves fall from the plane trees.
Gone are the sunny days so bright, oh!
Invaded by the long, long night.
I've left behind my years in bloom, oh!
And sink into deepening gloom.

Autumn warns us first by white dew, oh!
Winter's severe frost falls anew.
No more splendor of summer high, oh!
All are sickly and buried lie.
Discolored, leaves turn pale and fade, oh!
Branches criss-cross in disorderly shade.
Trees look languid and no longer fair, oh!
They yellow when their trunks turn bare.

蔚槮①之可哀兮，	可怜的树梢光秃秃的真是可怜，
形销铄而瘀伤。	病恹恹的树干在寒风中飘摇。
惟其纷糅而将落兮，	想到落叶衰草相杂糅，
恨其失时而无当。	怅恨好时光失去不正当时。
揽②骓辔而下节兮，	抓住缰绳我停下马鞭，
聊逍遥以相伴。	我缓缓而行暂且忘掉忧愁。
岁忽忽而遒尽兮，	岁月匆匆一年就将到头，
恐余寿之弗将。	恐怕我的寿命也长不了。
悼余生之不时兮，	可怜我此生生不逢时，
逢此世之侘傺③。	遇上这混乱的世道难以救药。
澹容与而独倚兮，	寂寞地靠在门柱上消磨时光，
蟋蟀鸣此西堂。	只听见西堂的蟋蟀鸣叫声声。
心怵惕④而震荡兮，	这叫声惊起了我心中的恐惧，
何所忧之多方。	为何百般事情缠绕着我不肯离去。
仰明月而太息兮，	仰望明月我长长叹息，
步列星而极明。	在星光下徘徊直到天明。
窃悲夫蕙华之曾敷兮，	暗自悲叹蕙花曾经开放，
纷旖旎乎都房。	千娇百媚地在华堂遍开。
何曾华之无实兮，	为何光开花没能结果，
从风雨而飞飏！	随着风雨的袭击狼藉纷纷啊！
以为君独服此蕙兮，	以为君王独爱佩这蕙花，
羌无以异于众芳。	谁知你将它视同一般花朵。

① 莳（shāo）：同"梢"，树梢。槮槮（xiāo sēn）：树枝光秃秃的孤立上耸。
② 揽（lǎn）：手拿着。
③ 侘（kuāng）傺：混乱的样子。
④ 怵惕：惊惧。

I grieve at sparse trees in this land, oh!
Like wounded skeletons they stand.
Their leaves and grasses wilt and wither, oh!
My time is also gone, but whither?
I seize the reins and use no whip, oh!
I rove as if on a pleasure trip.
But the end of the year draws near, oh!
I can't live to old age, I fear.
I mourn I was born in a wrong age, oh!
When the world is red-hot with rage.
I lean on rails in Western Hall for long, oh!
To hear alone the crickets' mournful song.
My heart trembles without relief, oh!
I have so much sorrow and grief.
Looking up, I sigh at the moon so bright, oh!
And pace beneath the stars till comes daylight.

I grieve for orchids once in bloom, oh!
Which beautify the capital room.
But no fruit is borne by the flower, oh!
Which flies away in wind and shower.
My lord prefers not orchid fair, oh!
To any other flower there.

闵奇思之不通兮，	可怜我曲折的心意难以通达，
将去君而高翔。	只好离开君王远飞高翔。
心闵怜之惨凄兮，	心中悲叹自己凄惨的遭遇，
愿一见而有明，	但愿能见君王一面倾诉衷肠。
重无怨而生离兮，	一次次想着自己无罪而被远放，
中结轸而增伤。	愁思郁结而更添悲伤。
岂不郁陶①而思君兮？	满腹悲愤哪能不深切思念君王啊？
君之门以九重！	君王的九重大门却将我层层阻挡。
猛犬狺狺②而迎吠兮，	猛犬相迎对着我狂吠，
关梁闭而不通。	关口和桥梁闭塞使我绝望。
皇天淫溢而秋霖兮，	皇天绵绵落着秋雨，
后土何时而得漧？	大地什么时候才能重见干燥土壤？
块独守此无泽兮，	我孑然一身守在荒芜的洼地，
仰浮云而永叹！	仰望浮云长久地叹息啊！
何时俗之工巧兮？	为何时俗那般工巧媚俗啊？
背绳墨而改错！	违背准绳而擅自改变法度。
却骐骥而不乘兮，	抛弃千里良骏不愿骑乘，
策驽骀而取路。	竟然鞭打着劣马慢慢地上路。
当世岂无骐骥兮？	当今世上难道少有骏马？
诚莫之能善御。	实在是无人能好好驾驭。
见执辔者非其人兮，	看到握缰绳的人不是驾驭能手，
故骈③跳而远去。	骏马也会蹦跳着挣脱束缚。

① 郁陶（táo）：忧思郁积的样子。
② 狺狺（yín）：狗叫声。
③ 骈：指跳跃。

My matchless thought I can't to him convey, oh!
So I leave him and fly away.
I pity myself sad and drear, oh!
I'd see him once to make all clear.
I cannot, but I won't complain, oh!
Although my heart is gnawed by pain.
Could I not long for my lord great? oh!
I can't go through his ninefold gate.
His fierce, snarling dogs bark and roar, oh!
None can pass the bridge and closed door.
High Heaven overflows with autumn rain, oh!
When will the Earth get dry again?
Alone by waterside I heave long sighs, oh!
And gaze at floating cloud with longing eyes.

The vulgar world's crafty and fine, oh!
They turn away from the ink-line.
They won't ride a swift horse, oh!
But take the road on a nag of weak force.
Is there in this age no fine steed? oh!
There is no man who can drive at full speed.
If a wrong rider takes the rein, oh!
The steed will bolt and run amain.

凫雁皆唼①夫梁藻兮，	野鸭大雁争着吃高粱水藻，
凤愈飘翔而高举。	凤凰却要展翅高翔。
圆凿而方枘②兮，	好比圆形的凿孔难以配上方形榫子，
吾固知其鉏铻③而难入。	我本来就知道它们格格不入。
众鸟皆有所登栖兮，	所有的鸟都有栖息的窝，
凤独遑遑而无所集。	唯独凤凰难寻安身之处。
愿衔枚④而无言兮，	但愿口中衔枚闭口不言，
尝被君之渥洽。	但想到曾受你的恩惠又不能不说。
太公九十乃显荣兮，	姜太公九十岁才声名显赫，
诚未遇其匹合。	因为他之前没有遇见投合的明君。
谓骐骥兮安归？	骏马啊应当去向何处？
谓凤凰兮安栖？	凤凰啊应当在何处栖息？
变古易俗兮世衰，	改变古老的传统啊世道大坏，
今之相者兮举肥。	现在相马人只喜欢马的肥腴。
骐骥伏匿而不见兮，	骏马隐匿再也见不到，
凤皇高飞而不下。	凤凰高高飞翔不愿回到故土。
鸟兽犹知怀德兮，	鸟兽也知道怀念有德的主人，
何云贤士之不处？	怎能怪贤良的士子隐居避世？
骥不骤进而求服兮，	骏马不急于求你任用，
凤亦不贪喂而妄食。	凤凰也不会贪婪地乱吃食物。
君弃远而不察兮，	君王毫不明察地放逐疏远贤士，
虽愿忠其焉得？	虽想尽忠又怎能施展抱负。

① 唼（shà）：拟声词，水鸟或鱼类吃食的样子。
② 枘（ruì）：榫子。
③ 鉏铻（jǔ yǔ）：不配合。
④ 衔枚：古时候行军大战，为了防止发出声音，每人口中衔一根筷子一样的木棍。

Wild ducks and geese eat water-weed, oh!
On which high-soaring phoenix will not feed.

If you put a square peg in a round hole, oh!
Can the peg fit and play its role?
The common birds all have a nest, oh!
Only the phoenix has nowhere to rest.
I'd gag my mouth and nothing say, oh!
Having received favor in former day.
Master Jiang throve at ninety years, oh!
Before then he'd not met his peers.
Where goes the fine steed in flight, oh!
Where will the phoenix alight?
The ways of the world become flat, oh!
The fancier of today like the fat.
The hidden steed will disappear, oh!
The flying phoenix won't come near.
Even birds and beats know their way, oh!
Why not good men choose where to stay?
Without good driver won't run a fine steed, oh!
Nor will phoenix take food for greed.
My lord neglected and rejected me, oh!
I wish to be loyal, how can I be?

欲寂漠而绝端兮，	我真想默默地与君王断绝往来，
窃不敢忘初之厚德。	却又不敢忘记当初你对我的知遇之恩。
独悲愁其伤人兮，	独自悲愁最是折磨人，
冯①郁郁其何极？	悲愤郁结何时才是尽头呢？
霜露惨凄而交下兮，	凉露寒霜交加备感悲凄，
心尚幸其弗济。	我心中还希望它们不能得逞。
霰雪雰糅其增加兮，	当雪珠雪花纷杂铺天盖地，
乃知遭命之将至。	才知道悲惨的命运即将到来。
愿徼幸而有待兮，	仍心存侥幸有所等待，
泊莽莽与野草同死。	在荒原中与野草一起萎枯。
愿自往而径游兮，	愿意直面君王陈诉是非，
路壅绝而不通。	可道路堵塞困难重重。
欲循道而平驱兮，	想沿着大道平稳驱车前行，
又未知其所从。	又茫茫然不知去向何方。
然中路而迷惑兮，	半路时就迷失了方向，
自压按而学诵。	强忍悲愤读《诗经》学习与人交往。
性愚陋以褊浅兮，	我生性愚笨且孤陋浅直，
信未达乎从容。	在困境之中做不到从容不迫。
窃美申包胥之气盛兮，	我暗自赞美申包胥的气概，
恐时世之不固。	恐怕时代不同古道全消。
何时俗之工巧兮？	为何如今世俗那么媚俗？
灭规矩而改凿！	抛弃前人的规矩改变法度吧！

① 冯（píng）：同"凭"，郁闷。

I'd be estranged from him without a word, oh!
But I can't forget the favor he conferred.
I suffer more without a friend, oh!
How can my sorrow have an end?

Bitter frost and dew fall along, oh!
My heart is glad they've done no wrong.
But when snow and sleet aggravate, oh!
I know my inevitable fate.
I'd wait for better chance from high, oh!
With vast expanse of grass I'd die.
Straight to my lord I wish to go, oh!
But the road is blocked high and low.
I wish to follow an easy way, oh!
But I can't find it night and day.
I stop midway in perplexity, oh!
What can I do but recite poetry?
But dull, I know not how to please, oh!
How can I recite verse with ease?
I love Shen's loyal sentiment, oh!
But fear the time is different.
The vulgar world is crafty and unfair, oh!
They destroy the compass and square.

独耿介而不随兮,	我耿介独立不随波逐流,
愿慕先圣之遗教。	愿意遵循前代圣人的教诲。
处浊世而显荣兮,	在污浊的世界而扬名显耀,
非余心之所乐。	并不是我心中所喜爱的。
与其无义而有名兮,	与其违背道义获取名声,
宁穷处而守高。	我宁愿遭受穷困保持高洁。
食不偷而为饱兮,	即便食不果腹我也满足,
衣不苟而为温。	衣不避寒我也不苟且媚俗。
窃慕诗人之遗风兮,	我暗自追慕诗人的遗风,
愿托志乎素餐。	以简朴的生活寄托怀抱。
蹇充倔而无端兮,	我心中充满委屈而毫无头绪,
泊莽莽而无垠。	只能流浪在无边无际的荒郊。
无衣裘以御冬兮,	没有皮袄来抵御寒冬,
恐溘死不得见乎阳春。	恐怕突然死去再见不到和煦的阳春。
静杪秋之遥夜兮,	寂静的寒秋漫漫长夜,
心缭悷①而有哀。	我心中萦绕着深深的哀愁。
春秋逴逴②而日高兮,	岁月悠悠我年岁渐老,
然惆怅而自悲。	也只能就这样惆怅自感悲凉。
四时遞来而卒岁兮,	四季相继一年又将到头,
阴阳不可与俪偕。	日月降落不能并存在天上。
白日晼晚其将入兮,	天色昏暗太阳将要落山,
明月销铄而减毁。	月亮消蚀而减少了清辉。

---

① 缭悷(lì):缠绕而郁结。
② 逴逴(chuō chuō):形容越走越远。

Staunch, I won't follow the age, oh!
But the teachings left by former sage.
In a foul world to appear bright, oh!
Won't give my heart the least delight.
I won't by foul means win a fame, oh!
But live poor and free from blame.
I may eat any food not bad, oh!
I need to be but warmly-clad.
I admire the old poet's style, oh!
I would be only worth my while.
Much grieved for no reason I stand, oh!
On this immense expanse of land.
I have no furs against winter's cold, oh!
I fear I'd die before spring I behold.

In lonely late autumn's long night, oh!
Tormented, my heart is in sad plight.
As spring and autumn alternate, oh!
I sadly grieve for my hard fate.
Four seasons come and go, a year will end, oh!
And light and dark will never blend.
The sun will rise and set again, oh!
The moon, however bright, will wane.

岁忽忽而遒尽兮，	岁月悠悠人生将近终点，
老冉冉而愈弛。	慢慢老去精力渐丧。
心摇悦而日幸兮，	动摇和喜悦让我每天都怀着侥幸，
然怊怅而无冀。	但总是满怀忧虑而失去希望。
中憯恻之凄怆兮，	心中惨痛凄怆欲绝，
长太息而增欷。	长长叹息又更添忧愁。
年洋洋以日往兮，	时光如水一天天流逝，
老嵺廓而无处。	老来备感空虚不知何处停留。
事亹亹①而觊进兮，	国事一天天在发生变化，
蹇淹留而踌躇。	我在荒原上停滞不前徒自彷徨。
何泛滥之浮云兮？	为什么浮云泛滥天空，
猋②壅蔽此明月。	追逐着遮蔽这一轮明月。
忠昭昭而愿见兮，	我只想表露忠心耿耿如月亮昭然，
然霠③曀而莫达。	可浓云阻隔令我难以逾越。
愿皓日之显行兮，	祈愿太阳能够朗照天地。
云蒙蒙而蔽之。	可云雾蒙蒙却把它遮蔽。
窃不自料而愿忠兮，	我不自量力只想着效忠君王，
或黕点④而污之。	有人竟用谗言把我的忠心污蔑。
尧舜之抗行兮，	尧和舜的品德多么高尚，
瞭冥冥而薄天。	光辉赫赫高与天齐。
何险巇之嫉妒兮，	为何也遭险恶小人的嫉妒，
被以不慈之伪名？	蒙受不慈的冤名竟难以申雪？

① 亹（wěi）亹：勤勉的样子。
② 猋（biāo）：狗跑的样子，引申为迅速。
③ 霠（yīn）：同"阴"。
④ 黕（dǎn）点：玷污，诬害。

The year will quickly pass away, oh!
Old age will come, all will decay.
Distraught, my heart still hopes for the best, oh!
Disappointed, I cannot rest.
Anguish and grief rise and rerise, oh!
What can I do but heave long sighs!
The years roll by from day to day, oh!
Where, old and lonely, can I stay?
Affairs press me to forward go, oh!
How can I hesitate in woe?

How does the Cloud overspread so soon, oh!
As to cover up the bright moon?
I wish my loyalty shine bright, oh!
But veiled in mist, it's out of royal sight.
I wish the bright sun to come out, oh!
But it is overcast all about.
I'll be loyal without thinking of fame, oh!
But others try to stain my name.
Kings Yao and Shun had virtues high, oh!
Their glory reaches to the sky.
But jealous persons backbite from behind, oh!
Defaming them as kings unkind.

彼日月之照明兮，	就像那日月光耀天地，
尚黯黮①而有瑕。	尚有昏暗见黑斑的时日。
何况一国之事兮，	何况一个国家的政事，
亦多端而胶加。	更是头绪纷繁多得错综纠结。

被荷裯之晏晏兮，	披着荷叶做的短衣很轻柔，
然潢洋②而不可带。	但太宽太松不能用带子系住。
既骄美而伐武兮，	你骄傲自满又夸耀武功，
负左右之耿介。	还以左右近臣所谓的正直自负。
憎愠怆之修美兮，	你憎恨忠诚之士的美德，
好夫人之慷慨。	却喜欢那些小人伪装的慷慨。
众踥蹀③而日进兮，	小人们碎步行进愈得意，
美超远而逾迈。	贤人却被放逐到远远的地方。
农夫辍耕而容与兮，	农夫停止耕作逍遥自在，
恐田野之芜秽。	就怕田野变得荒芜起来。
事绵绵而多私兮，	诸事琐细都充满私欲，
窃悼后之危败。	我暗自悲痛国家前途的危险。
世雷同而炫曜兮，	世俗小人都喜欢自我炫耀，
何毁誉之昧昧！	诋毁与赞誉多么混乱古怪啊！
今修饰而窥镜兮，	如今认真地照照镜子修饰打扮，
后尚可以窜藏。	以后还能藏身将祸患躲开。
愿寄言夫流星兮，	我希望流星做使者传话，
羌儵忽而难当。	它飞掠迅速难以托付。

---

① 黯黮（dǎn）：昏暗。
② 潢（huǎng）洋：衣服不贴身的样子。
③ 踥蹀（qiè dié）：小步快速行走的样子。

Bright as the sun and the moon are, oh!
Still neither is a flawless star,
Not to speak of the state affair, oh!
More complicated beyond compare.

A lotus coat is soft to wear, oh!
But too flimsy a girdle to bear.
If you are proud and boast of your might, oh!
None will be loyal to you left and right.
You dislike the straightforward beauty, oh!
And say the braggarts doing their duty.
They press forward and win each day more grace, oh!
True beauty's forced to far-off place.
If farmers idly put their plough down, oh!
The fields with weeds will be overgrown.
Preoccupied with private affair, oh!
Who of the State would take good care?
If blind, you just repeat what people says, oh!
Can you know whom to blame and whom to praise?
If you, adorned, look in the glass, oh!
You may hide your defects and pass.
I'd send my message by a shooting star, oh!
But soon it's away, I know not how far.

卒壅蔽此浮云兮,	日月终于被这片浮云遮挡,
下暗漠而无光。	下界就黑暗不见光彩。
尧舜皆有所举任兮,	尧和舜都能任用贤人,
故高枕而自适。	所以高枕无忧十分从容。
谅无怨于天下兮,	诚然不受天下人埋怨,
心焉取此怵惕?	他们的心中哪会有这种惊恐。
乘骐骥之浏浏兮,	骑着骏马就能畅快地奔驰,
驭安用夫强策?	何必用力扬鞭督促。
谅城郭之不足恃兮,	里城外城实在不足以依靠,
虽重介之何益?	即使重兵把守又有什么用?
遭^①翼翼而无终兮,	我一直谨慎地回旋不前没完了,
忳惛惛而愁约。	可忧郁愁思始终萦绕心胸。
生天地之若过兮,	人生在天地之间如同匆匆过客,
功不成而无效。	至今功业未成两手空空。
愿沉滞而不见兮,	我真想隐姓埋名不现身影,
尚欲布名乎天下。	难道还想在世上扬名取荣。
然潢洋而不遇兮,	然而我没有飘荡放浪一无所遇,
直怐愗^②而自苦。	只是愚昧不堪自找苦痛。
莽洋洋而无极兮,	荒野渺茫一片无尽头,
忽翱翔之焉薄?	我徘徊不定不知道去往何方?
国有骥而不知乘兮,	国内有骏马却不知道驾乘,
焉皇皇而更索?	惶惶然又要索求哪种?

① 遭(zhān):回旋不前。
② 怐(kòu)愗:愚昧。

At last the sky is veiled by floating cloud, oh!
The earth below is wrapped in a dark shroud.

Kings Yao and Shun used able men, oh!
They could sleep sound and carefree then.
None was against them here or there, oh!
Their hearts were free from fear and care.
If you ride your steed for a trip, oh!
Why should you force it with a whip?
You can't be safeguarded by town wall, oh!
What avails heavy armor at all?

Why am I worried endlessly, oh!
And gnawed by grave anxiety?
Passenger between earth and sky, oh!
I have accomplished nothing, why?
I will disappear and subside, oh!
Still I long for fame far and wide.
Look for connoisseur about, oh!
I wear myself foolishly out.
There's water everywhere below, oh!
Where can a wandering bird go?
None in the State can ride a fine steed, oh!
Yet they search for one fast in speed.

宁戚讴于车下兮，	宁戚在马车下敲着牛角唱歌，
桓公闻而知之。	齐桓公一听就知他才能出众。
无伯乐之善相兮，	如今再也没人有伯乐相马的好本领，
今谁使乎誉之？	谁能认出骏马的真相。
罔流涕以聊虑兮，	怅惘流泪你姑且思索一下，
惟著意而得之。	只有诚挚访求才能得到贤臣。
纷忳忳之愿忠兮，	我满怀热忱愿为君王尽忠心，
妒被离而障之。	却被小人们嫉妒阻挠。
愿赐不肖之躯而别离兮，	希望君王开恩让我这无用之身离去，
放游志乎云中。	任远游的意志翱翔在云中。
乘精气之抟抟兮，	乘着天地间一团团精气，
骛诸神之湛湛。	追随众多神灵在苍穹。
骖白霓之习习兮，	白虹做骖马驾车飞行，
历群灵之丰丰。	游历群神的一个个神宫。
左朱雀之茇茇兮，	南方朱雀在左面翩跹飞舞，
右苍龙之躣躣。	北方苍龙在右面奔行跃动。
属雷师之阗阗兮，	雷师咚咚敲鼓跟随在后，
通飞廉之衙衙。	风伯走在前面把路开辟。
前轻辌之锵锵兮，	前面有轻车铃声清脆，
后辎乘之从从。	后面有大车紧紧随从。
载云旗之委蛇兮，	车上载着云旗迎风飘扬，
扈屯骑之容容。	扈从的车骑多么密集蜂拥。
计专专之不可化兮，	我的一片忠心绝不改变，
愿遂推而为臧。	希望能得到施展为国所用。
赖皇天之厚德兮，	仰仗上天的深厚恩德，
还及君之无恙。	还要君王吉祥无凶。

When Duke Huan of Qi heard Ning's song, oh!
He knew Ning could make his State strong.
Without a connoisseur of horse, oh!
Who could discern one of great force?
I weep and brood over the day, oh!
I know where there's a will, there's a way.
I'll be loyal with a pure heart, oh!
But the jealous courtiers keep me apart.

If my worthless body allowed, oh!
My spirit to soar amid the cloud,
I'd ride the ether round on round, oh!
And race with gods sky-bound, sky-bound.
I'd drive the rainbow white, so white, oh!
And pass through the stars bright, so bright.
At left the Red Bird beats its wing on wing, oh!
At right the dragons green swing and swing.
The Lord of Thunder rumbles past, past, oh!
The Master of Wind flies ahead, fast, fast.
In front, light coaches ring bell on bell, oh!
Behind, the heavy waggons utter yell on yell.
Clouds undulate like banners serpentine, oh!
A train follows of horsemen fine.
I'll never change my loyal, loyal mind, oh!
My wish fulfilled, I will not be unkind.
If Heaven's favor should last long, oh!
I'd come back to see my lord free from wrong.

招魂

朕幼清以廉洁兮，　　我自幼秉赋清廉的品行，
身服义而未沬①。　　献身于道义而不敢漫不经心。
主此盛德兮，　　　　我坚持美德丝毫不偏离，
牵于俗而芜秽。　　　身处俗世而被横加诬陷。
上无所考此盛德兮，　君王不考察我的美德，
长离殃而愁苦。　　　长期遭受诬陷令我愁绪满怀。

帝告巫阳②曰：　　　上帝告诉巫阳说：
"有人在下，　　　　"有人在下界，
我欲辅之。　　　　　我想帮助他。
魂魄离散，　　　　　但他的魂魄已经离散，
汝筮予之。"　　　　你占卦将灵魂还给他。"

巫阳对曰：　　　　　巫阳回答说：
"掌梦，　　　　　　"占卦要找掌梦之官，
上帝其难从。　　　　上苍的命令恐怕难以遵从。
若必筮予之，　　　　如果你一定要占卦还魂给他，
恐后之谢，　　　　　只怕占卜完了他已谢世，
不能复用巫阳焉。"　巫阳招回来的魂魄也没有用。"

---

① 沬（mèi）：微暗。引申为消减。
② 帝：上帝。巫阳：古代神话中的巫师。

Requiem

While young, I was spotless and pure, oh!
To do what is right I was sure.
I served my lord with virtuous deeds, oh!
Entangled then amid vulgar weeds.
My lord of my deeds was not clear, oh!
I suffered and felt sad and drear.

The Lord God to the wizard said,
"To someone I'd give aid,
Whose soul's dispersed below.
To help him you should go."

The wizard said, "It seems
Hard to fulfil your dreams.
If you insist I should divine,
I'm afraid I could not decline."

乃下招曰: 于是下到人间开始招魂说:
"魂兮归来! "魂灵啊,回来吧!
去君之恒干, 为何离开你的躯体,
何为四方些? 去往四方随风飘荡?
舍君之乐处, 舍弃你安乐的住所,
而离彼不祥些。 偏要遭遇祸殃。

"魂兮归来! "魂灵啊,回来吧!
东方不可以托些。 东方不可以栖身。
长人千仞, 那里巨人身高千丈,
惟魂是索些。 只等着觅食你的魂灵。
十日代出, 十个太阳轮番出现,
流金铄石些。 金属石头都会熔化掉。
彼皆习之, 那些巨人都已经习惯,
魂往必释些。 而你的魂一去必成斋粉。
归来归来! 回来吧!
不可以托些。 千万不要在那里寄居。

"魂兮归来! "魂灵啊,回来吧!
南方不可以止些! 南方不可以栖止。
雕题黑齿①, 野人额头上刺花染着漆黑牙齿,
得人肉以祀, 他们专门用人肉作为祭祀,
以其骨为醢些。 还把骨头磨成浆滓。
蝮蛇蓁蓁, 那里蝮蛇成群遍地丛集,
封狐千里些。 大狐狸千里内遍地遨游。

---

① 雕题黑齿:额头上刻花纹,牙齿染成黑色。指南方未开化的野人。题,额头。

The wizard came down to play his role:
"Come back, O soul!
Why should you leave your breast
And roam north, south, east, west? oh!
Why desert your place of delight
And fall in a sad plight? oh!

O soul, come home!
Don't eastward roam, oh!
The eastern giants are nine fathoms tall;
They seek and catch souls they enthral, oh!
Ten suns together shine,
Melting stone and metal fine, oh!
The giants are accustomed to the day,
But you souls would melt away, oh!
Come home, come home!
Don't eastward roam, oh!

O soul, come back!
Don't stay with southerners whose teeth are black!
They have tattooed forehead;
They sacrifice the flesh of the dead,
Whose bones are pounded to shred, eh!
There huge serpents defile,
And foxes run from mile to mile, eh!

雄虺①九首，	凶残的虺蛇长着九个脑袋，
往来倏忽，	来来往往飘忽迅捷，
吞人以益其心些。	专门吞食人类滋补身心。
归来归来！	回来吧！
不可以久淫些！	千万不能在那里长久滞留。

"魂兮归来！	"魂灵啊，归来吧！
西方之害，	西方的大灾害很多，
流沙千里些！	流沙千里一片大漠。
旋入雷渊②，	如果被流沙卷进深渊，
麋③散而不可止些。	粉身碎骨无可奈何。
幸而得脱，	即便是侥幸摆脱，
其外旷宇些。	四外又是空旷死寂之域。
赤蚁若象，	红色蚂蚁如象一样庞大，
玄蜂若壶些。	黑蜂长得像葫芦。
五谷不生，	那里五谷都不生长，
藂菅④是食些。	只有丛丛野草可以充饥。
其土烂人，	沙土能把人烤烂，
求水无所得些。	无处取水解除口渴。
彷徉无所倚，	在那里彷徨往来没有依靠，
广大无所极些。	广漠无边没有终极。
归来兮，	回来吧！
恐自遗贼些。	恐怕自身遭受祸害。

① 雄虺（huǐ）：凶恶的毒蛇。
② 雷渊：神话中的深渊。
③ 麋（mí）：碎。
④ 藂（cóng）：聚集。菅（jiān）：一种野草，细叶绿花褐果。

The nine-headed snakes go
Swiftly to and fro
And swallow men high and low, eh!
Come back, come back!
Do not stay with those with teeth black, eh!

O soul, come back from the west vile
Where quicksands quake from mile to mile, eh!
If you fall in the thunderous whirlpool,
You would be swallowed by water cool, eh!
If you're by luck not drowned,
You'll find vast wilderness around, eh!
Where wasps are big as gourds; red ants
As huge as elephants, eh!
No grain grows there; man feeds
On dry and thorny reeds, eh!
The barren earth would make men rot;
No water could be got, eh!
You'll find no shelter near at hand
In such a boundless land, eh!
Come back!
Don't westward go,
Or you would fall in woe, eh!

"魂兮归来！　　　　　　　　"魂灵啊，回来吧！
北方不可以止些。　　　　　北方之地不可以停留。
增冰峨峨，　　　　　　　　那里层层冰封高耸如山峰，
飞雪千里些。　　　　　　　大雪飘飞千里洋洋洒洒。
归来归来！　　　　　　　　回来吧，
不可以久些！　　　　　　　千万不能够耽搁太久！

"魂兮归来！　　　　　　　　"魂灵啊，归来吧！
君无上天些。　　　　　　　你也不要往天上去。
虎豹九关，　　　　　　　　九重天的关口都有虎豹守候，
啄害下人些。　　　　　　　它们专门吞吃下界之人。
一夫九首，　　　　　　　　另有个妖怪一身九头，
拔木九千些。　　　　　　　能连根拔起九千棵大树。
豺狼从目，　　　　　　　　还有横眉怒目的豺狼，
往来侁侁①些。　　　　　　来来往往成群结队。
悬人以娭，　　　　　　　　把人吊起来当作游戏，
投之深渊些；　　　　　　　玩够了把他扔到不见底的深渊。
致命于帝，　　　　　　　　再向上帝报告完毕，
然后得瞑些。　　　　　　　然后你才会瞑目断气。
归来归来！　　　　　　　　回来吧？
往恐危身些！　　　　　　　上天去恐怕祸害自身！

---

① 侁（shēn）侁：众多貌。

O soul, come back, do not go forth!
You can't stay in the north, eh!
Where ice rises pile on pile
And snowflakes fly from mile to mile, eh!
Come back! Do not go forth!
You cannot stay long in the north, eh!

O soul, come back! Don't hie
Up to the sky, eh!
Where the man-eating tiger guards
The nine gates with leopards, eh!
The nine-headed monsters without cease
Pull up nine thousand trees, eh!
The wolves and jackals go
With hostile eyes to and fro, eh!
They hang out man for sport and throw
Him into the abyss below, eh!
They wait for orders from on high,
Then man may shut his eyes and die, eh!
Come back, come back at my call,
Or in danger you'll fall, eh!

"魂兮归来！	"魂灵啊，回来吧！
君无下此幽都些！	你不要下到阴曹地府。
土伯九约[1]，	那里有身扭九曲的土伯，
其角觺觺[2]些。	它头上长着尖角锐如刀凿。
敦脄[3]血拇，	脊背肥厚长爪沾血，
逐人駓駓[4]些。	追逐行人飞奔如梭。
参目虎首，	还有三只眼睛的虎头怪，
其身若牛些。	身体像牛一样壮硕。
此皆甘人，	这些怪物都以吃人为嗜好，
归来归来！	回来吧！
恐自遗灾些。	恐怕自己要招致灾祸。
"魂兮归来！	"魂灵啊，回来吧！
入修门[5]些！	快进入郢都的大城门。
工祝招君，	招魂的巫师在召唤你，
背行先些。	倒退行走一路先行引领。
秦篝齐缕[6]，	秦国的竹笼齐国的丝线，
郑绵络些。	做盖头的丝绵都来自郑国。
招具该备，	招魂的器具样样俱全，
永啸呼些。	招魂的呼唤声声相连。
魂兮归来！	魂灵啊，回来吧！
反故居些。	快快返回你的故乡。

[1] 土伯：地下王国的神灵。约：弯曲。一说，尾也。一说，肚下肉块。
[2] 觺（yí）觺：尖利。
[3] 敦脄（méi）：很厚的背肉。疑为神怪名。
[4] 駓（pī）駓：跑得很快的样子。
[5] 修门：郢都城南三门之一。
[6] 秦篝：秦国出产的竹笼，用以盛被招者的衣物。齐缕：齐国出产的丝线，用以装饰"篝"。

O soul, come back! Don't go
To the Hell down below, eh!
Its guardian has nine tails;
The horn on his head ails, eh!
With shoulders huge and bloody thumb,
He pursues men, fearsome, eh!
His three-eyed tiger's head
And bull-like body would cause dread, eh!
On human flesh he'd feed, eh!
Come back! Don't go below
Or you'll be lost in woe, eh!

O soul, come back! Do not be late
To enter the capital's gate, eh!
The wizard calling you will retreat
Backward to lead your feet, eh!
Basket and strings from east and west,
And central banners and the rest, eh!
Magic instruments ready one and all,
You hear the wizard's wailing call, eh!
O soul, come on your backward road
To your former abode, eh!

"天地四方，	"天上地下四面八方，
多贼奸些，	残害人的奸佞数不完。
像设君室，	仿照你的居室，
静闲安些。	清静闲适十分安宁。
高堂邃宇，	高高的大堂深邃的院落，
槛层轩些。	走廊重重栏杆围护。
层台累榭，	层层亭阁重重高台，
临高山些。	面对着崇山峻岭。
网户朱缀，	镂花大门涂抹着红色，
刻方连些。	门窗上刻着密密的方格图案。
冬有突①厦，	冬天有温暖的内厅，
夏室寒些。	夏天有凉爽的外室。
川谷径复，	山谷中小溪曲折，
流潺湲些。	溪流发出动听的声音。
光风转蕙，	丽日和风摇动蕙草，
泛崇兰些。	香兰丛丛散播芳香。
经堂入奥，	穿过大堂进入内屋，
朱尘筵些。	朱红色竹席铺陈。
砥室翠翘②，	光滑的石室装饰着翠羽，
挂曲琼些。	墙头挂着玉钩晶莹剔透。
翡翠珠被，	翡翠被褥镶嵌珠宝，
烂齐光些。	五彩缤纷艳丽动人。
蒻阿③拂壁，	细软的丝绸覆盖四壁，
罗帱张些。	罗纱帷帐高高悬挂在中庭。

① 突（yào）：深密。
② 砥室：形容地面、墙壁都磨平光亮像磨刀石一样。翠翘：翠鸟尾上的毛羽。
③ 蒻（ruò）阿：细软的缯帛。

No quarters of the world are paradise
But full of harm and vice, eh!
Think of the house of your own,
Quiet and reposeful up and down, eh!
Great halls and deep rooms on high ground
With railings on railings around, eh!
Pavilions and terraces far and nigh
Look on the mountains high, eh!
The lattice doors and crimson stairs
Are richly carved with squares on squares, eh!
Draughtless is the winter room;
The summer gallery is full of gloom, eh!
Streams murmur in and out
Of the gully and thereabout, eh!
The mililotus sway at ease
With lofty orchids steeped in breeze, eh!
The inner hall and rooms o'erspread
With floors and ceilings red, eh!
How bright the wall of polished stone looks
With hangings green on jasper hooks, eh!
The pearly kingfisher bedspread
Dazzles by the light those pearls shed, eh!
Walls are adorned with soft tapestries
And silken canopies, eh!

纂组绮缟①，	各色丝带缤纷艳丽，
结琦璜些。	系结着块块美玉和珍玩。

"室中之观，	"卧室中那些陈设景观，
多珍怪些。	珍宝众多奇形怪状。
兰膏②明烛，	香脂制成的蜡烛光焰通明，
华容备些。	佳人美女全都来到。
二八侍宿，	十六位侍女前来侍夜，
射递代些。	互相替代轮流伺候。
九侯淑女，	列国诸侯选送的淑美女子，
多迅众些。	超群脱俗人数众多。
盛鬋③不同制，	发式秀美各有千秋，
实满宫些。	后宫熙熙攘攘全部注满。
容态好比，	容貌姿态姣好互相比美，
顺弥代些。	真是风华绝代盖世无双。
弱颜固植，	面容娇媚身体康健，
謇其有意些。	脉脉含情令人心荡。
姱容修态，	身材娇小容颜俏丽，
絙洞房些。	幽深洞房中遍布。
蛾眉曼睩，	纤秀弯眉柔情万种，
目腾光些。	顾盼神飞秋波流光。

---

① 纂组绮缟：指四种颜色不同的丝带。纂，赤色丝带；组，杂色丝带；绮，带花纹丝织品；缟，白色丝织品。
② 兰膏：泛言有香气的油脂。
③ 盛鬋（jiǎn）：浓密的鬓发。鬋，下垂的鬓发。

Ribbons of varied hues displayed
With precious stone and jade, eh!

The sight in inner room is fair
With decorations rare, eh!
The orchid-perfumed candles shine
On flower-like faces fine, eh!
Young ladies of sixteen are brights;
In turn they share your bed at night, eh!
Noble maidens come from many a land;
Above other beauties they stand, eh!
With rich and varied headdress tall,
They throng the palace hall, eh!
Each has an unsurpassed fair face
And an unrivaled grace, eh!
Each slender body stands straight,
Silent but intimate, eh !
Their lovable, amorous looks
Illumine nuptial chamber nooks, eh!
Their moth-like brows and eyes bright
Glisten with gleams of light, eh!

靡颜腻理，	肤若凝脂如玉细腻，
遗视矊①些。	回眸一瞥意味深长。
离榭修幕，	离宫别馆的大幕中，
侍君之闲些。	美人们陪伴着你解闷消闲。

"翡帷翠帐，	"张挂起翡翠色的帷帐，
饰高堂些。	装饰那高高的厅堂。
红壁沙版，	红漆髹墙壁丹砂涂护版，
玄玉梁些。	黑玉宝石镶嵌的大屋梁。
仰观刻桷②，	抬头看那方椽上雕刻的图案，
画龙蛇些。	刻画的是龙与蛇的形象。
坐堂伏槛，	坐在堂上倚着栏杆，
临曲池些。	面向着弯弯曲曲的池塘。
芙蓉始发，	池中的荷花含苞待放，
杂芰荷些。	荷叶夹杂其间丰满肥壮。
紫茎屏风③，	小葵紫茎铺满水面，
文缘波些。	微风拂过碧波荡漾。
文异豹饰，	卫士身着文彩奇异的豹皮，
侍陂陁④些。	守卫在山丘坡岗之上。
轩辌既低⑤，	有篷有窗的卧车已到。
步骑罗些。	步兵骑兵随从分列两旁。

① 矊（miǎn）：目光深长。
② 桷（jué）：方的椽子。
③ 屏风：荇菜，又名水葵。一种水生植物。
④ 陂陁（pō tuó）：高低不平的山坡。
⑤ 辌（liáng）：可以卧息的安车。低，通"抵"，到达。

Their delicate flesh and soft skin
And seductive glances will ever win, eh!
In the tent or garden of pleasure,
They're waiting for your leisure, eh!

In lofty hall there hang curtain and screen
Adorned with kingfisher feathers green, eh!
Red walls with panels are inlaid
As the roof-beams with jet and jade, eh!
O'erhead the carved rafters wake
With painted dragon and snake, eh!
Seated in the hall, leaning on railings, you
May have a winding pool in view, eh!
The lotus begins its blooming hours,
Mingled with caltrop flowers, eh!
The purple-stemmed plants with grace
Ripple green water's face, eh!
Attendants in skins of leopard,
Ranged by the steps, stand guard, eh!
When you arrive in tilbury fine,
Footmen and riders wait in line, eh!

兰薄户树，	丛丛兰草种在门前，
琼木篱些。	玉树当作篱笆护墙。
魂兮归来！	魂灵啊，回来吧！
何远为些？	你为何还要去向远方？

"室家遂宗，	"家族聚会济济一堂，
食多方些。	食品丰富多种多样。
稻粢穱麦①，	大米小米和新麦，
挐黄粱些。	里面还掺杂着黄粱。
大苦咸酸，	有苦有咸又有酸，
辛甘行些。	辣的甜的也都用上。
肥牛之腱，	精选肥牛的大蹄筋，
臑②芳些。	炖得烂熟扑鼻香。
和酸若苦，	调和好酸味和苦味，
陈吴羹些。	摆上精致的吴国羹汤。
胹鳖炮羔③，	烧煮的甲鱼火烤的羔羊，
有柘浆④些。	再蘸上新鲜的甘蔗糖浆。
鹄酸膗⑤凫，	醋熘天鹅炖野鸭，
煎鸿鸧⑥些。	又煎大雁又烹小鸧。
露鸡臛蠵⑦，	熏鸡配上大龟熬的肉羹，
厉而不爽些。	味道虽浓却脾胃不伤。

① 粢（zī）：小米。穱（zhuō）：早熟麦。
② 臑（ér）：炖烂。若：与"而"意同。
③ 胹（ér）：煮。炮：烤。
④ 柘（zhè）浆：甘蔗汁。
⑤ 膗（juǎn）：肉羹。
⑥ 鸧（cāng）：鸧鸹，一种似鹤的水鸟。
⑦ 露：借为"卤"。一说借为"烙"。臛（huò）：肉羹。蠵（xī）：大龟。

Orchids carpet the ground about the door,
With hibiscus hedge-row before, eh!
O soul, come back! Why stay
So far away? eh!

Your household pays homage at your shrine
With all kinds of food and wine, eh!
With yellow millet, early wheat and rice
Offered in your sacrifice, eh!
Salt, bitter, sour and pepper hot,
Honey sweet and what not, eh!
The fatted beefsteak is so well
Cooked that it gives a nice smell, eh!
If you like ginger or vinegar,
There's soup of Southern connoisseur, eh!
You'll find stewed turtle and roast kid again
Served up with sauce of cane, eh!
Swans cooked in sour sauce, ducks side by side
With geese and big cranes fried, eh!
Seethed tortoise and chicken braised,
Delicious, not to spoil your taste, eh!

粔籹①蜜饵，	蜜饼和甜糕做点心，
有伥惶②些。	再浇上一些麦芽糖。
瑶浆蜜勺，	晶莹的美酒掺上蜂蜜，
实羽觞些。	斟满酒杯供人品尝。
挫糟冻饮，	除去酒糟再加上冰块，
酎③清凉些。	香醇可口又遍体清凉。
华酌既陈，	奢华的酒宴已经摆好，
有琼浆些。	有酒都是玉液琼浆。
归来反故室，	归来吧魂灵早回故居，
敬而无妨些。	恭敬有加保证无妨。

"肴羞未通，	"丰盛的酒席还未撤去，
女乐罗些。	舞女和乐队就纷纷登场。
陈钟按鼓，	撞起编钟敲起大鼓，
造新歌些。	唱起新歌多么悠扬。
《涉江》《采菱》，	《涉江》曲罢再唱《采菱》，
发《扬荷》些。	更有《阳阿》齐帮腔。
美人既醉，	美人都已经微醉，
朱颜酡④些。	红润的面庞胜海棠。
娭光眇视，	目光撩人含情脉脉，
目曾波些。	秋波流转水汪汪。
被文服纤，	身披着刺绣的罗衣，
丽而不奇些。	色彩华丽却很大方。

① 粔籹（jù nǚ）：用蜜和米面熬成的食品。
② 伥惶（zhāng huáng）：麦芽糖，也叫饴糖。
③ 酎（zhòu）：醇酒。
④ 酡（tuó）：因喝醉酒而脸红。

Fried honey-cakes of rice
And malt-sugar sweetmeats nice, eh!
The jade-like wine fills up
The bird-shaped cup, eh!
After wine strained of dregs and ice-cold drink,
Into refreshening coolness you'd sink, eh!
A sumptuous feast is displayed
With wine which looks like jade, eh!
Come home where you may expect
Nothing wrong but respect, eh!

The feast is in full swing;
Fair maidens come and dance and sing, eh!
Drums are beaten and bells are rung,
And newly composed songs are sung, eh!
"Gathering Caltrops, " "Crossing the Stream Wide, "
And "Sunny Riverside, " eh!
The beauties are drunk with wine;
Their rosy faces shine, eh!
Their flirting glances look
Like amorous waves in a brook, eh!
They are clad in silks fine,
Splendid without freak design, eh!

长发曼鬋，	长长的黑发双鬓柔美，
艳陆离些。	艳装浓抹艳丽非常。
二八齐容，	十六位美女形貌相当，
起郑舞些。	跳着郑国的舞蹈翩翩上场。
衽若交竿，	舞动衣襟如竹枝摇曳交叉，
抚案下些①。	弯腰垂手徐徐下场。
竽瑟狂会，	吹竽鼓瑟合奏疯狂，
搷②鸣鼓些。	猛敲大鼓咚咚作响。
宫庭震惊，	鼓乐齐鸣震撼宫廷，
发《激楚》些。	唱出的《激楚》声音高昂。
吴歈蔡讴③，	献上吴歌蔡谣，
奏大吕些。	演奏大吕调配合声腔。
士女杂坐，	男女纷杂交相坐下，
乱而不分些。	比肩嬉戏不分上下。
放陈组缨，	解下冠带随手放置，
班其相纷些。	色彩绚丽缤纷鲜亮。
郑、卫妖玩，	郑国、卫国的女子妖娆动人，
来杂陈些。	纷至沓来列队堂上。
《激楚》之结，	唱到《激楚》之歌的结尾，
独秀先些。	特别优美出色一时无两。

① 抚：通"拊"，拍击。案：同"按"。下：似指弯腰下屈的舞蹈动作。
② 搷（tián）：快速击打。
③ 吴歈（yú）：吴地之歌。蔡讴：蔡地之歌。

From chignon high falls their long hair
Adorned with jewels rare, eh!
The dancers in two rows of eight
Perform a dance of Central State, eh!
Their sleeves cross like bamboo stems
And come down bright with gems, eh!
In sound the pipes and zithers vie;
Thunderous drums run high, eh!
The palace walls tremble with fear
At the uproar they hear, eh!
Then songs are sung from west or east
And music played for the feast, eh!
Men sit by women's side;
In disorder they hide, eh!
The belts and strings untied
Run riot far and wide, eh!
Fair dancers come from east or west
Sit together with the guest, eh!
The songstress singing best
Finds favor o'er the rest, eh!

"菎蔽象棋[①],	"玉筹码象牙棋,
有六簙[②]些。	用来玩六簙棋游戏。
分曹并进,	分成两方对弈,
遒相迫些。	互相交手紧紧相逼。
成枭而牟[③],	掷彩成枭就取鱼得筹,
呼五白[④]些。	大呼五白收获胜利。
晋制犀比[⑤],	赢得了晋国制的犀带钩,
费白日些。	一日光阴耗尽不在意。
铿钟摇簴[⑥],	敲钟敲到钟架齐晃,
揳梓瑟[⑦]些。	梓木为瑟齐声弹奏。
娱酒不废,	饮酒娱乐不肯停歇,
沉日夜些。	沉醉其中日夜相续。
兰膏明烛,	带兰草香的明烛多灿烂,
华镫[⑧]错些。	华美的灯盏错落有致。
结撰至思,	酒后精心构思撰写文章,
兰芳假些。	文采绚丽可比幽兰之香。
人有所极,	人们高高兴兴快乐已极,
同心赋些。	一起赋诗表达心意。
酎饮尽欢,	酎饮醇酒尽情欢笑,
乐先故些。	也让先祖故旧快乐无比。
魂兮归来!	魂灵啊, 回来吧!
反故居些。"	快快返回故里家乡。"

① 菎(kūn)蔽: 饰玉的筹玛。赌博用具。象棋: 象牙棋子。六簙用具。
② 六簙(bó): 一种棋戏。可用以赌博。
③ 枭: 博戏术语。成枭棋则可取得棋局上的鱼, 得二筹。牟: 取。
④ 五白: 五颗骰子组成的特彩。得此可胜。
⑤ 犀比: 犀制的带钩, 用做赌胜负的彩注。一说用犀角制成的赌具。
⑥ 簴(jù): 挂钟的架子。
⑦ 揳(jiá): 抚。梓瑟: 梓木所制之瑟。
⑧ 镫(dēng): 蜡烛座子。

许渊冲译楚辞

Ivory chess with chips of jade,
The game of six pieces is played, eh!
The two divided sides commence
Their attack and defence, eh!
It's hard to win his fight;
The winner cries, "Five White!" eh!
He wins a rhino hook;
Bright as day it would look, eh!
Some strike the bell till its frame swings;
Some sweep the wooden zither's strings, eh!
Without cease they make merry and drink
Till days into nights sink, eh!
Candles of orchid-perfumed fat shed light
On their stands of carved bronze so bright, eh!
Guests rack their brain to make songs new,
Sweeter than orchid blooms in view, eh!
Each has his weak points and his strong!
Together they make a better song, eh!
When their pleasure reaches its height,
They drink to the departed with delight, eh!
O soul, come on your backward road
To your former abode, eh!

乱[1]曰：	尾声：
献岁发春兮，	新年开始春天到来，
汩吾南征。	我匆匆忙忙向南行。
菉[2]萍齐叶兮，	绿蓣长出齐齐的新叶，
白芷生。	白芷萌生出勃勃生机。
路贯庐江兮，	途中穿越庐江水，
左长薄。	左岸上是连绵的丛林。
倚沼畦瀛兮，	沿着沼泽和水田往前走，
遥望博。	遥望水乡广博无垠。
青骊结驷兮，	四匹青黑色马儿驾起一辆车，
齐千乘。	整整齐齐有千乘猎车。
悬火延起兮，	点起火把蔓延原野，
玄颜烝。	夜空里浓烟阵阵火光冲天。
步及骤处兮，	步行地赶到乘车的停留处，
诱骋先。	狩猎的向导又当先驰骋。
抑骛若通兮，	或停或行进退自如，
引车右还。	引车向右掉转车身。
与王趋梦兮，	与君王一起奔向云梦泽，
课后先。	看谁先到显本领。
君王亲发兮，	君王亲手发箭射猎，
惮青兕[3]。	射中青兕立即毙命。

① 乱：乱辞，尾声。
② 菉(lù)：一种水草，或以为通"绿"。
③ 青兕(sì)：古代犀牛一类的野兽，角为青色。

Epilogue

In the new year begins spring day, oh!
I hurry on my southward way.
Green duckweed sprouts in rows, oh!
And white clover grows.
I pass by River Lu, oh!
To my left stretches water blue.
I go along the waterside, oh!
And see an expanse far and wide.
The four black horses go along, oh!
Before a thousand chariots strong.
The wood is burned and flames rise high, oh!
A pall of smoke darkens the sky.
The footmen follow on the way, oh!
And vie to lure the hunted prey.
The steed is reined, the prey in sight, oh!
The chariot is turned to the right.
In Dream Lake with the king I'd race, oh!
To see who would win the first place.
The king himself shoots at the head, oh!
Of a rhino which falls dead.

朱明承夜兮,	黑夜之后旭日东升,
时不可淹。	时光飞逝从不肯停。
皋兰被径兮,	江边高地兰草长满路径,
斯路渐。	这条道已遮没不可寻。
湛湛江水兮,	湛湛江水潺潺流,
上有枫。	岸上一片枫树林。
目极千里兮,	纵目遥望千里之地,
伤春心。	满目春色引人伤心。
魂兮归来,	魂灵啊,回来吧,
哀江南。	故国江南堪哀难以忘情。

Dawn follows night on the run, oh!
Time and tide wait for none.
Covered by orchids and grass green, oh!
The waterside path can't be seen.
Deep, deep the river flows at ease, oh!
On rivershores stand maple trees.
I gaze for miles and miles with longing eyes, oh!
For spring could I not heave deep sighs?
"O soul, come back to southern shore, oh!
Over your homeland can you not deplore?"

大招

青春受谢，	四季交替新春伊始，
白日昭只。	阳光明媚灿烂辉煌。
春气奋发，	春意盎然生机勃勃，
万物遽只。	万物葱茏竞相生长。
冥凌浃行，	玄冥之神周游天下，
魂无逃只。	孤魂野魄无处逃亡。
魂魄归来！	魂灵啊请快快归来！
无远遥只。	别再漂泊切莫远行。
魂乎归来①！	魂灵，回来吧！
无东无西，	不要去那东方和西方，
无南无北只。	也不要去南方和北方。
东有大海，	东方有大海浩瀚无边，
溺水㴒㴒只②。	水势湍急万物被沉溺。
螭龙并流，	螭龙怪兽们顺流而行，
上下悠悠只。	上下出没着悠然自得。
雾雨淫淫，	雾气茫然淫雨绵绵，
白皓胶只。	白茫茫像冰冻凝结。
魂乎无东！	魂灵啊别去东方！
汤谷寂寥只。	旸谷寂寥空无人烟。

---

① 徕：同"来"。
② 溺水：水深容易沉溺万物。㴒㴒（yōu）：水流的样子。

Great Requiem

Green spring replaces winter drear;
The sun shines bright far and near, eh!
The breath of spring revives the earth
And quickens every creature's birth, eh!
Ice in the dark will melt by day;
The soul has nowhere to run away, eh!
O soul, come back to your own home!
Do not go far away and roam, eh!

O soul, come back and take a rest,
Don't go north or south, east or west, eh!
In the east there is the sea;
Its angry waves would drown you and me, eh!
The dragons swim side by side,
Up and down with the tide, eh!
The fog is mingled with the rain;
The sky appears one with the main, eh!
O soul, don't go to eastern state,
Where the valley is desolate, eh!

魂乎无南!	魂灵啊不要去南方!
南有炎火千里[①],	南方的烈焰绵延千里,
蝮蛇蜒只。	蝮蛇蜿蜒挡住道路。
山林险隘,	山林危险阻扰前程,
虎豹蜿只。	虎豹在那儿逡巡来往。
鰅鳙[②] 短狐。	怪兽都来害人,
王虺[③] 骞只,	大毒蛇王虺把头高昂。
魂乎无南!	魂灵啊别去南方!
蜮伤躬[④] 只。	鬼域含沙射影把人伤。
魂乎无西!	魂灵啊不要去西方!
西方流沙,	西方成片流沙堆积,
漭洋洋[⑤] 只。	苍茫千里漫无边际。
豕[⑥] 首纵目,	猪首妖怪眼睛巨长,
被发鬤[⑦] 只,	毛发散乱披在身上。
长爪踞牙[⑧],	长牙利爪令人恐惧,
诶笑狂只。	得意扬扬面露疯狂。
魂乎无西!	魂灵啊不要去西方!
多害伤只。	那儿很多妖孽把人伤。
魂乎无北!	魂灵啊不要去北方!

① 炎火千里:据《玄中记》记载,扶南国东有炎山。
② 鰅鳙(yú yōng):一种善于害人的怪物。
③ 王虺(huǐ):大毒蛇。
④ 蜮(yù):善于含沙射影的害人怪物。躬:身体。
⑤ 漭(mǎng):指水域广阔。漭洋洋,在这里形容沙漠的广袤无垠。
⑥ 豕(shǐ):猪。
⑦ 鬤(ráng):毛发散乱的样子。
⑧ 踞牙:踞,当作"锯"。锯牙,钢锯一般的牙齿,形容牙齿锋利。

O soul, don't go south for a while,
Where fire is burning from mile to mile
And coiling cobras beguile, eh!
In dangerous mountain and wood,
Tigers and leopards eat man as food, eh!
The cow-fish and spit-sand
And rearing serpents overrun the land, eh!
O soul, be not bewitched by southern charm!
The monsters would do you great harm, eh!

O soul, do not go to the western state,
Where the moving sands undulate
Like a boundless ocean great, eh!
The beasts with head like swine stare
With slanting eyes and shaggy hair, eh!
Their wild, mad laughter hides beneath
Their long claws and serrated teeth, eh!
O soul, do not go to the west
Infested with dangerous pest, eh!
O soul, do not go north, behold!

北有寒山，	北方的冰山高又寒，
逴龙赩只[1]。	烛龙的身体红亮亮。
代水[2]不可涉，	代水深深不可能过，
深不可测只。	水深无底难测量。
天白颢颢[3]，	天空飞雪一片茫茫，
寒凝凝只。	寒气凝结遍布四方。
魂乎无往！	魂灵不要去往北方啊！
盈北极只。	冰天雪地多么荒凉。
魂魄归来！	魂魄啊回来吧！
闲以静只。	这里悠闲自在宁静安详。
自恣荆楚，	荆楚故国到处自由自在，
安以定只。	安居乐业不再漂泊。
逞志究欲，	万事如意随心所欲，
心意安只。	无忧无虑心神安宁。
穷身永乐，	终生都能够保持快乐，
年寿延只。	延年益寿并万寿无疆。
魂乎归来！	魂魄啊回来吧！
乐不可言只。	这里欢乐说也说不尽。

---

[1] 逴（chuō）龙："烛龙"，古代神话传说中人面蛇身的怪物。赩（xī）：大红色。
[2] 代水：神话传说中的河水名。
[3] 颢（hào）颢：闪光的样子，这里指冰雪闪光。

Where tower frozen mountains cold,
And glares the red Torch Dragon old, eh!
The northern river's deep, we're at a loss
How we can go across, eh!
The sky is white with snow;
The earth congealed below, eh!
O soul, do not go forth
Beyond the extreme north, eh!

O soul, do come back please!
To enjoy leisure and ease, eh!
Do what you will in your southern state,
You'll be untroubled and sedate, eh!
Fulfil your wish, enjoy your best
And set your mind at rest, eh!
You will be happy and gay,
And live as long as you may, eh!
O soul, come back like birds,
You will be happy beyond words, eh!

五穀六仞，	五谷杂粮堆了十几丈，
设菰粱①只。	桌上摆满香喷喷的米饭。
鼎臑盈望②，	鼎中的熟肉满眼都是，
和致芳只。	调和五味是多么鲜美。
内鸧鸽鹄③，	各种飞禽都纳入盘中，
味豺羹只。	豺肉做羹再加入其间。
魂乎归来！	魂魄啊回来吧！
恣所尝只。	美食齐全任你品尝。
鲜蠵④甘鸡，	新鲜甘美的大龟和肥鸡，
和楚酪只。	烹调之后和上楚国酪浆。
醢⑤豚苦狗，	乳猪肉酱烧制苦味狗肉，
脍苴莼只⑥。	再撒上一些精细的香菜。
吴酸蒿蒌，	吴国的香蒿做成酸菜，
不沾薄只。	吃来不浓不淡口味纯。
魂兮归来！	魂魄啊回来吧！
恣所择只。	请任意选择这些佳肴。

① 菰（gū）粱：菰米饭。
② 臑（ér）：煮烂。盈望：满目都是。
③ 内：同"纳"，肥的意思。鸧（cāng）：鸧鹒，即黄鹂鸟。鸽：鹁鸠。鹄：天鹅。
④ 蠵（xī）：大龟。
⑤ 醢（hǎi）：肉酱。
⑥ 脍（kuài）：细肉，精肉，这里是切细的意思。苴莼（jū chún），一种香菜。

The five grains are heaped up high,
With corn of zizania near by, eh!
The cauldrons see the in view,
Sweetened with blended savors new, eh!
Plump waterbirds, geese and pigeons sweet,
Flavored with broth of jackal's meat, eh!
O soul, come back with delight!
Indulge your appetite, eh!

Fresh turtle, chicken succulent,
With southern sauces blent, eh!
Pickled pork, dog's meat dried,
With slices of zingiber beside, eh!
Sour salad of the South
Savory to the mouth, eh!
O soul, come back and rejoice
And indulge in your own choice, eh!

炙鸹烝凫[1]，	火烤乌鸦和清蒸野鸭，
煔[2]鹑陈只。	烫熟鹌鹑摆放在案头。
煎鰿膗[3]雀，	煎炸鲫鱼炖煨野黄雀，
遽[4]爽存只。	多么爽口啊口齿留香。
魂兮归来！	魂魄啊回来吧！
丽以先只。	回到故乡先尝尝美味。
四酎并孰[5]，	四器美酒一时间酿成，
不涩嗌[6]只。	不涩口也没有刺激性。
清馨冻饮，	冰镇的美酒清新飘香，
不歠役只[7]。	绝不能让仆役们偷饮。
吴醴白蘖[8]，	吴国的甜酒曲蘖酿制，
和楚沥只。	再把楚国的清酒掺进。
魂乎归来！	魂魄啊回来吧！
不遽惕只。	不要再恐惧战战兢兢。
代秦郑卫，	代秦郑卫四国的音乐，
鸣竽张只。	竽管齐鸣吹奏多响亮。
伏戏《驾辩》，	伏羲氏创作的乐曲《驾辩》，
楚《劳商》只。	楚国的乐曲还有《劳商》。

[1] 鸹（guā）：老鸹，乌鸦。烝：即"蒸"。凫（fú）：野鸭。
[2] 煔（qián）：把食物放入沸汤中烫熟。
[3] 鰿（jì）：鲫鱼。膗（huò）：肉羹。
[4] 遽（qú）：通"渠"，如此。
[5] 酎（zhòu）：醇酒。四酎，四重酿制之醇酒。孰：同"熟"。
[6] 涩嗌（sè yì）：涩口刺激咽喉。
[7] 歠（chuò）：饮。役：做杂役的微贱之人。
[8] 吴醴（lǐ）：吴国的甜酒。白蘖（niè）：白曲酒。

Roast crane is served up and quails boiled,
Stewed magpies and goose broiled, eh!
Duck is served up in steam,
Together with fried bream, eh!
O soul, come back and go ahead!
Before you choicest things are spread, eh!

Four kinds of matured wine
Won't rasp on your throat fine, eh!
Do not drink to excess with cheer
The fragrant ice-cooled liquor clear, eh!
White yeast is mixed with must of Wu
To make the clearest wine of Chu, eh!
O soul, come back, come here!
You may drink without fear, eh!

The Northern, Southern and Central Plains
Play their pipe music and refrains, eh!
And "Emperor Fu Xi's Defence"
And "Southern Grief" intense, eh!

讴和《扬阿》，	合唱《扬阿》这支楚名歌，
赵箫倡只。	赵国的洞箫率先吹响。
魂乎归来！	魂魄啊回来吧！
定空桑只。	为调理好宝瑟空桑。
二八接舞，	十六名美女轮流舞蹈，
投诗赋只。	舞步合着诗赋节奏飞扬。
叩钟调磬，	敲起钟磬声音悠远，
娱人乱只。	欢乐的人们如痴如狂。
四上竞气，	各国的音乐互相比美，
极声变只。	乐曲变化多端尽周详。
魂乎归来！	魂魄啊回来吧！
听歌譔只。	来欣赏各种舞乐歌唱。
朱唇皓齿，	美女个个朱唇皓齿，
嫭以姱只[①]。	花容月貌举世无双。
比德好闲，	德才兼备品行娴静，
习以都只。	技艺娴熟本领高强。
丰肉微骨，	体态丰盈弱骨纤纤，
调以娱只。	舞姿和谐举止安详。
魂乎归来！	魂魄啊回来吧！
安以舒只。	观赏歌舞忘掉忧伤。

---

① 嫭（hù）：美丽。姱（kuā）：美丽。

We chorus "Sunny Rivershore"
To Eastern flute songs of yore, eh!
O soul, come to hear the melody
Made by the lute of mulberry, eh!

Girls of sixteen join, in the dance;
The songs they sing entrance, eh!
Musicians strike the bells in time,
Sing the refrain and sound the chime, eh!
They vie in piping to satiety
And give a pleasing variety, eh!
O soul, come back and come along
To listen to your choicest song, eh!

With vermeil lips and teeth jade-white,
The girls are fair and bright, eh!
They're elegant with winning grace,
Accustomed to leisurely pace, eh!
With nicely rounded flesh and bones delicate,
They'll please and fascinate, eh!
O soul, do come back please!
You may enjoy comfort and ease, eh!

嫭①目宜笑，	美目含情顾盼神飞，
娥眉曼只。	娥眉娟秀曲美细长。
容则秀雅，	仪容娴雅容貌脱俗，
稚朱颜只。	朱颜温润天真烂漫。
魂乎归来！	魂魄啊回来吧！
静以安只。	你也会感到宁静安详。
姱修滂浩，	体态窈窕健美修长，
丽以佳只。	秀丽佳妙性情温良。
曾颊倚耳，	面颊饱满耳朵匀称，
曲眉规只。	弯弯眉毛犹如半圆。
滂心②绰态，	体态绰约心意宽广，
姣丽施只。	姣好艳丽打扮在行。
小腰秀颈，	腰肢细小秀颈颀长，
若鲜卑只。	装束就像鲜卑式样。
魂乎归来！	魂魄啊回来吧！
思怨移只。	美人让你忘记哀伤。

① 嫭（hù）：同"嫮"，美好的意思。
② 滂心：心意广大，风情万种，指能经得起调笑嬉戏。

Over their smiling dreamy eyes,
The long, smooth eyebrows rise, eh!
They look fresh, beautiful and nice,
Their rosy faces would entice, eh!
Richly adorned and slender,
They are lovely and tender, eh!
O soul, come back! It's good
To enjoy quietude, eh!
Their plump cheeks and small tilted ears,
The arched eyebrow like compass appears, eh!
Their bearing shows generous heart,
Their beauty brought out without art, eh!
The long slender neck and small waist
Would satisfy even foreign taste, eh!
O soul, come back! Don't lag behind!
Get rid of sorrow in your mind, eh!

易中利心，　　　　　　她们的心平气和，
以动作只。　　　　　　动作优美举止端庄。
粉白黛黑，　　　　　　粉面如玉黛眉似漆，
施芳泽只。　　　　　　涂上香脂香气袭人。
长袂拂面，　　　　　　轻舒长袖拂动善舞，
善留客只。　　　　　　殷勤留客热情大方。
魂乎归来！　　　　　　魂魄啊回来吧！
以娱昔只。　　　　　　长夜欢娱直到天亮。

青色直眉，　　　　　　美人眉毛如柳叶青青，
美目媔①只。　　　　　美丽的眼睛顾盼流光。
靥辅②奇牙，　　　　　迷人酒窝整齐的门牙，
宜笑嘕只。　　　　　　一颦一笑妩媚至极。
丰肉微骨，　　　　　　肤若凝脂软滑无力，
体便娟只。　　　　　　体态轻盈更显娇贵。
魂乎归来！　　　　　　魂魄啊回来吧！
恣所便只。　　　　　　佳丽服侍任你所为。

夏屋广大，　　　　　　这里的房屋高大宽敞，
沙堂秀只。　　　　　　朱砂描绘出秀丽厅堂。
南房小坛，　　　　　　南面厢房设置小平台，
观绝霤③只。　　　　　楼观的屋檐精致无比。
曲屋步壛，　　　　　　深邃屋宇狭长的回廊，
宜扰畜只。　　　　　　代步之马已经备好。

① 媔（mián）：眼睛美好，脉脉含情的样子。
② 靥（yè）辅：脸颊上的酒窝。
③ 霤（liǔ）：指屋檐。

The dancer fair has clever heart;
She's apt to act her part, eh!
Her eyebrow black and powder white
Give off a perfume light, eh!
Her face hidden behind sleeves long
Detains the guest like a song, eh!
O soul, come back! Don't stay away!
Make merry till night turns to day, eh!

Her straight black eyebrows rise
Over her captivating eyes, eh!
Her dimpled cheeks and fine teeth would beguile
The guest with bewitching smile, eh!
With plump flesh and bones delicate,
Her body would intoxicate, eh!
O soul, do come back please!
You may enjoy your ease, eh!

The northern hall is large with beams overspread
With woodwork painted red, eh!
Between pavilions and southern hall
There is a courtyard small, eh!
Beside the loggia long
Beasts are exercised in throng, eh!

腾驾步游，	或驾车或步行齐出游，
猎春囿①只。	若要射猎则还有春囿。
琼毂错衡②，	玉饰车毂金饰的车衡，
英华假只。	金碧辉煌啊光彩夺目。
茝兰桂树，	茝兰和桂树枝叶繁茂，
郁弥路只。	一路之上都香气弥漫。
魂乎归来！	魂魄啊回来吧！
恣志虑只。	如何游玩随您的意愿。
孔雀盈园，	孔雀聚集在园林之中，
畜鸾皇只。	还需养着鸾鸟和凤凰。
鹍③鸿群晨，	鹍鸡雁鹤在清晨啼叫，
杂鹙④鸧只。	水鹙鸧鹒鸣声杂其间。
鸿鹄代游，	鸿鹄在池中往来游戏，
曼鹔鹴只。	戏水鹔鹴翩翩飞来飞去。
魂乎归来！	魂魄啊回来吧！
凤凰翔只。	和凤凰一样在天空翱翔。

① 囿（yòu）：蓄养动物的园子。
② 琼毂（gǔ）：以玉饰毂。衡：车上横木。
③ 鹍（kūn）：鹍鸡。
④ 鹙（qiū）：水鸟名，据传似鹤而大，青苍色。

The horses gallop and hounds bark;
The hunters go to vernal park, eh!

The chariot has golden flowers inlaid
In wood and hubs of jade, eh!
Wild parsnip, orchid, cassia swing and sway,
So thick along the way, eh!
O soul, come back if you will!
You may enjoy your fill, eh!

Peacocks fill the garden wide;
Phoenixes are kept by their side, eh!
At dawn storks chorus with cranes,
And fowls sing the refrains, eh!
Large swans fly to and fro with ease;
All around wander green geese, eh!
O soul, why not come over?
See the phoenixes for you hover, eh!

曼泽怡面，　　　　　　润泽的脸上满是笑容，
血气盛只。　　　　　　血气充盛是多么健康。
永宜厥身，　　　　　　长期养生保养很得当，
保寿命只。　　　　　　保长命百岁益寿延年。
室家盈廷，　　　　　　家族中的人充满了朝廷，
爵禄盛只。　　　　　　享受的爵禄盛况空前。
魂乎归来！　　　　　　魂魄啊归来吧！
居室定只。　　　　　　安居的宫室确定不变。

接径千里，　　　　　　这里的道路绵延千里，
出若云只。　　　　　　人民出入如浮云舒卷。
三圭①重侯，　　　　　朝堂之上的诸位大臣，
听类神只。　　　　　　判断贤愚如天神明鉴。
察笃夭隐，　　　　　　认真体察夭亡疾病者，
孤寡存只。　　　　　　鳏寡孤独者皆有所养。
魂乎归来！　　　　　　魂魄啊归来吧！
正始昆只。　　　　　　仁政已经开始运行。

田邑千畛，　　　　　　田地与城邑阡陌纵横，
人阜昌只。　　　　　　人口众多生活富足。
美冒众流，　　　　　　教化惠及黎民苍生，
德泽章只。　　　　　　德政和恩泽日益昭彰。
先威后文，　　　　　　先施威严尔后行仁政，
善美明只。　　　　　　政治清廉美好又光明。
魂乎归来！　　　　　　魂魄啊归来吧！

① 三圭：指国家的重臣。

Your face is beaming with delight
of sanguine health at the height, eh!
To preserve life your body's fit,
Its lamp of life ever lit, eh!
Your family and household fill the court
In high rank of every sort, eh!
O soul, come back! Don't go away!
It's better in your house to stay, eh!

For miles and miles the crowd
Comes back and forth like cloud, eh!
Lords of three sceptres in a line
Listen to orders divine, eh!
They watch over and uphold
Orphans and widows, young and old, eh!
O soul, come and defend
The weak from beginning to end, eh!

You have thousands of fields by the stream,
Where people prosper and teem, eh!
You'll reign all over the state
By virtue and favor great, eh!
You'll rule first by might and then by right,
With goodness at its height, eh!
O soul, come back anew!

赏罚当只。	赏罚分明没有不公平。
名声若日,	名声就像辉煌的太阳,
照四海只。	光辉照耀这五方四海。
德誉配天,	功德和荣誉可配天地,
万民理只。	妥善治理天下的万民。
北至幽陵,	北方到幽州的边塞,
南交阯只;	南方抵达交趾地带。
西薄羊肠,	西方近羊肠的险隘,
东穷海只。	东方尽头至穷人迹的所在。
魂乎归来!	魂魄啊回来吧!
尚贤士只。	这里尊重贤良之才。

发政献行,	发布政令施行德政,
禁苛暴只。	禁止苛政暴虐百姓。
举杰压陛,	推举豪杰坐镇朝廷,
诛讥罢只。	罢免无德庸劣之臣。
直赢在位,	忠直之人居于高位,
近禹麾只。	使他们辅国君近前。
豪杰执政,	豪杰当国牢握权柄,
流泽施只。	广布恩泽百姓感恩。
魂乎归来!	魂魄啊归来吧!
国家为只。	为国家做贤良之臣子。

Here punishment and reward are due, eh!
Your fame as bright as the sun
Shines over everyone, eh!
Your virtue rises heaven-high,
Well-known to people far and nigh, eh!
It spreads from northern frontier
To southern countries far and near, eh!
From the narrow western Gorge free
To the farthest eastern sea, eh!
O soul, come back if you would
Revere the wise and the good, eh!

Proclaim your rule and act!
Restrain oppressors with tact, eh!
Raise to power the brave and keen,
And get rid of the mean, eh!
The good and just reign in the land
Most like King Yu in his command, eh!
The brave and wise hold sway in capital;
From them flows favor over all, eh!
O soul, come back! Don't hesitate!
Come back for the good of the State, eh!

雄雄赫赫，	国家的威势雄雄赫赫，
天德明只。	上天的神德万古彪炳。
三公^①穆穆，	三公庄严肃穆互尊重，
登降堂只。	上上下下进出在朝廷。
诸侯毕极，	各地诸侯都位极人臣，
立九卿^②只。	设立九卿辅佐君王。
昭质既设，	箭靶已树起鲜明标志，
大侯张只。	其上悬挂大幅的布侯。
执弓挟矢，	射手们个个持弓挟箭，
揖辞让^③只。	相互揖让全遵从礼仪。
魂乎归来！	魂魄啊归来吧！
尚三王^④只。	崇尚和效法三王之治。

① 三公：太师、太傅和太保。
② 九卿：冢宰、司徒、宗伯、司马、司寇、司空、少师、少傅、少保。
③ 揖辞让：古代射礼，射者执弓挟矢以相据，又相辞让，而后升射。
④ 三王：楚三王，《离骚》中的"三后"，指句亶王、鄂王、越章王。或禹、汤、文武。

Majestic you appear
With Heaven's virtue clear, eh!
The stately dukes one and all
Ascend and descend in the hall, eh!
The princes come all with their maces,
The nine ministers in their places, eh!
White targets are set up there
Where is stretched the leather of bear, eh!
Bow under arm, arrow in hand,
On ceremony they stand, eh!
O soul, come back to your own door!
Revive the ways of the Three Kings of yore, eh!

图书在版编目（CIP）数据

许渊冲译楚辞：汉文、英文 /（战国）屈原著；许渊冲译. -- 北京：中译出版社，2021.1（2024.4重印）
（许渊冲英译作品）
ISBN 978-7-5001-6444-9

Ⅰ. ①许… Ⅱ. ①屈… ②许… Ⅲ. ①古典诗歌－诗集－中国－战国时代－汉、英 Ⅳ. ①I222.3

中国版本图书馆CIP数据核字（2020）第242950号

出版发行	中译出版社
地　　址	北京市西城区车公庄大街甲4号物华大厦6层
电　　话	(010)68359719
邮　　编	100044
电子邮箱	book@ctph.com.cn
网　　址	http://www.ctph.com.cn
出 版 人	乔卫兵
总 策 划	刘永淳
责任编辑	刘香玲　张　旭
文字编辑	王秋璎　张莞嘉　赵浠彤
营销编辑	毕竞方　顾　问
中文注释	张　华
封面制作	刘　哲
内文制作	黄　浩　冯　兴
印　　刷	中煤（北京）印务有限公司
经　　销	新华书店
规　　格	840mm×1092mm　1/32
印　　张	9.75
字　　数	360千
版　　次	2021年1月第1版
印　　次	2024年4月第3次

ISBN 978-7-5001-6444-9　　定价：59.00元

版权所有　侵权必究

中 译 出 版 社